GIRLS
FROM DA HOOD 4

GIRLS
FROM DA HOOD 4

ASHLEY & JAQUAVIS,
AYANA ELLIS

www.urbanbooks.net

Urban Books
1199 Straight Path
West Babylon, NY 11704

Prada Plan © copyright 2008 Ashley
Real Bitches Do Real Things © copyright 2008 Jaquavis Coleman
The Last Woman Standing © copyright 2008 Ayana Ellis

ISBN-13: 978-1-60162-043-9
ISBN-10: 1-60162-043-8

First Printing March 2008
Printed in the United States of America

10 9 8 7 6 5 4 3

This is a work of fiction. Any references or similarities to actual events, real people, living, or dead, or to real locales are intended to give the novel a sense of reality. Any similarity in other names, characters, places, and incidents is entirely coincidental.

Submit Wholesale Orders to:
Kensington Publishing Corp.
C/O Penguin Group (USA) Inc.
Attention: Order Processing
405 Murray Hill Parkway
East Rutherford, NJ 07073-2316
Phone: 1-800-526-0275
Fax: 1-800-227-9604

Ashley "Da Street Diva"
Acknowledgments

Hey, everybody! This is only a short story, so I'm going to follow the script and keep my acknowledgments short and sweet. I want to thank . . .

*__God__ for allowing me to learn from the negative in my life and overcome my past by turning it into something positive and life-changing. These stories are truly a reflection of me and I am so grateful to have been blessed with the talent to share myself with the world through my pen.

*__Carl Weber__ for continuing to believe in my craft and for expanding my knowledge of the literary industry. You are giving me an opportunity to learn the business and become a prominent figure in this game.

*__JaQuavis Coleman__ for all that you do. May we continue to do big business together and get this money like only we can.

*__All of my loved ones__, family and friends alike for your continued support. I love you!

*__Denard, Natalie, and the entire Urban Books Family__ for all of your hard work and support.

*__Keisha Ervin__, for reaching out and showing me so much love. I don't deal with people that ain't like me and you are truly one of a kind, girl. Real bitches keep real friends, lol. Love ya.

*<u>**Sharonda from Augusta, Georgia**</u>. I believe that you truly are my #1 fan. Your email truly touched me and it is because of you that I am positive that these books need to be read by young people. I was just you a few years ago, so I am honored that you look up to me in the way that you do.

*<u>**Last, but definitely not least to the readers and book clubs**</u> that have supported JaQuavis and me thus far. Your opinions are the ones that matter the most. We do this for you and I hope that you all enjoy my first solo venture. Don't worry, Ashley JaQuavis ain't going nowhere. JaQuavis and I will always write together. We're just expanding so that you can get to know us individually as well. Anyway, I hope y'all enjoy! I guess it wasn't short, but it was most definitely sweet. Make sure you hit me up at www.ashleyjaquavis.com with your reviews.

 Ash

Acknowledgments

I want to thank any and everyone who had a hand in my literary success and it's very much appreciated. I want thank God first and foremost for giving me the talent to paint pictures with words. I also want to thank Ashley Snell for being my biggest critique and best friend. You know how we do. Thank you to my brother, my nigga Denard Breland for being a stand-up dude. Thank you to Carl Weber for mentoring and helping me become a better businessman and writer. A big thanks goes to Natalie Weber for helping me in this journey and making everything run smoothly. I truly appreciate your time and patience. I want to THANK YOU, MARIA, for being the best editor ever and making sure my work is on point. Last, but not least, I want to thank the readers for continued support. You guys make all of this possible.

One,
JaQuavis Coleman

www.ashleyjaquavis.com

Acknowledgments

First and foremost, I'd like to thank God for giving me this gift of visual writing. I want to thank Urban Books for giving me a voice and a chance to bring "class to hood literature." I want to thank my agent and friend, Tracy Brown, for being my #1 fan and always being honest with me about my work. I want to thank my girl Carmen Bautista for believing in me so much that she introduced me to Tracy, who in my opinion is just the bomb! I want to thank the "hood" for being my inspiration behind so many things that I write. I want to thank "the struggle" for pushing me to want more and do better. I believe in expression through experience, which allows my work to come off as real because I write about what I know. I want to personally thank my friends and family that constantly push me and give me their blessings. I want to thank my mother for the tough love. If I had it easy, I'd probably be lazy. My oldest brother, Courtney, for always being a fan and believer, and my twin and other brother, Taff (Black), for just being my sidekick . . . (we ride we ride we riiiiide LOL) my only sister, Tana (mah-kee-dah-dah) (we K-ci and Jo-jo for life) and the rest of the breakfast club (Knisha, Wendy, Kherra and Pilot) for keeping me laughing on emails all day. (Gotchya Bit**es!LOL) My girl, Evette Maisonet, for being the angel on my shoulder, Tamara Jolly for listening to everything I write and recite, Dale Robinson for being my little sis and friend, Lorraine Stanislaus for pushing me out of New York, Eneida and Sybil (London Fischer) for being the realest co-workers a girl could have, Hughette Jasper and Felicia Jasper (40 Granite) I love you both so much. You held me down when I couldn't hold myself and I will always love you both for being a mother and grandmother to me and my daughter even when you didn't have to. And last but not least, I want to thank my ladybug, my daughter Nia. You are my hero and I'm doing it all for you, li'l mama. Thank you, everyone for your support in advance. To everyone else that I did not mention, blame it on the mind not the heart.

Ayana Ellis

"Prada Plan"

By
Ashley

Chapter One

"Baby!" Disaya called out as she walked through the Harlem brownstone. The house had an old Harlem Renaissance flavor to it, and the deep shades of brown, orange, and cream complemented her style perfectly. She had always dreamed of owning something just like it, and her dreams became a reality when she received the keys to it the day her baby proposed to her. It had been completely renovated, and the house was exactly what she wanted it to be. Disaya was completely in love with her home and the man that she shared it with.

"Indie, baby, are you home?" she called out as she walked from room to room, unloading the many bags that she had purchased from her shopping trip earlier that day.

"Yo, I'm downstairs. Come here for a minute, ma. I got to holla at you about something," he yelled from the basement.

Disaya took off her Baby Phat thigh-high boots and eased herself out of her jeans. She hated wearing clothes, and when she was in her own home she seldom wore them. Her turquoise Victoria's Secret thong was swallowed by her voluptuous behind as she switched her hips, a habit she practiced even when she didn't have an audience.

"Here I come," she yelled back. She walked over to the refrigerator and grabbed a bottle of water and a Smirnoff. She also grabbed the Blockbuster tapes that she had gotten on her way home and then made her way to the fully furnished basement. She smiled as she descended the steps. "I picked up some movies on my way home. I've been shopping all day. I just want to sit back with you and chill." She approached him and kissed him lightly on the lips as she handed him the drink. She then walked over to the big screen and bent over seductively. She looked back at Indie as he stood and sipped at the Smirnoff.

He eyed her thick behind and the butterfly tattoo that was printed on it as she loaded the DVD into the player.

Disaya stood up and, before she could even turn around, felt the sting of the glass break against her face as Indie slammed his Smirnoff bottle into her head with full force.

"Aghh!" she cried out as her hands went up to protect her face. Blood seeped through her fingers and onto the white carpet.

"You fucking sheisty ho." Indie snatched her by the hair and pulled her back to her feet.

"Indie, stop it. Baby, you're hurting me," she screamed loudly as she clawed at his strong hands now wrapped around her delicate neck.

He held her away from his body with one arm and pointed his finger in her face with the other. "You dirty-ass bitch, I treat you good. I took your stanking ass out of the ghetto and you try to pull some okey-doke type shit on me!"

"What are you talking about?" Disaya asked in tears as she struggled to breathe.

"Don't fucking sit in my face and lie!" he yelled as he slammed her against the wall repeatedly. Tears built up in his eyes, and his stomach felt hollow from her deception. He looked at the engagement ring that he had given her and snatched it roughly from her finger, almost breaking it.

"Indie, no!" she cried as he took the most important thing in the world from her. "Baby, I don't know what you heard, but I haven't lied to you. I wouldn't lie to you. I've kept it real with you since the beginning. Baby, I love you."

She was pleading with him to believe her, and her eyes seemed sincere. He wanted to pull her into his arms and tell her that he could forgive her, that he could look past her disloyalty, but he knew that he couldn't. A major player in the drug game for years, he'd promised himself that he would never let a bitch knock him off his square, and this included her.

"YaYa, you could have had anything. I would've given you the world," he whispered as the pain of her actions set in.

"Baby, I didn't do anything," she cried as she struggled to breathe.

Indie's facial expression changed, and he loosened his grip on her neck. "YaYa," he said, calling her by her nickname, "I'm gon' ask you a question. I'm only gon' ask you this one time. I want you to think real hard before you answer me, okay?"

Disaya tried to think of what she could have done to deserve this treatment from him. "Okay," she whispered in reply.

"Have you ever done anything to hurt me? Have you ever lied to me?"

"I swear to God on our unborn child I haven't," she said convincingly as she touched her stomach.

Her words reminded Indie of the seed that she carried inside of her. They had just found out that she was six weeks pregnant. He remembered when she first told him that. He was the happiest man in the world. He had never felt more love for a person than he did that day, but now all of his love turned to hate as he stared at Disaya in contempt. Before he could think about his actions, he raised his foot and kicked her with all his might. His foot collided with her stomach, and she dropped to her knees in excruciating pain.

"Aghh!" she screamed in agony. *God, please let my baby be okay,* she thought. It was the first thing that crossed her mind. She was in disbelief. She would have never imagined that Indie would try to hurt her or do anything to hurt their child.

"Bitch, shut up! All this time, it was you. You sat back and watched me go through that shit, and all along you were behind it."

"What are you talking about? I didn't do shit!" she screamed. She held her stomach as she began to spit up blood.

"Oh, you didn't do shit, huh?" He grabbed her

roughly and pulled her over to the wooden dinette set that occupied space in the basement. He sat her down forcefully and yelled, "Well, how do you explain this?" He stormed over to the entertainment center and pressed play on the VHS player. He had discovered the one thing that she had tried so hard to hide from him. "Explain it, YaYa," he repeated as he watched her betrayal on tape.

As soon as the tape began to play, tears filled her eyes. *Oh my God! Where did he get this from?* she thought to herself as she watched in horror. She was at a loss for words. She couldn't explain herself because in her heart she knew that there was no talking her way out of the situation. She closed her eyes as the hot tears streamed down her face.

"Uh-uh. Bitch, don't close your eyes. Watch it. I've already seen it from beginning to end. I've been watching the shit over and over again for the past five hours hoping my eyes were playing tricks on me."

Disaya couldn't bring herself to open her eyes but was forced to when Indie's fist collided with her face. She knew that the video only got worse, but she opened her eyes and watched it anyway to avoid him striking her again.

"I want you to watch this, so you'll know exactly why you are going to die," he whispered as his heart broke into two as he watched Disaya's triple-X performance.

I wish I could go back. I should have told him myself. It's not what it looks like. I could have explained to him how it really went down, she told herself as her mind wandered back to when it all began.

Chapter Two

Disaya stepped into the club and smiled when she noticed how packed it was that night. *Tips gon' be on point tonight,* she thought to herself as she made her way toward the bar. Her skintight Rocawear jeans and gold halter only added to her sex appeal, which she knew would increase her value that night.

"Hey, YaYa, where you been? You been missing crazy money tonight," her best friend Mona stated.

YaYa hopped onto the bar and twirled her legs around so that she could get to work. "Straight? These niggas working with deep pockets tonight?"

"Shit! Deep enough. I've already made a buck fifty and it ain't even eleven o'clock." Mona flipped a tequila bottle in the air before filling two shot glasses with the liquor. Mona was a tall, high-yellow girl with sandy hair that cascaded down her back. She was average in the face, but most dudes were willing to look past what she lacked in beauty because she made up for it with a set of perky D-cups that she always kept on display.

She was in no way comparable to Disaya however. With her caramel-colored skin, green eyes, and shoulder-length layered hair, Disaya made sure she stayed fly. Her 5 foot 7 frame was perfectly proportioned, and she had a figure that most women would kill for. Disaya always seemed to demand the attention of the room, and tonight in the club was no different.

"Yo, let me get a bottle of Mo-mo, baby girl," a dude stated as he slapped his hand on the bar counter repeatedly. He had walked straight up to the bar, disregarding the people who were waiting in line for their drink orders to be filled.

Disaya kept taking orders from the rest of the line, while Mona went to take care of the man.

"Nah, ma. I was talking to ol' girl. I want her to hook me up," he stated with an intoxicated slur.

Disaya overheard the guy and turned around as she continued to work the entire bar. "Yo, my man, my girl here gon' get you right. Just give her your order and she'll take care of you," Disaya said with a smile. "That'll be six dollars," Disaya stated to another customer as she continued to serve her busy clientele.

"That's all right. I'm-a wait for you," the dude said with a slick smile.

Mona walked up to Disaya and whispered, "You might want to take care of him, girl. That's Ronnie B."

"Ronnie B?" Disaya repeated in confusion.

"Bitch, Ronnie B. Elite Entertainment. Word is he throwing this party to scout for more models for his company. I hear they be getting crazy paid too."

Disaya didn't give a damn who the dude was. She'd heard about his entertainment company though, and word on the streets was that anybody associated with him was getting paid. She strutted over to the dude sitting at the end of the bar and peeped him from head to toe as she approached. She could tell by the Audemars Piguet that he sported on his wrist that he was working with more chips than the average dude.

"What can I get for you?" she asked him.

"What's your name?" he inquired, completely ignoring her question.

"YaYa," she replied as she shifted her weight to one side.

"YaYa . . . what is someone as attractive as you doing working behind a bar?"

"Paying the bills," she replied with a quick tongue.

YaYa wasn't the type of chick to front like she had more than what met the eye. She was a real chick and wouldn't claim to be anything more than what she was. She knew that she was a Rocawear ho, but she was looking to be upgraded and was determined to get her paper up so that she could graduate from hood-rich clothing lines to high-end designers. She knew that most niggas in the hood had hustle plans, but she wasn't trying to compete in their games. She wasn't built for the coke game, but she did have all the right assets to get what she wanted. She had a seductive and natural beauty that was so rare in the hood. That was the advantage that she had on all of the other girls from her neighborhood. She was strikingly gorgeous, and she knew it. She flipped the game and turned what a dude would call his hustle plan into her "Prada plan," which was to use what she had to get what she wanted.

The man sitting before her was about to become her

meal ticket and didn't even know it. *I'll be rocking Prada in no time if I can get down with his company*, she thought to herself.

"Your man ain't taking care of home?" he asked.

"Is that your slick way of asking me if I have one?" She placed one hand on her hip, her arched eyebrows furrowed, as she waited for him to reply.

"I guess that wasn't all that smooth, huh?" he asked jokingly with a smile.

YaYa smiled too. She could tell that he was embarrassed from the whack line he'd just thrown her way. "You straight. Your game just need a little work, that's all," she replied with a laugh.

He nodded his head and lifted his glass. "Blame it on the liquor."

"Well, you're running a little low on that, so what can I get you?"

"Have one of the waitresses bring a couple bottles of Mo and Cris up to VIP." He went into his pocket and pulled out a wad of money and a business card. He placed them both on the counter top.

Disaya picked up the green and the card then counted out one thousand dollars as he began to walk away.

"Hey, you gave me way too much!" she shouted after him as he continued to maneuver through the crowd.

He stopped in his tracks, turned around and said, "That's your tip! Come to the address on the card tomorrow if you trying to make more," he replied.

YaYa looked at the card that she held in her hand. She was about to respond, but when she looked back up, Ronnie B had already disappeared into the crowd. She looked back at Mona, who was eagerly watching the entire encounter.

When Disaya returned to her side, Mona asked, "What he say?"

Disaya passed her the card. "The nigga gave me a five-hundred-dollar tip and told me to get at him if I wanted to make more."

"What!" Mona yelled. "YaYa, do you know how hard it is to get down with Elite? He just up and told you to come through. You going, right?"

"Hell yeah. I'm gon' go, but you got to come with me. I ain't trying to be up in there by myself."

"You know I'm down. If I can get with Elite, I can finally make some real cash and stop fucking with these cats with shallow means," Mona muttered while thinking about her current situation. "I'm tired of messing with these niggas with play money."

Disaya burst into laughter. "What the hell is play money?"

Mona began to laugh too as she replied, "You know, play money. Niggas be walking around here with 22's and chromed-out cars, but don't have no real cash. They be parking them shits at they mama's crib at the end of the night because they grown as hell, still living at home."

"Or they be wrapping rubber bands around a stack of ones with a hundred-dollar bill on top to make it look like they balling," Disaya added through her laughter.

"Hell yeah! Them fronting-ass, no-money-getting niggas be talking about, 'Girl, I will keep your hair done.' I be wanting to say, 'Nigga, please . . . I can do that myself.'"

Disaya couldn't stop herself from laughing because she knew her girl was telling the truth. "All jokes aside though, I'm not fucking with no more broke niggas. If he can't buy me that brownstone in Manhattan, I ain't fucking with him. It's time to step into the big leagues."

"Well, it doesn't get any bigger than that." Mona motioned her head toward the VIP balcony where Ronnie B was.

His eyes were glued on Disaya. He lifted his glass in the air and nodded to her.

Disaya smiled seductively as she returned his stare.

"Excuse me! Can I get a rum and Coke?" a girl asked, snapping Disaya out of her daze.

Disaya turned around and got back to work as she thought to herself, *I'm about to get this money. These niggas getting they grind on. It's time to pull out the Prada plan and make this cake.*

Chapter Three

Disaya tossed clothes all over her studio apartment as she debated with herself about what to put on. She had seen some of the girls that worked for Elite Entertainment and they were all model-type chicks. She didn't want to walk into the place half-stepping. She knew that whatever she wore, she had to be on point, and none of the clothes inside of her closet were going to get the job done. "Damn!" she yelled in frustration.

She picked up her phone and quickly dialed Mona's number.

"Hello?" her friend answered in a whisper.

"Bitch, why are you whispering?" Disaya asked in confusion.

"I'm shopping on West Thirty-fourth," she replied, still whispering.

"You must have read my mind. Meet me at Macy's in an hour."

Disaya quickly threw on some Seven jeans, a Bob Marley T-shirt, and some Force One's, and an hour later, she met Mona in front of the store.

"You bring your bag?" Mona asked.

"You know I did. This is more valuable than a Visa," she joked as she patted the black book bag that she carried in her hand.

"You want to create the distraction, or you want me to?" Mona asked.

"You do the distraction. I'll take care of the rest."

The girls walked into the store and headed their separate ways. This was a routine that they'd gotten used to, so they were both confident that they would be in and out in less than twenty minutes. Disaya pulled out a red pen and marked stars on the tags of the clothes that she liked the best. They both knew that they needed to look fly for the night. Ronnie B wouldn't even look twice at them if they weren't dressed to impress. She peeked over at Mona, who was a couple aisles down. The two girls didn't even speak to each other, they were so busy concentrating on the task at hand.

Once Disaya had marked all the clothes that she liked the best, she asked for assistance from one of the salespeople. "Excuse me, do you have this dress in white, and a size eight?" she asked the white red-headed woman who was trying to keep tabs on Mona. The woman's eyes cut low in the corners as she watched Mona closely.

"Excuse me?" Disaya stated again, this time with a little more attitude.

"Oh, umm, let me check in the back for you," she said as she reluctantly turned her back on Mona.

The saleswoman walked to the back of the store, and in less than two minutes flat, Mona had walked around the entire department and boosted all the clothes that Disaya had tagged. She discreetly stuffed them into the black book bag and then walked into the restroom, where she proceeded to remove the alarm sensors from the clothes.

The saleswoman came back with the dress just as Mona was exiting the bathroom. The woman then ran behind the counter and picked up the phone and called security. She didn't even think about handing Disaya the dress. "Hey! Excuse me, miss!" She yelled across the store just as Mona reached the exit. "I'm going to have to check your bag!"

"What!" Mona yelled out. "Bitch, I ain't got to steal from your store!" She made sure to raise her voice, to attract the attention of the other patrons in the store.

Disaya smirked as she watched the entire scene.

Security arrived with the manager. "Excuse me, miss," the manager stated. "We are going to have to check your bag."

"What? Because I'm black I can't afford to shop in this store? You think I got to steal?"

"I saw her putting clothes into the bag, sir," the saleswoman told her manager.

As Mona continued to argue with the staff, Disaya walked into the restroom where Mona had swapped bags and picked up the black book bag full of designer clothes. Disaya had tagged everything from Dior to Fendi, which would cause the store to take a hell of a loss. She carried the bag at her side as she walked right past Mona and the group of people.

Mona winked her eye and gave her a quick smile before Disaya strolled out the front door, merchandise in hand. They had just gone on another one of their shopping sprees. They never spent a dime, yet they always made it happen and stepped out fresh.

Disaya waited outside and burst out laughing when she watched through the window as the manager opened Mona's book bag to find nothing in it but an old quilt. The look on the saleswoman's face was priceless.

When Mona walked out of the store, she met Disaya up the block. She had three large Macy's bags in her hand.

"What is all that?" Disaya asked.

Mona was laughing hysterically. "I raised so much hell, they gave me store credit just for accusing me." She handed one of the bags over to her girl. "Here are the shoes you were looking at."

"Bitch, those were some seven-hundred-dollar shoes! How much store credit did they give you?" Disaya asked in astonishment.

"Twenty-five hundred," Mona replied in a nonchalant tone.

Disaya slapped hands with her friend. "You's a bad bitch."

"No, you's a bad bitch," Mona replied. "We about to put this Prada plan of yours into action."

Disaya could feel the butterflies fluttering in her stomach as she approached the large warehouse where Ronnie B hosted some of his infamous parties. She was fly in her cream Dolce & Gabbana jacket. The cropped style of the jacket stopped just at her waist and matched the cream knee-high leather boots she was rocking. Her designer jeans suffocated her wide hips and thick thighs. *Can't nobody tell me shit,* she thought as she stepped seductively into the building. There were girls scattered throughout the lower level of the building, and a group of dudes mingled on the second level of the loft-style warehouse. Disaya turned toward Mona and said, "What the fuck is all this about?"

Mona shrugged her shoulders and continued to follow Disaya through the room.

Before she could answer, one of the girls made her way upstairs and clapped her hands to get everybody's attention. "Excuse me!" she stated loudly.

Disaya looked up at the chocolate-colored girl. She had the beauty of a supermodel. She was slim, and her long, jet-black hair was held off her face with a pair of Dior sunglasses. Ronnie B stood behind her, one hand wrapped around her waist. "Ladies, welcome to Elite Entertainment. All of y'all are here for the same reason. Y'all are trying to get down. As you can see, you have to be perfect, or damn near close to it in order to get down with us. We don't need no simple-minded, stuck-up-ass bitches in here either. I'm gon' tell y'all the truth right now. You will fuck, suck, and please whoever you are asked to. It don't matter if the nigga is fat, ugly, white, black, whatever. If he got that cake to put up, we will take care of him. The cut will be seventy-thirty. Don't get big-headed and think that you can do this on your own, because you can't. Some of the most hood-rich niggas in New York request our services. We deal with niggas so big, you can't even get them to look your way, let alone become wifey. So drop them gold-diggin'-ass tactics that y'all been using. If you ain't afraid of money and you trying to get it with us, I need y'all to get in line one by one so we can start the interviews."

"Fuck this bitch think she is?" Mona whispered in Disaya's ear as she looked up at the landing where the girl stood.

"Ain't no telling, but I don't know if I'm down with this. I didn't know Ronnie B was getting down like this. I was thinking he was on some model management type stuff. Seventy-thirty split—I know this nigga didn't ask me to come here so he could pimp my ass." Disaya frowned, her perfectly arched eyebrows showing her distress.

Ronnie B noticed her disposition as he approached. "What up, mama?" He looked her up and down, licking his lips in lust.

Disaya didn't respond. She crossed her arms and looked at him with an attitude before turning her attention toward Mona. "You ready?"

"Whoa! Hold up. What up? I thought we had a good conversation the other night. You're getting ready to bounce just like that. You ain't been here ten minutes," Ronnie B told her.

"Look, this ain't for me. I'm not one of your little groupie broads. I don't get pimped. If I sell my pussy, believe me, I better be profiting one hundred percent," Disaya said as she walked away.

Ronnie walked after her and grabbed her arm lightly. "Yo, Disaya, just hear me out, okay. I need you, ma. You got everything I'm looking for. I only fuck with the baddest bitches in New York, and you one of 'em. I'm not trying to pimp you, ma. I'm trying to feed you. Working with me, you'll get money. Yeah, I'll be taking a cut, but that's simply a small finder's fee. You'll be caked up and living like you want to be living, you feel me?"

"Come on, YaYa . . . the Prada plan, remember?" Mona said, trying to convince her friend to at least give it a chance.

Ronnie B picked up on the comment and said, "Yeah, YaYa, the Prada plan. See, your girl down. Now, all I need is you on the team and I'm good. Money gon' flow like water."

"Fine, but I ain't standing in this long-ass line."

Ronnie B took Disaya's hand, and she grabbed Mona's as they maneuvered their way to the front of the line. Disaya could hear the smart comments and smacking lips of the other girls waiting in line as they made their way to the front of the line.

"You're next," Ronnie whispered in her ear. He opened the door and walked inside.

Disaya waited in line for a half an hour, and finally the door opened. She stepped inside and strutted into the room. Her body language displayed confidence as she stood in the middle of the room. She stood in front of a table of six people, one of them being the dark-skinned girl who had addressed the group of wannabes earlier.

"I'm Leah, and you are?" the girl asked.

"I'm YaYa." Disaya shifted her all her weight on one leg, giving her hips an enticing shape.

One of the dudes that was sitting at the table said, "Turn around, ma."

A half-smile crossed Disaya's face as she turned around slowly, pausing so that they could take all of her in. She clapped her cheeks together discreetly, showing how she could work her ass muscles.

"Damn, baby girl, you hurting 'em," the guy commented.

Ronnie B just sat back and observed Disaya. He wanted to see how she handled herself under pressure.

"So tell us about yourself, YaYa," Leah said.

"Ain't too much to tell. What you see is exactly what you get."

"Well, why do you want to be down with Elite?"

Disaya frowned. "I don't. I was asked to come here. I'm just trying to see what y'all got to offer."

"We ain't offering shit. You got to show us why you should be down." Leah got up and walked over to Disaya and circled her, eyeing her up and down. "Are you down for whatever?"

"I'm down to make money," YaYa replied.

Leah stopped in front of YaYa and stood directly in her face. She stood so close to her that Disaya could smell the peppermint scent on her breath. Leah kissed her softly on the lips.

YaYa was hesitant at first but decided to see where the kiss would lead. She knew that Ronnie and his crew were testing her to see if she was really ready for the lifestyle that they led. She realized that if she joined Elite Entertainment she'd have to do a lot more than kiss another woman. So, to prove herself, she tongued Leah back passionately. To YaYa's surprise, she felt her pussy get wet. She wasn't bisexual and had never expe-

rienced a sexual encounter with a woman, but just the
fact that she had a roomful of men lusting after her
while she kissed another girl made her body tremble.

"Damn, shorty right," one of the dudes said to Ronnie B as they slapped hands.

"That's why I chose her," he replied.

When the girls ended their kiss, Leah nodded her
head in approval. "She's in," she said as she switched
back to her seat and sat down.

"Here you go, baby girl." Ronnie B held out a Sidekick for her.

She walked toward him and accepted it.

"Keep this on you at all times. Only use it to contact
one of the Elite members. All of our numbers are pro-
grammed in there. I'll hit you up when I need you."

Leah pulled an envelope out of her purse and passed
it to Disaya. "Go get yourself fresh. I can see by the way
that you're dressed that you don't really need the help
in the clothes department, but buy yourself something
new anyway. Consider it a signing bonus."

Disaya began to walk out of the room. Before she
opened the door, Ronnie B yelled, "Send your girl in."

Chapter Four

Disaya couldn't wait to make that fast money. She knew that this was her chance to come up in a big way. Her clientele was about to shoot through the roof. Now that she was down with Elite, she would be introduced to some of the most hood-rich niggas the East Coast had ever produced. And she was hoping that she would be able to find a nigga to take care of her.

She counted the money that Leah had given her. It was five stacks, and she planned on using that to put a down payment on a new whip. She was currently driving a 2003 Mazda and decided that it was time for an upgrade. She knew that she couldn't really afford the car, but she figured that she should treat herself. YaYa had champagne tastes with beer money and was tired of riding around in her five-year-old car. She wanted an upgrade and didn't care if she didn't have a job to pay for it.

She drove her car down to the dealership. As soon as she stepped out of the car, she was surrounded by salesmen. They thought that she was a naïve woman that they would be able to swindle. They had no idea that she planned on hustling them out of the best car on the lot. She had on a short jean Azzuré skirt and a knit sweater that hung loosely off one shoulder. Her stiletto heels clicked on the pavement as she made her way into the dealership. She had a trail of salesmen following behind her, but she knew who she was looking for. She didn't even want to waste her time with the employees. She wanted to deal with the owner.

She walked directly to the rear of the building and opened a door that had the name *Bill Perkins* engraved on it. An attractive, older black man wearing a pair of reading glasses sat behind the desk.

"Hello, Bill. I need a car," she said.

He looked up at her and then at the swarm of salesmen standing idly in the hallway, watching her every move. His eyes then did a once-over of the beautiful girl that stood before him. "Excuse me," he said as he got up and walked past her. "All right, gentlemen, get back to work!" Bill then turned around to see Disaya sitting on the edge of his desk, her legs crossed. Her skirt was so short, he could see her black lace panties underneath.

"What can I do for you, Ms. . . . ." Bill paused when he realized he hadn't caught her name.

"Jessica. Jessica Simpson," YaYa said with a smirk, giving him a ridiculously false name.

"Well, Jessica, what can I do for you?"

"I need a car," she repeated.

"Is there a specific price range that you're trying to stay in?"

"No, sir. I want the best car on this lot."

He raised an eyebrow at the young woman. "The best car on my car lot is a dark blue Dodge Magnum with a Hemi engine. That's a big car for such a small, pretty, young lady like yourself. It also has a big sticker price to go along with it."

"Well, Mr. Perkins, I like riding on big things, if you know what I mean. I've got five thousand in cash and an *O*-three Mazda to use as a trade-in."

The man laughed and shook his head. "That's not going to get you a forty-thousand-dollar car, young lady."

Disaya leaned back on his desk and spread her legs seductively. "We should be able to work something out. I've got something that's worth more than gold."

Bill Perkins shut his door and closed the blinds to his office window. When he turned around, Disaya could see the bulge in his slacks. *I'm getting ready to start tricking niggas for a living anyway. I might as well start with him,* she thought to herself.

The dealer actually wasn't a bad-looking man. He appeared to be in his early fifties, and his graying facial hair gave him a mature look. She stuck one finger in her pussy and then lifted her finger to his lips. "Come taste me," she said, licking her sweet, glossy lips.

He licked her wetness off her fingers as he grinded his hardness against her body. "Hmm," he moaned. He began to nibble gently on her neck.

The man's hands sent a tingle up Disaya's spine. He moved with the expertise of a Casanova. Disaya knew that he had to have seduced many women in his day. He knelt down on one knee and slipped his tongue into her pussy, twirling it in circles inside of her. She moaned so loudly that she was sure the entire establishment knew what was taking place inside the office. His head game was on point, and she couldn't help but enjoy it. The man inserted two fingers into her opening as his tongue tap-danced on her clitoris. She moved her hips like a belly dancer, pressing her vagina firmly against his mouth. He was giving her so much pleasure, she couldn't help but grind back.

He put his hands underneath her skirt and gripped both of her ass cheeks. He massaged them as he helped her grind her pussy on his tongue. He reached down with one hand and began to stroke himself while he pleasured her.

Disaya looked down and saw the thick, juicy eight inches he was working with. *Damn, I should've brought some condoms,* she thought as she watched his hand move up and down his shaft. The look of pleasure on his face brought her to a climax, and she felt herself cum. He didn't seem to mind, and seconds later he grunted loudly as he erupted.

Disaya stood up and fixed her skirt. "Is that payment enough for you?" she asked.

The sexually suppressed man looked up at her and then climbed to his feet. It had been a long time since he had done something freaky. His wife was an older, more reserved woman who had already been through menopause. Disaya had no clue how much joy she'd just given him.

"Just let me draw up the paperwork. I do have to warn you, I can get you off the lot today with, say, half of the bill taken care of. You'll still have to make payments on the car every month until the remaining balance is taken care of."

Once I roll the car off the lot, it's mine anyway. The repo man won't be able to find my ass, let alone my car, she thought. "I understand," she said aloud.

Bill Perkins gave her a credit of twenty-five thousand for the Dodge Magnum and then drew up the paperwork in Jessica Simpson's name. Disaya couldn't help the smile that spread across her face when he handed her the keys.

He walked her to the car and opened the door for her. "Don't hesitate to stop by if you ever need a tune-up," he offered with a wink as he wiped his beard.

Without responding, she put the car into drive and peeled out of the parking lot.

Disaya and Mona sat in the Magnum with the windows down, singing along with Young Berg and bouncing in their seats to the beat. The parking lot of the car wash was packed as everyone pulled up trying to show off what they were riding in. It was the middle of August, and everybody who was anybody in Harlem knew that this was the place to be on a Friday night. Disaya's new car sparkled underneath the street lights that illuminated the lot. She was proud of herself because she knew that she was hanging with the big boys, as far as her whip was concerned.

The girls stepped out of the car, dressed to impress, and they both hopped onto the hood of the car.

"Bitch, don't fuck up my paint job." YaYa eased her body onto her hood. Her factory speakers were turned up to the max, and both girls grooved to the mix CD that was pumping from the car.

There were people everywhere getting their smoke and drink on. Half-naked girls walked from one end of the parking lot to the other, trying to grab attention from the local hustlers, and dudes were falling for the bait. Everybody was chilling, though, having a good time.

Disaya and Mona sparked up a blunt and then fell into a puff-puff-pass rotation, the weed taking their minds to another level.

A car pulled up beside them, and a familiar voice shouted out, "Yo, let me get some of that."

Mona looked over at the black-on-black Lincoln Navigator, and a smile spread across her face. "What up, Bay?" she said loudly. She hopped off the car and stepped to his window.

He nodded his head at YaYa. "What up, YaYa, girl? Don't be acting all new like you don't know nobody," he said playfully.

YaYa threw up the peace sign, leaned back on her hood, and continued to get blunted.

"I see you shining, baby girl," he yelled, laughter in his voice as he noticed her new car. Bay owned the car wash that everyone was parlaying. He was a hustler and was getting big money around town. He was smart, though, and opened up several front businesses with his dirty money, the car wash being one of many.

"Just a little bit," she replied with a smile. She inhaled the smoke and held it down for a minute before blowing it out.

"Y'all trying to get into something?" he asked.

Mona and Bay had been fucking around since forever. They were each other's jump-off, and YaYa always felt out of place when she was around them. "Hell no, Bay," YaYa told him. "Every time we chill with you, y'all mu'fuckas be all hugged up and shit, leaving me feeling like the ugly friend and shit. I ain't no damn third wheel."

"Come on now, YaYa. You know you far from ugly. You got these chickens beat by a mile. Besides, I'm supposed to be meeting my man at the spot, so we can all just chill. I got some Goose at the crib. Baby, you know that's your juice."

Disaya smiled at Bay as she shook her head from side to side. She had to admit that the nigga knew her well. They had grown up in the same hood together and had always been cool. She had taken her first sip of alcohol with him when she was fifteen. He had gotten her pissy off Grey Goose, and she was hurling for days.

"Whatever, Bay. You and Mona, go do y'all thing. I can't mess with y'all tonight," she said as she continued to lean back on her car.

"YaYa, come on, girl." Mona gave her best friend the sad face. She knew that YaYa wouldn't be able to tell her no.

"All right, damn. You know you ain't right for pulling out that damn face. I'll follow y'all over there. Bay, this nigga better not be ugly!" Disaya got down off her car and threw the roach onto the ground.

She was feeling the effects of the weed as she followed closely behind Bay's car. When she pulled onto his street, she noticed that there was a pearl white Cadillac STS sitting in front of Bay's crib. *At least the nigga riding right,* she thought to herself as she stepped out of her car. She wore long khaki gauchos and a peach-colored strapless top. Her heels tied around her ankles and showed off her perfectly French-manicured toes, and defined calf muscles. She watched as a tall, brown-skinned dude stepped out of the vehicle. He wore light denim Evisu shorts. They were baggy, but not to the point where his ass was showing, and matched the white Bape polo shirt he was rocking. He was fly, and the way he wore his fitted NY Yankees hat low over his eyes gave him a mysterious look.

Mona whispered to Disaya, "He ain't ugly."

"Nah. He definitely ain't that," she said as he approached.

The girls watched as Bay slapped hands with the dude. They both walked over, and the introductions began.

"Yo, this my dude Indie." Bay unlocked his door and pulled Mona's hand, practically dragging her into the house.

Before she fully disappeared into the house, she yelled, "It was nice to meet you, Indie. I'm Mona. This is my girl—" Before she could even finish her sentence, she disappeared up the steps, headed to Bay's bedroom.

Disaya shook her head. She knew that they were going to leave her hanging like that, which was why she didn't want to come.

Indie looked down at Disaya. "And you are?"

"I'm YaYa." She stepped inside the house, walked straight into the kitchen, and went for Bay's liquor cabinet.

Indie sat down at the kitchen table and watched the beautiful girl in front of him.

"You want something to drink?" She tiptoed, trying to reach the top shelf, but Indie came behind her, reached up, and grabbed the bottle with ease.

"Thanks." YaYa looked up at him. *Damn, this nigga is fine.*

She grabbed two glasses and took the Grey Goose bottle into the living room. Bay's place was decked out with a 72-inch big screen and Italian leather furniture. Indie followed behind her and took a seat next to her on the couch. They were both silent as they sat side by side not knowing what to say to one another.

Disaya wasn't normally the shy type, but for some reason she was at a loss for words. "Okay," she said with a laugh, "this is awkward."

"We need to do something about that," he replied with a smile that was so gorgeous, he should've been on toothpaste commercials.

"Okay, I'm gon' keep it real with you. Bay and Mona are always hooking me up with these ugly, crazy mu'fuckas, so I'm a little reluctant to fuck with you. It's obvious that you ain't ugly, but I got a couple questions for you."

Indie smiled at her blunt nature and sat back. "Shoot."

"You got kids?"

"Nah, no kids." Indie leaned back on the couch and extended one leg out, to make himself more comfortable.

"Is that your mama's car you driving?"

Indie started to laugh.

Disaya hit him softly with one of the couch pillows. "I'm serious. Answer the question."

"Let me just clear this up for you right now, ma. I don't know what type of niggas you used to fucking

with, but I'm not one of 'em. I'm a good dude. I don't
drive nothing I don't own. I don't have any kids or crazy
baby mother running around here. If I did have a
shorty, you would know it because I'm a man. And when
I do have kids, I plan on having them with my wife. I
handle my business, I don't lie, and I'm not for the bullshit. I'm straight-up with everybody that I encounter."

Disaya nodded her head in approval. "Okay, I hear
you. Let me ask you this, though. If your shit is tight all
like that, why you ain't got a girl?"

Indie smiled. "Because I'm looking for a woman." He
took a sip of the Grey Goose. "Now, can I get to know
the beautiful woman that is sitting in front of me?"

"I think I can make that happen. But can I ask you
one more question? I promise this will be the last one."

"What up?" he asked with a sexy smirk.

"Are you gay . . . because you seem to be too perfect?"
YaYa burst out laughing.

It was his turn to throw a pillow at her. "Nah, I'm a
hundred percent. That's something you will learn in
time, if you lucky."

Indie and Disaya sat in the living room talking all
night. They practically cleared out Bay's liquor cabinet.
Disaya was impressed with him. He seemed to have his
shit together. He was a real dude, and she enjoyed
being in his company. They even pulled out Bay's Mo-
nopoly game and got it popping.

For the first time, Mona and Bay had hooked her up
with somebody she was actually interested in. They
chilled until four in the morning until they both became tired.

"This bitch is still upstairs with this nigga. I'm about to go home before I pass out," Disaya said with a slur in her voice. She stood up and grabbed her keys. She was tipsy, and her balance was off, causing her to stumble.

"Yo, ma, you can't drive anywhere tonight," Indie said. "Come here." He motioned for YaYa, and she grabbed his hand so he could pull her onto his lap.

"I got to get to the crib," she said, laying her head on his shoulder.

"We'll crash here for tonight. In the morning we'll grab some breakfast, and then I'll make sure you make it home safely." Indie rubbed the top of her head. "That's okay with you?"

"Yeah," she replied, closing her eyes.

Indie chuckled at her as she curled her legs up on the couch. She reminded him of a child as she fell into a light sleep. She was gorgeous. He could tell that she was a little rough around the edges, but he liked her feistiness and was going to make sure that he saw her again.

Bay and Mona came downstairs the next morning and saw their friends laid up together on the couch.

Mona noticed all the empty liquor bottles on the floor. "Looks like she liked him."

"This mu'fucka get all the hoes." Bay chuckled, amazed that Indie was able to charm YaYa.

"YaYa, girl, get up," Mona called out.

"Umm, I'm up. And who you calling a ho, Bay?" she asked drowsily as she began to stir out of her comfortable sleep.

"You know I ain't mean it like that." Bay slapped Disaya hard on her thigh, waking her up fully.

The commotion awakened Indie as well. He gently stroked the top of her head and asked, "You feel better?"

"I feel worse." YaYa moaned. Her stomach was queasy, and her head felt like it would explode from the pounding headache.

"You ready to go?" Mona asked.

"I don't think I can get up right now, Mo," YaYa told her.

"Yo, YaYa, you can crash here for a couple hours until you get yourself together. From the looks of it, you drank yourself into the grave last night. I got to make a couple moves, but you can let yourself out once you straight," Bay offered.

"I'm a little fucked-up myself. I'll crash with you, if that ain't a problem," Indie added.

"Nah, that ain't a problem." Disaya tossed her keys to Mona. "Mo, don't fuck my shit up."

"Bye, girl. Call me when you make it home." Mona kissed Bay on the cheek. "Don't do anything I wouldn't do!" she yelled as she walked out the door.

Bay left shortly after her, leaving Indie and YaYa alone.

"How you feel?" Indie asked her.

She was still lying on his chest, and it felt good to be in the arms of a man. It had been so long since she was seriously attracted to someone. "My stomach is killing me. What about you?"

"I'm good. I don't get too fucked-up. I can handle my liquor. I just wanted to make sure you were straight."

She sat up and looked at him in the eyes. "You seem like you're a good dude."

"Why do you sound surprised?"

She shrugged her shoulders. "I don't know. Niggas ain't built right these days. You just seem different."

"I'll take that as a compliment," he said. "You hungry?"

She nodded and then slowly rose to her feet. She excused herself and went to the bathroom. *Damn, I look tore up.* She stared in the mirror at her disheveled appearance. She opened Bay's medicine cabinet and squeezed some toothpaste on her finger. She tried her best to get her teeth clean without a toothbrush, not wanting to be all in Indie's face with stank breath. She straightened her hair with her fingers. It wasn't that bad. It had a wild look to it, but she figured it would have to do.

Let me go back downstairs before he think I'm up here shitting or something. She hurried back to the living room.

"You ready?"

"Yeah, we can go." YaYa followed him to his car, and to her surprise, he opened the door for her. *Yeah, this dude is definitely different than most. His game is nice. I might have to give him the goodies.*

They drove to IHOP and ate breakfast together. Disaya ordered an omelet and pancakes to soak up some of the liquor from the night before. Disaya was tearing into her food when she noticed Indie laughing at her. "What's so funny?" she asked with a mouthful of food.

"You killing that omelet."

"What, you thought I was one of them girls that don't eat?" YaYa laughed. She looked at Indie and wondered what it would be like to be his woman. She knew that he would treat her right. She could just vibe with him. They clicked in a major way, but she knew that at that moment in her life there was only room for one love—the love for money. She had just gotten down with Elite and was trying to get her paper up. And that was her first priority.

After breakfast Indie dropped her off at her apartment. She was reluctant to get out of the car because she was having such a good time. "Thanks for breakfast, Indie. I had a good time with you."

"You ain't got to thank me, ma. Get at me if you want to do it again."

"I just might do that," she replied in a seductive tone.

He got out of the car and opened her car door.

"Why do you do stuff like that?" she asked in a sincere tone. She'd never met a man like Indie. His swagger was hood, he dressed like a hood nigga, walked like a hood nigga, and it was obvious that he was getting money like a hood nigga, but he wasn't the average dude. The way he treated her had her open. He was a gentleman, and that was something she'd never encountered.

He touched her chin. "Because you deserve it."

She wanted to reach up and kiss him, but she knew her breath was foul. Instead, she put her arms around him and stood on her tiptoes to hug him. "Thank you, Indie. I had fun." She pulled a pen out of her purse and wrote her number on the inside of his hand. "Call me," she said, making eye contact with him. She walked away, letting the natural sway of her hips hypnotize him. She turned around just before she disappeared through the doors. He was watching her, just as she knew he would be. She smiled and waved before closing the door behind her.

Disaya was on cloud nine as she walked into her apartment. She couldn't stop thinking about Indie. He was perfect, and she was feeling him to the fullest. She reluctantly took a long hot shower. She didn't want to rinse the smell of his Issey Miyake off her, but she knew that she had to. She crawled into bed and drifted into a mind-numbing sleep.

Just as she began to dream, she felt the vibration of her Sidekick. She thought that maybe it was Indie, so she jumped up to answer her phone. She saw that she had a message from Ronnie B, and her mind quickly refocused on money. *Hell yeah, it's about damn time,* she thought. She had expected to get right to work, but it had been almost a week since she had linked up with Elite. She flipped up the Sidekick and read the message: *I got a job for you. Come to the Marriott on Lexington and 51st tonight at 11 P.M. It's time.*

Chapter Five

Disaya and Mona stepped into the building. Each girl had their own thoughts racing through their minds. They didn't know what to expect and were silent as they made their way to the top floor of the hotel.

"I'm nervous, YaYa," Mona said, as they watched the numbers to the elevator slowly change.

"Me too. We'll be all right, though. Let's just go in here and make the money. Don't let the money make you. You don't have to do anything that you don't want to. If you start getting uncomfortable, we'll dip, okay?" Disaya said, trying to reassure Mona just as much as herself.

"Okay." Mona nervously took a deep breath to calm her nerves.

Disaya stepped off the elevator first and was amazed when she saw that the entire top floor of the hotel was one huge presidential suite. She was even more shocked to see the Miami Heat basketball team lounging around the room. The first familiar face that she noticed was Leah's.

Leah was chilling with the star center for the team. She walked over to them and smiled. "Y'all ready?"

Mona and Disaya didn't respond verbally, but they nodded their heads to signal yes.

Leah chuckled seductively as she looked them both up and down. She recognized their nervousness. "Calm down," she said. "This is easy. These are the easiest clients to please. Professional ballplayers can't get too freaky because they're in the spotlight. They're only in town for the night. They just came back from the Garden, so they're really just trying to kick back. All you really have to do is be good company, you know, show them a good time. Mona, you start over there with some of the other girls. YaYa, you can come with me."

Disaya followed Leah over to the sectional sofa, where the starting five players were. Disaya fit in nicely with the group as she joined in on their casual conversation. The longer she was there, the easier it got. She began to feel like she was having a good time with close friends instead of a group of people she barely knew.

Disaya noticed that one of the players was distant. He didn't talk much. When he got up and headed out to the balcony, she decided to follow him. She got up and slid open the glass door that led to the balcony. She walked over to him with two champagne flutes in her hand. "You look like you need this." She handed him one of the glasses. The midnight air was cool against her skin, and the atmosphere on the balcony was much quieter than inside the suite.

He turned around and looked down at her. "Thanks." He guzzled the expensive champagne.

"I'm a big fan, Mr. MVP," she said with a smile.

He looked her up and down as he licked his lips. "I wouldn't expect someone like you to follow sports."

"I don't follow sports, just you." She slid her body between him and the railing to the balcony.

He smiled. "I heard about y'all New Yitty chicks."

"Oh yeah? Well, what exactly did you hear? I can tell you if it's true or not," she said, obviously flirting. She sipped her champagne.

"You don't have to tell me. I can see that it's true just by looking at you."

Disaya replied with a sexy laugh. "Oh, you really got to tell me what you heard now, since you claim I fit the description."

"It's nothing bad. I just hear that y'all some go-getters up here. Y'all see what y'all want and y'all go after it. I hear it ain't nothing like a New York woman. Y'all know how to put it down."

"That's true, at least in my case."

He whispered in her ear, "See you trying to get me in trouble," and showed her his wedding band.

"I would never do that. I'm not trying to come between that. I just want to show you a good time, let you know that you've got something warm to get into when you come to such a cold city." Seduction oozed off of YaYa's every word, and she could feel the bulge grow in his Armani slacks. "You know you want to," she whispered in his ear, letting her tongue wet his earlobe as she pulled away. "If you didn't, you wouldn't be here."

He put his arms around her waist and palmed her ass tightly, pulling her into his crotch. A small moan escaped his lips.

When he lifted her onto the railing of the balcony, her heart began to pound frantically, and she could feel her womanhood creaming in anticipation. "What are you doing?" she asked nervously as she looked down twenty stories.

"Shh. Trust me," he said.

He began to kiss on her neck and massage her breasts, making her pussy instantly drip with wetness. She couldn't believe she was getting ready to have sex with one of the most talented players in the NBA. She spread her legs, and he put his hands underneath her Prada dress. Then she unzipped his pants and pulled his manhood out of its confinement. *Damn,* she thought to herself as she looked down at his length. She pulled a condom out of her bra and gently slid it onto him. "See, I'm not trying to trap you. I just want to please you, daddy." She moaned as he maneuvered himself into her.

He easily filled the space between her legs with his nine inches. He pushed her head back as he moved in and out of her, using deep, passionate thrusts.

Seeing how high up she was as her upper body hung over the balcony filled her heart with fear, not to mention she was having sex out in the open on a balcony where people could see her. The situation caused her body to tremble uncontrollably. She rotated her hips and threw the pussy back at him with a vengeance as he fucked her proper. The street lights below had her in a daze as their lustful encounter took place under the stars.

Oh my God! she thought to herself. She didn't know that dick could be so good. She could feel every muscle in his body working as his athletic frame moved in and out of her. He pulled her up and stayed inside of her as he put her against the balcony window. Her back hit the glass with a thud, causing everyone inside of the presidential suite to focus their attention on the couple outside.

Disaya didn't give a damn who was watching her, though. The nigga was fucking her so right, she was losing her mind. Every time he entered her, he paused deep inside her and rotated his hips, creating friction against her clitoris. She rolled her hips furiously, wrapping her arms around his neck to keep her balance.

Leah looked on in lust at the scene taking place on the balcony. She had definitely underestimated Disaya. She'd thought that YaYa would be afraid to get down for hers, but it was obvious that she had what it took to be down with Elite. Disaya's ass cheeks were pressed against the balcony door, and everyone in the room was in awe of her voluptuous body. *Damn,* Leah thought to herself as he let her hands slip between her crossed legs. She discreetly slipped her middle finger into her pussy and rubbed her clit with her thumb. "Ohh," she moaned quietly. She couldn't take her eyes off of them, nor could anyone else in the suite.

Mona stood in the middle of the room watching her friend get down on the balcony. She wanted to get busy with the player she was chilling with all night, but didn't want Disaya or anyone else to think that she was a ho. But witnessing Disaya in the act, she figured it was okay to get it popping.

One of the players gripped himself through his pants. He asked Mona, "Damn, do you get down like your girl?"

Without saying a word, she grabbed his hand and led him into the bedroom.

Disaya moaned as she felt his dick begin to throb inside of her. "Right there." He pumped in and out of her so hard, she came harder than she ever had in her life.

He finally put her down and kissed her on the lips. "Aww shit, we got an audience," he said as he turned her around.

Disaya's mouth fell open when she realized that she'd just put on a show. She hid her face in his chest as they both stepped back inside the room to an eruption of hoots and hollers.

"Oh my goodness," she mumbled.

"Don't be shy. You're a celebrity now."

They enjoyed the rest of the night with each other, and as promised, Disaya made him feel like he had someone in New York who he could call on the next time he visited.

Disaya had to admit he was mad cool, and the sex was on point. She honestly wouldn't mind if he did get at her the next time he came up.

At the end of the night, he walked her to her car. "How much do I owe you?" He pulled out a checkbook from his pants pocket.

"How much was it worth?"

He shook his head in amazement. He had never encountered a chick like her and knew that she was worth the twenty-thousand-dollar check he was about to write her. He handed it to her and then took off his chain with the number *3* on it and put it around her neck.

Her mouth almost dropped to the floor when she felt the weight of the many carats that sat around her neck.

"Make sure you get at me if you ever come to Miami," he said. He opened her car door, and she got in.

"I will, Mr. MVP." She closed the door and pulled up to the entrance of the hotel, where Mona, Leah, and some of the other girls were standing around saying their goodbyes.

Mona and Leah approached her car. Mona hopped into the back seat, and Leah sat in the passenger side.

"I didn't drive here tonight," Leah said. "You mind if I ride with you?"

Without responding, Disaya sped out of the parking lot, leaving tire tracks on the pavement.

Leah turned toward YaYa. "What the fuck! Bitch, you got game," she said, nodding her head in approval. "I gots to give it to you. You put it down in there for real. I've got to admit, I'm impressed."

Mona noticed the bling around her girlfriend's neck. "Yeah, and you got that nigga to give you his chain."

Leah looked over at the necklace. "Just a word of advice—Don't wear that shit when we go into the spot to meet Ronnie. He'll want a cut of that too. I always keep it one hundred percent when it comes to the cash, but as far as I'm concerned, the extra shit is my tip, feel me?"

Disaya nodded as she pulled into the parking lot of the warehouse. The two-story loft-style warehouse served as the office space and meeting spot for Elite. Disaya removed the chain from her neck and put it in her glove box before stepping out of the car, and they all walked into the building, where they met some of the other girls who had already arrived. She did the math in her head and calculated that she would get six stacks of the twenty-thousand-dollar check in her hand. She frowned when she realized how small her cut actually was, but it didn't matter because the chain in her car was worth at least thirty large.

She walked up the steps to the top of the loft, and the three girls entered Ronnie's office. He had the money that he'd made that night neatly sorted out in thousand-dollar stacks on his desk.

"What's good, baby? How'd it go?" he asked Leah as they sat down across from him.

"Everything was everything. Same shit, different day. We got a new superstar on our hands, though," she said enthusiastically.

He looked over at Disaya and smiled. "So how much did you pull in?"

Disaya put the check in front of her face. "Twenty G's."

Ronnie B nodded his head, excitement filling his eyes. "That's what the fuck I'm talking about!" He took the check and gave her six of the thousand-dollar stacks that sat on his desk. He collected his cut from Mona and Leah then they all got up to leave.

"I'm coming to your crib," Mona told YaYa as they walked out of the building.

"What y'all bitches getting ready to get into?" Leah asked.

"Nothing. Mona ass practically lives at my house. We don't really be doing shit, though, just chilling. Why? You coming through?"

Leah didn't usually chill with females, especially chicks

from Elite, but she didn't have a problem chilling with Mona and YaYa because their hustler's mentality was similar to her own. "Yeah, I'll roll," she said.

The girls headed back to Disaya's, and they instantly vibed. It was weird because Disaya and Mona had never let another chick into their circle, but Leah seemed to fit right in.

"Girl, that nigga had you assed-out on the balcony," Mona teased.

"Hell yeah. Everybody got a peek at that fat ass."

Disaya was so embarrassed, she didn't know what to say. "I couldn't help it. That boy had me in the zone. The dick was so right. I didn't even realize everybody was watching." She asked Leah, "Do you think I went too far?"

"Hell no! I wish I had a damn camcorder. We could've taped that shit and then sold them bitches for like ten dollars apiece."

"Girl, please. I'm not trying to be out here on no-body's tape." Disaya dismissed the thought with a wave of her hand.

They all stayed up clowning and joking until they passed out on the living room floor.

The ringing of Leah's Sidekick woke them up the next morning. She flipped up her screen and read the message that Ronnie B had just sent her: *Leah, I got a job for you and YaYa. This nigga out of DC coming up and he want a* ménage à trois *with two of the best. I don't know if Disaya is down with that girl-on-girl action, but he gon' want to see a lot of it. He's paying big money. Make sure that she's ready. Be at the Marriott in Manhattan tonight at 9.*

Disaya looked around the apartment. "Where's Mo?" She saw a note on the couch.

Leah reached over and grabbed it. She read it aloud. "Bay called me after y'all went to sleep, so I bounced with him. I will catch up with y'all later."

Disaya flipped her hand. "I should've known."

"Who's Bay?"

"This dude we grew up with. Him and Mo been fucking around for a minute, and every chance they get, they hook up." Disaya could still smell the sex on her body and got up and began taking off her clothes. "I'm about to hop in the shower."

Leah realized that she hadn't taken a shower after the previous night's escapades. "You mind if I take one after you?"

"Nah, girl. Make yourself at home. But unless you want to take a shower in ice water, you better just jump in there as soon as I get out. I'll make sure I make it quick."

As Disaya removed the rest of her clothing, Leah watched her as she walked into the bathroom. "Girl, your body is banging," she said. "I wish I wasn't so skinny."

"Leah, please . . . your ass look like a model. You ain't got nothing to worry about. I wish I was your size. Everything I eat goes straight to my ass and hips."

Disaya and Leah made their way into the bathroom and hopped in.

"So how long have you been down with Elite?" YaYa asked, yelling over the sound of the loud shower pipes as she lathered her loofah and spread the suds all over her body.

"A couple years now."

Leah stood in front of the mirror in the bathroom. She looked through YaYa's clear shower curtain, and the silhouette of her body made her moist between the legs. Disaya's curves were perfect. Leah sat down on the toilet and enjoyed the enticing view. She removed the dress that she'd worn the night before. She couldn't stop her hands from making their way to her pussy. She played with her clit with one hand and rolled her nipples between her fingers with the other, while she watched Disaya wash her naked body. She loved playing with herself. No one could make her cum the way she could make herself cum.

The feeling mounting inside of her finally became too much to bear, and she had to see what Disaya's skin felt like. She stood up and pulled back the shower curtain slowly as she stepped inside.

"Whoo!" Disaya yelled out in surprise. "Girl, you scared the shit out of me. What you doing?"

"You said the water get cold quick."

"I'll step out. Let me rinse off," Disaya said.

"Here, let me wash your back."

Disaya handed her the loofah, and Leah rubbed her back gently. Disaya's breath became shallow as she felt Leah's soft hands caress her back.

"YaYa, you are tense, girl." Leah started at the top and rubbed the soap lower and lower until she reached YaYa's ass. She dropped the loofah and began to rub her hands all over Disaya's back. "I give killer back rubs. This should loosen you up."

The feeling of Leah's hands on her body made Disaya's nipples hard. She wasn't sure what was going on between the two of them. *Is this bitch gay?* Disaya didn't say anything. She simply allowed Leah to massage her back. Leah's hands traveled south and ended up massaging YaYa's ass cheeks.

Disaya felt her pussy get wet. She whispered, "What are you doing?"

"Relax, girl. I'm just loosening you up," Leah replied sweetly. She moved her hands around the front of YaYa's body and caressed her breasts. Her nipples were on point, and Leah pinched them gently, causing tingles to shoot up and down YaYa's spine. "You want me to stop?"

"No." YaYa didn't know what the hell had taken over her. She was far from gay, but Leah did something to her. Her touch felt different than any man's.

Leah turned her around, and they stood breast to breast and shared a kiss as the water from the shower sprayed down on them. Leah's mouth found Disaya's nipples, and she suckled on them slowly, rolling her tongue over Disaya's breasts. Leah put her hand between YaYa's legs and felt that her clitoris was hard. She began to grind her own clitoris against YaYa's.

YaYa moaned in a pleasurable tone. "What are you doing to me?"

Leah didn't respond. She simply got on her knees and tantalized YaYa's love button with her tongue until YaYa had an explosive orgasm.

YaYa rinsed her body and hopped out of the shower. A little embarrassed by what had just taken place, she anxiously wrapped a towel around her body. Leah, on the other hand, couldn't have been happier. A bisexual, she was attracted to YaYa since the first day she'd met her. Ronnie B just gave her an excuse to seduce her.

"Are you gay?" YaYa asked her, finally breaking the silence between them.

"No, I'm not gay. I love dick, YaYa, but every once in a while I do like to get my pussy licked right. The only people that I find can do it the way I like it is a woman. Have you ever felt anything like what I did for you in there?"

"No."

"Did you like it?"

"Yeah, I did," YaYa said in an unsure tone.

"Well, then that's that. What we just did don't make you gay. You love dick, but every once in a while, I'll get you right and eat your pussy for you. Truthfully, I had to break you in. There is a lot of girl-on-girl stuff that goes down in Elite. In fact, tonight we're going to the Benjamin for a threesome with this DC cat. He gon' want to see me and you doing our thing anyway, so just consider what we just did practice. Ronnie B couldn't have you going in there looking like an amateur, so he asked me to make sure that you're ready. This is the business, baby. I just happen to be good at it."

With those words, Leah walked her naked body over to Disaya and unwrapped the towel from around her body. "Now, let me get you ready for tonight." Leah lifted one of Disaya's breasts and devoured it. She pushed Disaya down on the bed and climbed on top of her. She smiled when she felt YaYa's clit get hard once again. She rubbed their clits together and kissed Disaya on the lips.

"Wait," Disaya moaned, unsure of what she was doing.

"It's all in the game, YaYa," Leah whispered in her
ear, as they continued to bump coochies.

"It's just business?" Disaya asked as she grinded back.

"That's it, just business, YaYa. Now, just lay here and
let me make you cum like you never have before."

YaYa and Leah stepped in the lobby of the luxurious
Benjamin Hotel wearing nothing but trench coats.
Their stilettos clicked across the floor as they made
their way to the elevator. They took it to Room 222 and
knocked. A fat, sloppy-looking dude opened the door
and invited them in.

They walked in, and he immediately pounced on
them. Sweating profusely, he was already pissy drunk,
and Disaya could smell the 151 reeking from his pores.
He had nothing on but a pair of boxers, his penis dangling out of the slit in the front, and was stroking himself in anticipation.

He tried to kiss Leah in the mouth, but she felt as if
she would gag from the stench. She wanted to get him
as far away from her as she could. She pushed him off.
"Lie on the bed and enjoy the show."

Disaya looked down at the drunken mess that lay on
the bed. Then she looked at dude in disgust. *This big,
fat, nasty-looking mu'fucka.* "What type of shit is this?" she
mouthed to Leah.

Never having encountered a client like this, Leah
shrugged in a state of confusion. She knew he had to be
working with big chips, though, if Ronnie B was mess-

ing with him. "Let's freshen up real quick." She hurriedly pulled YaYa into the bathroom.

"Call Ronnie right now," Disaya whispered.

Leah pulled out her Sidekick and dialed his number. "He's not picking up," she said nervously. "Look, this dude must have some money, so let's just do the job and get up out of here."

"Fine by me."

They headed back into the room.

"Hurry up and show me something," the dude said.

Both girls dropped their coats. Before he could touch them, they began kissing each other. It wasn't sensual like it had been earlier, but rushed and exaggerated. They just wanted to give him a show, so he would take care of himself and they could get paid then go home.

"Let me join in." He pulled Disaya down onto the bed and prepared to enter her.

Disaya stopped him. "Hold up, dude! You ain't going in me raw. You better put on a condom."

"What! I told Ron B I don't do condoms. I paid that nigga extra for it too," he said aggressively as he prepared to stick himself inside her.

Leah pulled the guy off YaYa. "Hold up! We don't go without protection. And what do you mean, you already paid Ron B?"

"He asked for twenty stacks up front, ma. He charged me extra to go in raw."

"Look, you need to take your problem up with Ronnie B. We don't get down like that. Let's go, YaYa."

They put on their trench coats.

"What the fuck you mean, let's go? I paid cash money

for y'all stank bitches. I'm about to get something from somebody!" he yelled.

"Okay, daddy, fuck it. We game," Leah said, trying to calm the guy down. "Lay down, baby," she told him.

He calmed down and lay on the bed, with his dick in his hand.

"You want me to suck it for you?" she asked in a seductive, whiny voice. "Can I put it in my mouth?"

"Yeah, put it in your mouth, baby girl," he moaned, closing his eyes.

Disaya threw up in her mouth a little bit when she saw Leah take him into her mouth.

Leah sucked on it seductively while he pushed her head down on him forcefully, his eyes still closed. Out of nowhere, she bit down on him with all her might.

"Awww!"

"Oh shit!"

"Bitch, let's go!" Leah yelled.

They both scrambled into their coats and rushed out of the room. Down the hallway, they heard ol' boy screaming into his cell phone and assumed he was talking to Ronnie.

Both girls were furious as they drove toward the Elite warehouse. "I know Ronnie ain't trying to pull dirty on me," Leah said. "He knows that the money supposed to go through our hands first."

They slammed their car doors as they arrived and raced up the stairs to Ronnie B's office. "What the fuck is wrong with you?" Leah yelled as soon as she saw him.

Ronnie B didn't say anything. But he did haul off and slap the shit out of her. Blood flew from her mouth from the force of the blow. "Bitch, you walked out on one of my clients. You damn near took his dick off! That nigga paid ten large to fuck with y'all bitches and you just gon' walk out? You making me look bad," he said as Leah held her face in shock.

"Fuck you, Ronnie! You already know that ain't no nigga running in me raw. I'm not about to be out here catching AIDS for your ass. Then the nigga paid you— What the fuck he paying you for, huh? You ain't the one opening your legs for the fat, sloppy mu'fucka. You said he paid ten?"

"Yeah, bitch, he paid ten!" Ronnie yelled back.

"You lying, dirty-ass nigga, he already told us he gave you double that."

"I'll pay y'all bitches what I want to." He walked away from her and sat back down at the table.

"No, Ronnie, you gon' pay us what you owe us. The cut already seventy-thirty, which is some bullshit for what you do—As a matter of fact, fuck you. I don't need you. I know half of your clientele personally anyway. I don't need you pimping me. I can get my own gwop!" Leah stormed out of the room and left Disaya standing there staring at Ronnie B.

"So what you gon' do, YaYa? We don't need her. That bitch pussy drying up anyway."

Disaya thought to herself, *Nah, her pussy far from dry.*

"You can take her place as the *HBIC*," Ronnie offered.

Disaya shook her head and walked away. She couldn't believe that she had thought being down with Elite was where the money was at. Leah was right. They could branch out on their own and make a hundred percent of the profits. They didn't need Ronnie B.

Mona was standing at the bottom of the stairs with a couple other members of Elite when Disaya came racing down the steps. "YaYa, you okay?" she asked in concern.

"Yeah, I'm good. Get your stuff. We out." Disaya looked behind her, to see Ronnie B standing at the top of the loft.

"What you mean, we out?" Mo asked.

"We don't need this nigga. We can get this money on our own."

Ronnie B came down the stairs and stood next to Mona. He put his arm around her. "Come on, ma, don't listen to these hoes. You can run all of this. You can take Leah's place at the top. You the head bitch of Elite now. You gon' give all that up to go back to how you used to live?"

"Mo, don't listen to him. He's grimy," Disaya pleaded.

Ronnie B pulled out a wad of hundred-dollar bills and handed them to Mona. "Can you get this much money anywhere else?" he asked her.

Mona took the money. "I'm staying, YaYa."

"Mo!" Disaya yelled out to her friend.

Mona never looked back as she ascended the steps with Ronnie B.

Chapter Six

Six Months Later . . .

Disaya decided to treat herself to a day of shopping. She had been stressing out over Mona for the past few months. Leah found out that Ronnie B was messed up behind them leaving, becoming violent and controlling, to prevent any of his other girls from leaving. He was making all of his girls take ecstasy on a daily, so that they would be even freakier for his clients. He even decreased their cut to twenty percent, so a lot of his girls, including Mona began to turn tricks on the side. Leah had even told YaYa that she'd seen Mona walking the ho stroll, just to make extra money.

Ronnie B was having a hard time competing with Disaya and Leah. Money was indeed flowing like water. They discovered that word of mouth was the best marketing scheme, and they also took advantage of the Internet. They set up their own website called www.prada

panties.com, and they became a hot commodity online. They were getting thousands of hits each day, and everybody from rappers, hustlers, and ballplayers were recruiting their services. They took professional pictures in seductive poses and posted them on their site. They also had live chats for 20 minutes for $19.99. They were making bank for real and living the life. Disaya's Prada plan was actually coming true. She now had money coming in consistently and stayed laced in her favorite designers. It sometimes bothered her that she had to spread her legs and drop her morals to achieve her dreams, but the constant flow of money clouded her judgment and made everything that she was doing seem worth it.

Disaya walked out of her house and got into her Magnum. She drove over to Fifth Avenue and Fifty-seventh Street to her favorite jewelry store, Tiffany's. She was getting ready to lace herself in diamonds because she felt like she deserved it.

She walked into the store and stopped at the first display. It displayed dozens of diamond engagement rings. She traced her hand over the top of the display as she admired the beautiful jewelry.

"Shopping for that special ring?" a blond salesman asked. He had a feminine tone to his voice.

Disaya immediately noticed his gay swagger. "Oh no . . . I was just looking," she said.

"Would you like to try one on?" he asked.

Before Disaya could reply, the salesman had taken out the canary yellow 2 ½-carat diamond ring. "Is this the one that you had your eye on?" he asked.

Disaya nodded as she held out her finger. He slid it on for her, and she admired the flawless quality of the stone. "Damn!" she exclaimed in a whisper. She could see herself rocking that ring one day.

"It's almost as beautiful as the woman that's wearing it," a voice behind her said.

She turned around and smiled when she saw the familiar face. She hadn't heard from him since they had chilled together at Bay's house, but he looked just as good as the last time she'd seen him.

"It looks like I'm too late, huh?" Indie nodded toward the ring she was trying on.

"What? Oh no! I was just trying it on," she said, embarrassed. She took it off and handed it back to the salesman.

"How have you been?"

He still had the same gangster swagger and was fresh in Sean John jeans and a black button-up with a matching fitted cap.

"I've been all right. Don't be acting like you interested now. You never called," she said sweetly.

"Nah, ma, it's not even like that. I've had a lot to handle, you know. Business first, shorty."

When they walked out of the store, she noticed that he was gripping a different car this time, riding in a burgundy Nissan Maxima.

"Well, it was good to see you again, but I got business to take care of," she stated smartly as she walked toward her car.

"Whoa, whoa!" He grabbed her arm gently, stopping her from walking away. "Okay, I deserve that. Let me make it up to you."

"I'm straight. I don't fuck with niggas that don't put me first. I got to be a priority," she said, moving her neck with every word, her arms folded across her chest.

"You know you sexy when you mad. I noticed that when I first met you. When you're upset about something, you chew on your bottom lip," he said. "I don't want to be the reason why you hot, ma. Let me take you out."

Disaya rolled her eyes at him, but she couldn't help but to forgive him. *The nigga got an A game. I got to give him that,* she thought. "Okay, you can take me out, but you got some making up to do."

She parked her car in a parking garage around the corner and then hopped into the car with him. They continued their day of shopping along Fifth and Madison Avenue. She purchased so many clothes and shoes that she had a hard time carrying everything. She quickly found out that Indie loved to shop just as much as her. She was clocking his pockets too. He was working with major chips, and a part of her wondered how he made it. The nigga even had the audacity to whip out a black card to purchase his items. *Those joints are invitation only. This nigga is definitely paid,* she thought to herself as she admired the sexy man in front of her.

"So what is it that you do?" she asked him as they walked down the block.

Indie didn't respond right away. He stopped walking and looked down at her. "I peep your style, YaYa. I know you ain't new to game. You not one of these little naïve chicks out here, so I'm gon' keep it real with you. I'm not proud of what I do, but it's all I know how to do. I'm getting money. You know, me and Bay, we doing our thing right now. I don't plan on being in this spot forever, but right now it is what it is."

"You don't have to explain that to me, Indie. I'm not exactly where I want to be in life either. I understand you doing what you got to do to stay on top. I respect that."

They continued walking until they got back to his car. As he put all of her bags into the trunk, she couldn't stop staring at him.

"What you looking at?"

"You." She reached up to kiss him, and he put his arm around her waist and pulled her close as they continued to kiss.

"Indie, I like you, but you ain't ready for a girl like me." Disaya pulled away from him.

"You something else. You know that, right? Let me get to know you. Come away with me for the weekend. We'll fly out to Vegas and do it big."

"What's in Vegas?" she asked skeptically.

"The De La Hoya-Mayweather fight. You don't have to worry about money or nothing. I got you. Just come with me."

Leah lay across Disaya's bed as she watched her girl pack her clothes. She was jealous that she was going to Vegas without her. "Who is this dude you going with?" she asked.

"His name's Indie. I met him a while back."

"Well, how long are you going to be gone? You know the website is popping. We got dudes lined up to fuck with us."

"We'll only be gone for a couple days, so I'll be back in time."

"All right, girl. Well, you want me to tighten you up before you go?" Leah licked her lips seductively, thinking about how sweet YaYa tasted.

One of the reasons why she loved being in business with Disaya was because she loved the way her pussy tasted. Disaya didn't know it, but Leah was becoming attached to her in a big way, and she didn't like the fact that Disaya was so geeked over her weekend getaway with Indie. *I'm gon' have to get rid of this nigga,* she thought to herself.

"He's a real dude, Leah. He don't bullshit or try to game me. He keep it one hundred with me. That's why I like him."

On the inside Leah was steamed. "You think he's feeling you the same way?" she asked, pretending to be happy for her. Even though YaYa only let her get the goodies when they were making money, Leah still didn't want to share it with some dude, especially if he wasn't paying.

"I don't know, but we'll see this weekend."

Disaya stepped off the plane and fell in love with the city of Las Vegas, Nevada almost instantly, with its palm trees and slot machines everywhere. It felt good to be in a completely different atmosphere.

"You wait for the bags. I'll go grab a rental." Indie kissed Disaya softly on the lips before leaving her side.

She couldn't believe she was here with him and couldn't wait to get out of the airport. After about twenty minutes, their bags finally arrived. She picked them up and then stepped outside, where Indie was waiting curbside with a rented Hummer.

"Are you serious? This is where we staying?" she asked in disbelief when they arrived at the Bellagio Hotel and Casino. She looked up at the gorgeous hotel to see the lit-up fountain spraying straight into the air.

Indie laughed at her. "This is it, shorty. What? This ain't good enough?"

"Hell yeah, this good enough. I've never stayed in anything better than the Holiday Inn, so I'm in heaven right now."

They made their way up to the deluxe suite, where Disaya collapsed onto the bed. "Oh my goodness. I love Vegas. I love this room. I love this life." She sat up and looked at him. "I could live like this, for real."

Indie made his way over to her and sat next to her. He opened one of his suitcases, which contained nothing but money.

"Indie, you brought all that money for four days?"

"Yeah. It's only a hundred stacks. You got to do it big while you're in Vegas. Ain't no half-stepping. Besides, half of it is yours."

"Don't lie!" she yelled.

"I don't lie. I want you to have a good time." He pulled stacks of money out of the suitcase and set it in front of her. "This is yours."

She reached over to him and kissed him passionately on the lips, and he kissed her back. Then she tried to ease in between his legs.

He stopped her. "You don't have to do that. I'm not trying to buy you, YaYa. I brought you here so that I could get to know you better. I'm feeling you, and I'm at a point in my life where I'm looking for one chick to be with."

YaYa blushed. "You think that chick is me?"

He cleared the hair from her face. "I don't know. That's what I'm trying to find out." He got up and opened a door that led to another room. "This is your room. I'll be right next door if you need me."

"You're not sleeping in here with me?" she asked with a pout.

"Nah, ma. You ain't just a jump-off to me. I respect you, so I'm gon' treat you like a woman. Let me ask you something." He walked back over to where she was sitting. "Could you see yourself being with me?"

"I don't know. I want to see myself being with you. I want to be with you. It just seems like your expectations are so high." YaYa could feel the tears welling in her eyes. She knew Indie would never mess with her if he knew what she did to get by.

"Let me give you some game, Disaya. You are beautiful, but you don't respect yourself. You flaunt your sexuality, and believe me, ma, I see you. But I also want to get inside your head. I don't want to fuck you. I fuck hoes. I want to get to know you, and I want to learn to love you. Yeah, I want to know your body, because you was definitely blessed in that department. But if you gon' be wifey one day, I got to respect you first. You a little rough around the edges, and I'm willing to groom you, yo, but you got to let me know that this is what you want to do." He wiped the tears from her face and kissed her on the lips. "These tears let me know that you want to change."

"You don't know how badly," she mumbled to herself. It was the first time that she had actually began to regret how she was living her life. Indie pulled out strange emotions from within her. Being around him, a man who respected her so much, made her want to respect herself.

Indie stood up and headed for the door. "Get gorgeous, shorty. There's a dress for you in the closet. I'm about to hit the casino. The fight starts at nine. I'll meet you downstairs, all right?"

Disaya nodded her head and watched him as he walked out of the room. He had given her a lot to think about. His words almost made her feel ashamed. It was almost like Indie could see right through her. *If I tell him about what I've been through, will he be able to look past it?*

She put on a black Valentino baby doll dress. It flowed when she walked and gave a subtle view of her Coke-bottle figure. She put on matching heels and added her Tiffany accessories to accent the beautiful dress. She had never dressed up like that before, and she was in awe of herself as she stood in front of the mirror. She actually felt like a lady. She pulled her hair up in a loose ponytail that was held up by a diamond-studded clip. She applied a light bronzer to her face and a neutral-colored eye shadow to her eyes, giving her a striking appearance.

A tear slipped down her face as she turned around in the mirror. She stepped out of the room and made her way down toward the casino. She was eager for Indie to see her like this. She hoped that she could change his perception of her. She stepped into the casino and sparkled underneath the dim lights. As she walked toward the craps table, all the men standing around it focused their attention on her.

She smiled at the way Indie shook the dice close to

his ear as he prepared to toss the ivory. She stood at the opposite end of the table from him.

When he finally looked up, his jaw dropped in surprise. He paused for a second as he admired her transformation. A sly smile spread across his lips. He finally threw the dice, and the dealers yelled, "Yo! Eleven winner!"

When she walked over to him, he pulled her in front of him. He stood behind her and wrapped his arms around her waist. "This is how I want my wifey to be," he whispered in her ear as he kissed her neck.

The dealers brought the dice back toward Indie.

"Shoot something, lil' mama," he challenged her, whispering the words in her ear.

YaYa then picked up the dice and tossed them onto the table.

Leah lay in her bed and played in her pussy, with the phone to her ear. She was talking to Nanzi, a go-getter in Harlem who was getting money. She had contacted him a couple days earlier to see if he was interested in what she and Disaya had to offer him. He was game and was willing to pay big money for a night of fun with the two girls. He'd heard that they were skilled in the art of seduction and was trying to see how they got down.

Leah couldn't go through with the meeting without Disaya. She needed her to be there. Her plans for him wouldn't work if Disaya wasn't there. She was trying to keep the nigga at bay until YaYa got back into town, so she gave him her number so they could talk.

"You got my pussy wet with all that you talking," Leah said seductively over the phone. She had been having

phone sex with Nanzi for a couple days, trying to keep
him interested in her proposition. She wanted him to
know that she was a freak and had promised that she
would turn him out as soon as Disaya could join in.

"Why don't you let me come handle that for you?"
Nanzi asked.

"Nah, I got to wait for my girl. Don't worry though.
She comes home in a couple days. It's gon' be worth
the wait. Her head game is on point. Believe me, I
know."

"Y'all get down like that? With each other?" he asked,
intrigued.

"Yeah, daddy. We get down however you want us to
get down."

She couldn't wait until Disaya came back from Vegas.
She knew that Nanzi was the answer to all of her problems. She was about to get paid.

Disaya and Indie were having a great time at the
casino. Indie was infatuated with her and made her feel
like she was worth something.

"Can I tell you something?" Disaya asked.

"What up, baby?"

"I think I want to change for you."

"Show me, ma. That's all I ask. A lot of people talk,
and I hear what you're saying, but actions speak louder
than words. Now can I tell you something?"

She didn't respond, so he took it as his cue to continue speaking.

"I'm feeling you, and if you let me, I want to take care
of you."

Disaya smiled graciously as her heartbeat sped up. She was speechless. She really didn't know what to say.

Indie changed the subject as he looked at his phone and noticed that it was almost time for the fight to begin. "You ready to see a mu'fucka get knocked out?" Indie asked as he led her through the casino and out onto the busy streets.

The Las Vegas strip looked like a carnival. The lights and attractions from the different casinos were quite a sight.

"I heard 50 Cent supposed to be walking Mayweather out," Disaya shouted as they entered the MGM. She could barely hear herself above all of the chatter in the arena.

"Yeah, I heard that too. You know that's a flashy-ass nigga. He about to give it to De la Hoya," Indie commented as they found their seats.

Disaya noticed how close they were to the ring. She looked to her right and noticed that they were seated among the stars. She knew that Indie had broken bread for the seats. They would have a perfect view of the fight. Disaya didn't really care for sports, but just the fact that she was sitting next to Indie made her night enjoyable. She tried to imagine what life would be like if she chose to take him up on his offer. *He wants to take care of me.* She looked at the gorgeous man sitting to her right. She tried not to think about anything but the present, as she enjoyed herself.

After the fight, they resumed their casino antics and did it real big at the craps tables.

Indie and Disaya retired to their room at four A.M.

She stopped in the hallway because she was unsure where he was going to sleep. She finally gathered the nerve to ask him, "Will you sleep with me tonight?"

He opened the door for her, and they went inside. He unzipped the back of her dress and eased it off of her shoulders. With his arms wrapped around her waist, he kissed the nape of her neck and guided her to the bed. He stripped down to his boxers and then lay on the bed. He grabbed YaYa's hand and pulled her down next to him.

Disaya's head found a comfortable place on his chest, and she closed her eyes as he stroked her hair until she fell asleep.

Disaya woke up the next morning and found Indie sleeping soundly beside her. He was so damn fine to her, and she was really hoping that he could see a future with her. He made her feel so special the night before, made her realize that she was worth so much more. She was selling her soul to the devil just to make some quick cash, and without even knowing it, he had given her the strength to change her life. For that alone, she was in love with the man. All she had to do now was get him to love her back.

She kissed his chest and worked her way down until she reached his manhood, and took that morning hard-on all into her mouth.

Indie stirred in his sleep and awoke to the pleasure that she was giving him. "Yo, what you doing?" he asked groggily.

His protests quickly turned into moans, as she put her professional head game into effect. His muscular frame tightened up as she pleased him, and he felt like he would explode at any moment. He curled his toes, trying to stop the pressure that was building up in his body.

"Hold up," he said, switching into the 69 position. He stuck his tongue between her legs and licked her pussy gently, almost like a cat drinking milk, and Disaya moved her hips and head in unison as she sucked him like a lollipop.

Indie slipped his tongue into her asshole, causing her to cum instantly. She was always disgusted by dudes who wanted to play with her ass, but Indie was the exception. He made her feel so good that she was throwing her ass back on his tongue like it was a hard dick.

Disaya got up and rode him backwards, so he could get a view of her ass. She bounced up and down on him, grinding slowly as she rode his shaft. He licked his fingers and stuck one in her ass. The feeling was so erotic, she lost her mind. She massaged his balls and rode him, while he fingered her ass with one hand and rubbed her cheeks with the other.

She was feeling so horny, she invited him to do something that she was terrified of. She got on all fours and said, "Fuck me, Indie."

He got on his knees and stuck the tip of his long, thick dick in her wet pussy. He then removed it and wet her ass with it.

She tensed up, bracing herself for the pain she was expecting to feel.

"Relax, ma. I won't hurt you," he whispered in her ear.

Disaya tried to relax her muscles, but when he eased himself into her ass, she felt like he was ripping her apart. *Oh shit!* She closed her eyes and gritted her teeth.

He began to grind slowly, and once he was inside of her, the pain subsided and the orgasms came one after the other. He fucked her slowly and reached around to finger her at the same time, his thumb dancing on her clit while his middle finger ventured inside her pussy walls. He maneuvered his dick in and out of her ass, and it felt so good, she was speaking in tongues.

"Indie!" she called loudly over and over again.

He finally pulled himself out of her ass and stuck his dick into her pussy. His pumps grew more and more powerful until he erupted inside of her.

She turned around and laughed lightly when she saw his eyes roll in the back of his head.

"Damn, girl," he exclaimed. "You got that wet-wet."

"I know. And I'm ready to let it be yours if you want it."

He touched the side of her face. "I want it. I want you."

They got up and took a shower together and continued their lovemaking for another hour.

The ringing of Indie's cell phone interrupted them, and they both got out and entered the room.

Indie looked at his caller ID. "Damn! That was Bay." He dialed Bay's number and waited as the phone rang. "What up, dude?" he said when Bay finally picked up.

"Yo, is YaYa with you?" he asked.

Indie frowned. "Yeah, she right here. Hold up." He handed Disaya the phone.

She displayed a look of confusion as she took the cell phone from him. "Hey, Bay," she said.

"Yo, YaYa, I'm gon' kill your mu'fuckin' friend when I see her. That bitch foul! I swear on my mother, I'm murking that ho when I catch her."

Disaya's facial expression immediately dropped and fear entered her heart. "Yo, Bay, you need to chill out with all them threats. What the fuck are you so hot for?"

"That nasty bitch gave me HIV. Word is bond, she's dead when I catch her!"

With those words he hung up in her face. Tears of shock, fear, and disbelief formed in her eyes as she looked up at Indie hopelessly. They graced her face as she broke down crying on the middle of the hotel room floor.

Indie knelt down and wrapped his arms around her, in his attempt to comfort her. "What's wrong? What happened?"

"Mona gave Bay HIV. My best friend is dying," she said as she cried on his chest. "I wasn't there for her," Disaya uttered in disbelief as she thought about Mona's inevitable fate.

Damn, that's fucked-up, he thought to himself. Mona was so young and was probably one of the last chicks he would've expected to have the virus. Her beauty had been deceiving and he was disappointed to hear that another beautiful sister had let her promiscuity lead to her death. Mona was lost in her chase for money, and now her recklessness had affected one of his closest friends. He knew that birds of a feather usually flocked together, but he hoped and prayed that Disaya was nothing like her friend.

Chapter Seven

The news about Mona had definitely ruined Disaya's spirits. All she could think about was the fact that Mona had contracted HIV. *That could have been me,* she thought to herself. No matter how hard she tried, she couldn't get the tears to stop falling from her eyes.

She looked out of the airplane window to avoid facing Indie. He didn't say anything, and he gave her some space to think. He did however hold on to her hand to let her know that he was there if she wanted to talk. The flight seemed to take forever. All she wanted to do was go check on her friend. *God, please let this be a big misunderstanding. How can she have AIDS? She's a good person. Please don't take her away from me,* she prayed silently. Disaya had never experienced a relationship with God before, but she desperately felt the need to ask Him for help. She knew that the reason she was hurting so badly was because she was just as lost as Mona. They had been leading the same lifestyle, doing the same things, and she realized that the shoe could have easily been on the other foot.

When they finally arrived back in New York, Disaya rushed to get her baggage. "I have to get to her," she said, quickly locating her bags and heading for the car.

"Tell me what you need me to do." Indie opened the car door for her.

She dropped her chin to her chest and closed her eyes. "I just need you to take me home. Right now, that's all you can do," she said sadly.

"Okay." Indie could see she was hurting, and he wanted to help her, but he knew that she wasn't ready to let him in. They sat silently in the car as he drove her to her apartment.

"I'm sorry about the trip," she said in a low tone.

"Don't worry about that. You go do what you got to do. Call me if you need me."

She nodded her head and opened the door to get out. She didn't even bother going up to her apartment. She headed straight to her car and drove away.

She walked into the Elite warehouse and immediately noticed how much it had changed. The smell of stank pussy was everywhere, and it looked more like a crack-house than a place of business. "Mo!" she yelled as she rushed up the stairs.

There were girls spread throughout the building. They all looked worn out. Disaya was shocked. Elite used to have some of the hottest chicks in New York, and now they looked like used-up prostitutes.

She knocked on Ronnie B's office door. "Mo!"

Ronnie pulled open the door and licked his lips

when he saw Disaya standing there. "So you finally came back to daddy, huh?"

"Not hardly, nigga. Where's Mona?" YaYa pushed past him and entered his office. She saw a naked Mona laid out on Ronnie's desk and another girl licking away between her legs. YaYa's sadness quickly turned into rage. "Mona, get up! Do you even know what you're doing?" She looked around at the ecstasy pills scattered all over the desk. It was no wonder Mona had contracted HIV. Ronnie had turned her out on ex and Elite into a sex shop. Girls who used to be well-paid escorts had been converted into low-class prostitutes. There was no telling what type of dudes he had Mona tricking with. She pulled Mona up by her hair. "Put on some clothes and let's go!"

Ronnie snatched Disaya's arm and pulled her away from Mona. "She ain't going nowhere. This my bitch. She's good right here."

"Don't put your fucking hands on me. I don't give a damn what you say. She's leaving here with me." Disaya pulled Mona up and off the desktop.

"Why are you tripping, YaYa?"

"Shut up, Mona. Let's go." As Disaya dragged Mona into the hall, she held on to the rail of the loft. Disaya could hear the girls at the bottom of the loft talking shit.

"She don't want to go. You ain't her mama. Let the bitch go! I told you that she wasn't leaving up out of here!" Ronnie shouted.

"Fuck you, Ronnie! She already done caught AIDS fucking around with you. I'm not about to let you pimp her until she's too sick to make you money."

"AIDS? Bitch, you got AIDS?" Ronnie shouted. "I been fucking you and you infected?" He grabbed Mona by the face and had her leaning over the edge of the railing.

"Stop it!" Disaya screamed, clawing at his arms, trying to get him to release her friend.

"I don't, Ronnie. I swear, I don't!" Mona pleaded.

Disaya looked in her friend's eyes and saw that she really believed herself. *She doesn't even know she's infected,* Disaya thought.

Before she could do anything to stop him, Ronnie B violently shoved Mona over the edge of the railing.

Everything seemed to move in slow motion as she watched Mona fall three flights down to the concrete floor below. "No!" she screamed.

The frightened screams of the other girls were deafening.

Disaya took off down the stairs. "Mona!" she yelled as she ran to her friend's side. There was blood leaking from the back of Mona's head.

"YaYa?" Mona called out to her.

There was so much blood around Mona, Disaya was afraid to go near her.

"I'm here, Mo," she yelled to her from a couple feet away.

An excruciating current was flowing through Mona's entire body, and she couldn't move. The pain was so great that tears built up in her eyes. "Is it true? Do I have AIDS?"

"Don't think about that right now, Mo," Disaya said in a panic as she pulled out her Sidekick. She frantically dialed 9-1-1. "Please help me!" she cried. "My friend was pushed over a ledge. There's blood everywhere."

The building quickly cleared out as everyone scrambled to get away from the scene.

After giving the operator the address to the building, Disaya looked down at her friend. "Mo, hold on, girl. The ambulance is coming."

"YaYa, I want to see you," Mona cried, tears flowing freely down her face. "I don't want to die alone."

Disaya's heart was pounding from fear of contracting the deadly disease, but she knew her friend needed her. She walked over to her and knelt down beside her. Disaya was afraid of touching Mona, but she was even more afraid of losing her best friend in the world. She was sure that it was probably in her head, but she could smell the infectious blood as it poured from Mona and soaked through her jeans. Disaya tensed up as she felt her skin become moist from the contact. She gripped Mona's hand tightly as she rubbed her hair softly. "Just hold on, Mo. You's a bad bitch, Mo. Come on, Mo, bad bitches don't die."

Mo chuckled half-heartedly as she felt her eyes close. "I'm sorry," she replied before her eyes shut against her will.

Leah arrived at the hospital to see Disaya sitting on the floor in the hallway, still covered in Mona's blood. "Is she okay?" Leah rushed and hugged her friend. She could see that YaYa was distraught. A twinge of jealousy ran through her as she realized how much YaYa truly cared for Mona. The feeling quickly passed, and she sat on the floor next to her and held her as she cried hysterically in her arms.

"I knew I shouldn't have left her with Ronnie B. If she would've just left when we did—"

"This is not on you, YaYa. Mona is a grown woman. We couldn't control what she did. She chose to stay down with Elite. This is not your fault. The only thing that we can do is be here for her now."

Disaya nodded her head. "I know you're right, but I still can't help but feel guilty. She got that shit, Leah."

"What shit? AIDS?"

"HIV," Disaya corrected, a thick sadness in her voice.

"Damn, that's fucked-up," Leah mumbled in disbelief. She'd heard of different chicks getting caught up by the virus but had never been this close to the disease. She always thought that she protected herself enough not to worry about catching HIV, but now that Mona had contracted it, she wasn't so sure. If she had stayed down with Elite, she could have easily fucked behind Mona or even had sex with her, which would have put her life on a permanent countdown.

There was a long silence between the two girls as they both got lost in their own thoughts.

"See, that's why we need to hit it big one time. We need to quit fucking with all these different niggas. We need to do it big one time. I got the perfect dude lined up too."

"What?" Disaya asked in disbelief.

"Look, just hear me out. This dude named Nanzi hit us up on the site. He's working with some major money. He wants to get down with us. He wants to do it at his crib, because he don't trust anybody. The payoff is large too. More than we ever made before. We can do this one last time and be set for a minute."

Disaya shook her head. "I can't believe you're even thinking about that right now."

"Excuse me, Ms. Morgan," a nurse said, calling Disaya by her last name.

"Yes?" Disaya responded eagerly. She and Leah stood up.

"There is a social worker here to see you regarding your friend's condition." The nurse pointed to a white woman in a blue pants suit. The woman looked uncomfortable in the hospital as she approached Disaya.

"Hello. I'm Ms. Tillman," the white woman said, introducing herself. She didn't even wait to hear Disaya's name. "Your friend is injured very badly. Upon running some blood tests we also discovered that she's HIV-positive. Does your friend have any medical coverage?"

"No, I don't think so," YaYa replied.

"The treatment she needs is very expensive. The fall that she took damaged her spinal cord, and she is hemorrhaging. The pressure from the blood is putting strain on her damaged spinal cord. If we don't operate in the next couple days, she will be paralyzed."

"How much are we talking?" YaYa asked.

"The surgery and recuperation costs total out to three hundred thousand. We need a ten-percent down payment before the hospital can even get her on the operating table."

"Thirty thousand." Disaya thought about the money that Indie had given her in Vegas. She was in such a rush to get to Mona, she had left it in his car and didn't even think about taking it with her.

"One last time and we can pay Mona's down payment. After that, you'll still be set for a minute," Leah whispered in Disaya's ear.

"I'll come up with the money. I'll have it by tomorrow." She didn't want to do it. She wished that she could be the woman that Indie wanted her to be, but her friend needed her. *I have to get this money,* she thought.

Disaya sent Indie to voice mail for the fifth time that night. She closed her eyes and leaned over the sink, dreading what she was about to do. Indie had made her realize that she needed to respect herself. While they were in Vegas he made her feel something that she had never felt before. Love. She felt love from him, but also, for the first time in a long time, she was loving herself. But what she was about to do went against everything that he wanted her to be. A part of her wanted to walk out and run to him, but she knew that she needed to do this for Mona. Mona always had her back, and she couldn't leave her hanging without at least attempting to help her.

Disaya walked out of the bathroom wearing a black lace camisole and saw Leah standing across the room behind Nanzi. Nanzi had a camcorder in his hand and had it aimed at Disaya's body. He got excited as he zoomed in on her curves, and he lusted for her when he focused on the fat lips between her legs.

"What is he doing?" Disaya asked. "You didn't say shit about being on tape."

"Yo, just chill, ma," Nanzi told her.

Disaya noticed that Leah had cut her hair into a shoulder-length wrap similar to her own.

"Do a dance for me." Nanzi put the camcorder on the tripod and ran over to his surround sound stereo system and pressed play. Young Jeezy bumped throughout the room.

Disaya closed her eyes as a tear slid down her face. *"You got to respect yourself, ma."* She heard Indie's words playing over and over in her head as she moved her body to the beat of the song. She kept her eyes closed as she felt Nanzi's lips on her neck.

Nanzi wasn't a bad-looking dude, and it was obvious he was caked up. A year ago, Disaya would have been all over him, but she had grown up since then. She now realized that everything that glitters isn't gold.

She opened her eyes and saw Leah watching her behind the camera. She felt dirty and cheap, but she continued with the thought of saving Mona on her mind.

"Why I got to pay for this pussy, ma? A bitch like you supposed to be taken care of," he whispered. Nanzi stuck one finger in her pussy, brought it to her face, and pushed it forcefully in her mouth.

Indie's face flashed in her mind. "I can't do this," she whispered. She pulled her straps back onto her shoulders and rushed out of the room.

"Yo, what's up wit' ya girl?" Nanzi asked impatiently.

"Nothing. She's cool. I'll be right back." Leah rushed after Disaya and grabbed her arm when they got into the hallway. "What the fuck is up?"

"I can't do this, Leah."

Leah put her hands on her face and kissed her. She stuck her tongue down her throat sloppily. She whispered, "Save this pussy for me, YaYa. I'll take care of him."

Disaya backed up from Leah and pushed her off. "Leah, go on with that shit! I can't do this anymore. This ain't for me. I'm better than this."

"Look, just calm down," Leah told her. "I'll go and take care of Nanzi then we'll get what we're owed and bounce. Just work the camera."

When both girls walked back into the room, Disaya stayed behind the camera and watched as Leah stripped, her mouth instantly finding its place around Nanzi's shaft. Her head was in his lap, and her ass was in the air, facing the camera. She clapped her fat ass cheeks together and fingered herself as she gave Nanzi the best head job of his life.

Once her pussy was good and wet, she climbed on top of Nanzi, who was rock-hard, and began to ride him slowly.

Disaya frowned when she saw the pink butterfly tattoo on Leah's right ass cheek. *What the fuck? This bitch got her hair cut like mines, and she got the same tattoo as I do.*

Nanzi, his eyes closed, looked like he was in heaven, his hands planted firmly on Leah's ass as he picked her up and pounded her down onto his shaft. Disaya noticed Leah reaching for something at the headboard of the bed. *What the hell is she doing?*

Disaya was clueless, but Leah knew exactly what she was doing. She had planned that night perfectly. She knew what her purpose was and was determined to get what she had come for.

Disaya's eyes bugged out when she saw Leah pull the chrome handgun from behind the pillow.

Boom! Nanzi never saw it coming.

Blood as red as wine poured onto the white sheets. Disaya couldn't stop the scream that escaped from her throat.

Leah walked backwards to where Disaya was standing and shut the camera off.

"What did you do? What the fuck did you do?"

"What I had to. This is our only way to hit the safe. This dumb nigga been flashing his cash all in the streets, talking about his safe, and how he untouchable because he sleep with his pistol underneath his pillow. I knew he would have that mu'fucka right where I needed it to be. He didn't expect me to use his own gun on him. Now, we can go somewhere away from all this, YaYa, just me and you." She rubbed the side of Disaya's face.

"Bitch, are you crazy? You just fucking killed somebody!"

"I did it for us, so we could take the money and be together. Come on, help me unload this safe," Leah said as she quickly put her clothes back on.

She went over to the safe and shot the steel lock with Nanzi's .45, opening it up.

Disaya watched Leah unload the money. *This bitch is nuts.*

"It's like two hundred fifty grand in here," Leah said excitedly as she divided the money into two different duffle bags. She wiped the room down to eradicate any evidence that they'd been there. She swiped the camcorder off the tripod then tossed Disaya one of the bags.

"One hundred twenty-five grand. Tell me this wasn't worth it."

Disaya was in shock and felt horrible for the man that lay slumped inside the room. She hurried and ran out of the house.

"Disaya, now we can be together," Leah said again.

"Why you keep talking this 'be-together' shit, Leah? I'm not gay. I don't want to be with a woman. That shit is never going to happen, so kill that noise you talking. You are fucking looney! I thought it was just business to you, but your ass is really obsessed with me."

"I'm not, YaYa. I just want us to have the best of everything. Now you can stop messing with that nigga Indie. I know you were with him because of the money. Now we have money, you and me, boo," she said, a crazed look in her eye.

This bitch has lost it, Disaya thought. "Bitch, there is no *we.* There is only me. I'm not fucking with you like that. As a matter of fact, I'm not fucking with you at all. I love Indie. I've never loved you. We were girls who got money together, that's it. Yeah, we had to do some freaky shit in order to get paid, but that's all it was about to me— the money."

"You don't mean that. You just tripping right now."

"Yeah, I am tripping. Bitch, you just blew that nigga brains out. I'm not fucking with you, Leah. Now, let me out the fucking car, you fucking dyke."

Leah pulled over the car in a rage. "Fine, bitch. Get out!"

Disaya stepped out of the car and began to walk in the opposite direction.

Leah shouted as she walked away, "Where would you be without me, Disaya? Nowhere! You wouldn't be shit, but a broke bitch with some good pussy!"

YaYa gripped the bag of money. *I should've never fucked with her like that. This money ain't worth it.*

Chapter Eight

Disaya walked for miles in a slow daze until she reached the hospital. Her face was so pale, she looked like a zombie. She kept seeing the look on Nanzi's face when he was shot. The guilt was eating at her, but she still tried to convince herself that his death was worth Mona's life. She dropped the thirty G's that Mona needed for her surgery off at the nurses' station and, just as quickly as she had come, left.

She picked up her phone and called the only person that she knew could make her feel better.

"Hello," Indie answered.

"I need you," she said desperately.

"Where are you? You sound like something's wrong."

"I'm at the hospital," she whispered. She didn't have the energy to speak loudly. She was drained mentally, physically, and emotionally. She hung up the phone and stood outside of the emergency room. She didn't know if he would show up. She just sat on the curb and waited, thinking about all the foul shit she'd done.

Indie finally pulled into the parking lot and jumped out when he saw Disaya sitting on the curb. Her face was stained with white ash from her dried-up tears. He ran up to her. Her hair was disheveled, and her eyes were red and puffy from crying. "What happened to you?"

She didn't respond.

"YaYa, talk to me, ma. Who did this to you?"

She wrapped her arms underneath her legs and balled up as she placed her head on top of her knees.

The sound that erupted from her body expressed true pain, and it broke Indie's heart to see her like that. He picked her up from the ground and placed her gently in the passenger side of his car. He pulled off and took her to his condo on the Upper East Side of Manhattan. She didn't speak the entire way there. He didn't know what had happened to her, but she was sure traumatized.

He carried her into his home and laid her down on his bed. "Who hurt you?"

"The world," she replied in a whisper. She told him about Mona and how Ronnie B had thrown her over the top floor of the warehouse, leaving out the rest of the events that took place that night.

Indie was enraged. He knew what type of business Ronnie B ran. He pimped chicks because he couldn't pimp the streets. He didn't have the heart to take on the streets like the real get-money niggas, so he recruited bitches to make money for him. Ronnie B festered on lost souls, so that he could feel like a man.

"Don't worry about that. I'll handle that," he told her. "You shouldn't have been around that nigga in the first place. If he had hurt *you,* I would've had to kill him."

He took her clothes off of her and went and got a sponge and a large bowl with hot soapy water in it. He rubbed her body down and then kissed her passionately as he lay beside her.

"Don't leave me," Disaya said out of the blue.

"I love you, ma," he whispered in her ear. "I'm not going anywhere."

"I love you too."

It had been weeks since Disaya had spoken to Leah, and she was glad that she didn't try to contact her. Leah didn't have it all, and Disaya wanted nothing to do with her. Disaya had been staying over Indie's house for almost a month, and they were getting along well. He had practically moved Disaya in with him. Most of her things were at his house, and he made her feel at home.

The more time she spent around Indie, the deeper her love grew for him. She wanted to tell him the full story of what had happened to her the night he'd picked her up from the hospital, but she didn't know how he would react. She wasn't willing to risk his love by telling him the truth.

She walked from his kitchen with a plate fit for a king. She woke up extra early just to fix him breakfast. As she walked back toward the room, she heard him talking in a low tone on the phone. His back was toward her, so he couldn't see her standing in the doorway to his bedroom.

"Ma, it's not like that. I got company, so that's why I haven't been over in a while. I promise you, I'll be there tonight. I got something special planned anyway. Look, I got to go. I don't want her to hear me. I'll see you later." Indie hung up the phone. When he turned around, he was surprised to see her standing there.

Her feelings were hurt more than anything, but all he saw was anger in her eyes.

She stood there with a look that said, *Yeah, nigga, I heard you,* her eyebrows arched as she waited for an explanation.

"It ain't what you think, yo," he explained as he walked toward her. "Is this for me?" He reached to kiss the side of her face.

"It depends on who that was on the phone," she said, dodging his kiss.

"That was my mother, yo."

"Your mother?" YaYa twisted up her lips in a disbelieving smirk.

"Yeah. What? A brother can't talk to his mama?"

Disaya realized she was tripping and handed him his food. Embarrassed, she said, "I'm sorry."

"What did I tell you, huh? I would never hurt you," he said, his mouth full of food.

"I know," she said with a smile.

"Trust me. Oh yeah, and we going to my parents' crib for dinner tonight. My moms want to meet you."

"Meet me for what? How she know about me?"

"Don't worry about all that. I got some shit I need to take care of today, so you on your own. Just be ready by six o'clock."

Indie finished his breakfast, got dressed, and was out the door, leaving YaYa to her own thoughts.

Disaya hated being left alone. It gave her too much

time to think. She tried to block the guilt out of her mind by concentrating on the one good thing in her life. Indie. He was everything that she wanted. *Now all I got to do is impress his mama,* she thought as she looked in the closet to choose something to wear.

Disaya gripped Indie's hand as she stood outside of his parents' New Jersey home right across the bridge. The size of their suburban home let Disaya know that they came from money.

A middle-aged woman answered the door and hugged on Indie tightly. "My baby!"

"Hey, Ma." Indie kissed her on the cheek and then turned to Disaya. "This is—"

"I know who this is. This is the girl that my baby boy can't stop talking about," she said as she embraced Disaya too.

The woman made her feel welcome, and Disaya immediately fell in love with her.

"It's so good to meet you, baby. You are just as pretty as he said you were."

Disaya blushed. "It's nice to meet you too, Mrs. Perkins."

"Chile, please. Call me Elaine. Come on in," she said as they walked inside of the house.

"Where's Pops?" Indie asked.

"He's in the den watching that damn football," Elaine said. "Go on back there with him. You know you want to. I don't know if your brother is coming. I've been calling him, but he doesn't like to answer the phone for his old bird."

"He'll probably show up. You know how he is." Indie turned to Disaya. "You gon' be all right?"

"Boy! Yeah, she gon' be all right. I'm not going to scare the girl off." Elaine hit Indie with the kitchen towel.

Disaya laughed and nodded her head in agreement. "I'll be fine."

Indie kissed her on the cheek and then looked at his mother. "Be easy on her, Ma." He made his way to the back of the house, leaving Disaya with his mother.

"Come on, Disaya, you can help me in the kitchen," Elaine said.

"Call me YaYa."

Elaine and Disaya clicked instantly. She grilled Disaya about everything under the sun and seemed to approve of her.

When Indie entered the kitchen again, Disaya was pulling the macaroni and cheese out of the oven. He said, "Disaya, I want you to meet my father."

Disaya turned around, and when she saw the man's face, the casserole dish fell from her hands and onto the floor. "Oh!" Disaya said as the hot dish crashed at her feet. She panicked as she bent down to clean up the mess. "I am so sorry, Elaine," she said, her eyes glued to the floor, to avoid looking Indie's father in the eyes.

Indie bent down to help her. "You okay?"

"I'm fine. The pan was just too hot." YaYa couldn't believe her luck. Indie's father was the car dealer that she'd let suck on her pussy to get her car. *Perkins . . . Bill Perkins,* she thought to herself. *Ain't this about a bitch?* A dinner party had just turned into a very uncomfortable situation for Disaya. "Excuse me," she said. "I think I burned my hand."

"The bathroom's up the stairs to your right," Indie told her.

Disaya practically ran up the steps, ascending them two at a time, until she found refuge inside the bathroom. She frantically splashed her face with water as she tried to calm herself down. She was sure that her little indiscretion would come out. She shook her hands nervously as she tried to think of an explanation for Indie. Suddenly, an overwhelming nausea overcame her, and she leaned over the toilet and violently heaved up the contents of her stomach. *Just breathe,* she told herself.

YaYa finally made her way downstairs, where everyone was seated at the dinner table.

"Are you okay, sweetheart?" Elaine asked.

"Yes, I'm fine," she replied with a weak smile.

Indie stood up and pulled her chair out for her as she sat next to him. "You all right?" he whispered to her.

She nodded and grabbed his hand under the table. She was nervous throughout the entire dinner. She could feel his father's eyes on her as she talked and was overcome with guilt. *That was a long time ago. I'm a different person now,* she told herself.

"I think she's perfect, Indie," Elaine said. "I'd be proud to have a daughter-in-law like her. Plus, I haven't seen you this happy in a long time."

Disaya turned toward Indie in confusion. "Daughter-in-law?"

Before she could say anything more, Indie pulled out a small black gift bag.

"What's this?" she asked him.

"Look and see."

Disaya reached into the bag and pulled out a key. "That's the key to our new brownstone in Harlem."

"What?"

"Keep looking."

Disaya pulled out a small Tiffany's box and opened it. She gasped when she saw the canary yellow diamond that she'd tried on months earlier.

Indie smiled. "You ready to make this official?"

Disaya looked around the table, her mouth hung open. Her eyes stopped on his father, and she was quickly forced back to reality. Tears filled her eyes. *I can't marry this man,* she thought.

To her surprise, Mr. Perkins nodded his head in approval.

Disaya quickly answered, "Like a referee with a whistle."

Elated to see her baby boy choose a woman to spend the rest of his life with, Elaine laughed and clapped loudly.

"It took you long enough, ma. You sure?" Indie lifted her chin with one finger. "Will you marry me?"

"Yes, Indie. Yes, yes!" she yelled, smiling from ear to ear.

Bill Perkins nodded. "You're a lucky man, son," he said as Indie slipped the ring on YaYa's finger.

Disaya mouthed the words, "Thank you," to his father. She knew he would keep their little secret, and she was forever grateful to him for that.

The doorbell chimed, interrupting the joyous occasion.

Elaine said, "Let me go get that."

Indie picked Disaya up and hugged her tight, spinning her around the room. "I love you, girl."

"I love you, Indie. I can't wait until Mona's ass gets better, so I can show off my rock!" Disaya held her hand away from her body and admired the ring.

They all heard Elaine scream from the front foyer, "Oh God! No!"

As everybody took off toward the front door, Disaya could see the lights from the squad car in the driveway.

"Fuck is all this?" Indie asked as he joined his mother's side.

"It's your brother, Indie. They say he's been killed!" Sobbing heavily, Elaine collapsed into her husband's arms.

Disaya saw Indie's facial expression change instantly. A silent rage took over his face.

"Indie?" she called out to him as she put her hands on his face.

Indie pressed his forehead against hers as he shook his head in distress.

"Indie, baby, talk to me," she pleaded as she saw the tears fall down his cheeks.

Indie punched the front door to his parents' house, putting his fist through it. He then rushed out of the house.

YaYa watched helplessly as he got into his car and sped away. "Indie!" she yelled. But the only sound that she could hear was the sobbing of his mother and the breaking of her heart as she imagined how devastated her future husband must be.

Chapter Nine

Disaya waited days before she saw Indie again. His parents dropped her back off at his apartment, and the only thing she could think of doing was to wait patiently until he came home. She blew his cell phone up constantly. She just wanted to know that he was okay.

Disaya cleaned the apartment from top to bottom and made dinner, hoping that Indie would decide to come home that night. She stared restlessly at the clock as she watched the hours pass. Nine became ten, and ten changed to eleven, as she sat at the candlelit table in her Victoria's Secret lingerie. *God, please let my baby be okay. You just brought my soul mate to me. Don't take him away so quickly.*

Eventually she rested her head on top of the table and dozed off.

Indie walked into the house at five A.M. and saw Disaya sleeping at the dinner table. He saw that she had prepared dinner for him. His grief was at its peak, and he wasn't trying to hurt her, but the only thing he could think about was his older brother. He staggered over to Disaya and stood over her for a while, watching her sleep. She was beautiful, and he was lucky to have her by his side. He got down on both knees and laid his head in her laps as he cried for his brother.

Disaya woke up and rested her hand on Indie's face. She massaged his tense neck muscles.

"Baby. Oh, Indie, I love you so much. I'm so sorry about your brother."

"He was my heart, yo," Indie replied through sobs. "I swear on everything I love that I'm-a murk whoever is responsible for this. Nigga's gon' feel it."

YaYa could see the vengeance in his eyes. "Indie, please don't do anything right now," she said. "Just think about it. I don't want anything to happen to you. It would kill me if something happened to you." Seeing him like this tore Disaya up on the inside. He was always so strong and assertive. Now he was hurting badly and needed her support.

Indie didn't respond.

He did stay locked inside his condo until the funeral. He didn't want anyone to see him weak. The only comfort he got was seeing Disaya's face. Every time she smiled at him, she took a little bit of the pain away. He almost felt guilty for loving her at a time like this, and sometimes he pushed her away unintentionally.

YaYa was patient with him, though, and understood that he needed to grieve. He didn't talk to her at all. She knew that he was fighting his own battles in his heart and mind, so she didn't mind the silence.

Indie held on tight to her every time he was around her. He felt like he was under water and couldn't come up for air. He was drowning in sorrow.

For his entire life his older brother had been there for him, but now he was gone. He planned on murdering whoever was responsible for his brother's death. He just didn't have the strength to execute his plan. He knew that his heart would be weak for a while. He would give himself time to heal, and then he would hit the streets to find out exactly what had happened to his brother.

Indie wore a black-on-black Armani suit to the funeral. He looked like he had stepped off of the cover of *GQ*, with his VVS cufflinks, purple lapel neck accent, and the platinum Cartier tie clip. He looked at himself in the mirror and took a deep breath as he prepared to send his brother off.

Disaya sat on the bed in a snug black Prada dress that cut in a low V near her breast line and was also cut low in the back. And she wore a huge black hat that covered her eyes. Her satin Prada gloves made her look as if she was born and raised with elegance and class.

"Are you sure you want me to come?" Disaya felt like she would be out of place at the funeral. "I mean, it's going to be your family and, er, I don't think that—"

"YaYa, you're part of my family now. You're about to be my wife. I need you by my side today," he said.

Disaya felt the flutter in her stomach. She knew exactly what it was. She was pregnant with Indie's baby but was reluctant to tell him because so much was going on with him already. She wasn't exactly sure how far along she was. They'd never used a condom during sex, so she was clueless as to when it happened. She thought that it happened while she was in Vegas with him but wasn't exactly sure. She stared off into space as she thought about the child that was growing inside of her. She was engaged and pregnant. She couldn't believe how much her life had changed in such a short period of time. *I was just trying to hustle niggas out of money. I was chasing a Prada plan and ended up getting something worth way more valuable than money.*

"You okay?" Indie asked her.

She snapped out of her daze and nodded. *I should wait until after the funeral to tell him.*

"What's on your mind?"

"Nothing."

Indie could tell from the look in her eyes that she was lying. "Don't lie to me, ma. I never want us to keep anything from each other. Promise me that you gon' always keep it real with me."

A tear slipped down her face. "I promise."

"Now, tell me what's wrong?"

"I'm pregnant," she said, her head down.

"You're what?" he asked loudly. He lifted her chin. "For real?"

She nodded as tears flowed down her cheeks.

"What you crying for, baby? You just made me the happiest man on this earth. You just gave me a reason to keep living. I'm having a shorty," he said in excitement and disbelief.

Seeing him that excited made her smile. "Is this really okay?" she asked with uncertainty in her voice.

"You ain't got to worry about nothing, YaYa. You're about to be my wife. You're carrying my child. You gon' always be taken care of. My family will never want for anything," he assured her. "I just need you to do one thing."

"What's that?"

"Help me through my brother's funeral. I need you to be strong for me today."

"I can do that," she replied, and she kissed him on the forehead.

The funeral was packed, family members and friends all showing up to pay their final respect. Indie's parents walked into the sanctuary first. They were followed by Indie and Disaya. Disaya felt out of place, but she wanted to be there for her man. She held on to him as she walked down the long aisle of the church. An ivory-and-gold casket sat at the head of the aisle. The entire room was covered in lilies.

The closer they got to the casket, the tighter Indie gripped her hand. He hadn't shed any tears yet, and she knew that he would never do it in public, but she knew he was hurting inside. She placed his hand on her stomach, to remind him that he still had two people who loved and needed him. He rubbed it gently before pulling his hand away.

It was their turn to view the body, and Indie couldn't move his feet. Elaine broke down to her knees when she saw her son's body lying there. Her sobs were so loud that they silenced everyone else. Bill picked her up from her knees and helped her to the first pew of the church.

"It'll be okay," Disaya whispered as she stepped forward with Indie. She walked up to the casket, and her heart stopped when she saw his brother's face. *Nanzi?* Her breaths became shallow. *Oh my God, I did this to him. I did this to Indie. Leah killed Indie's brother.* She couldn't suck enough air for her lungs. *Oh my God.* Disaya felt the room spin underneath her. Suddenly, her legs could no longer hold her up, and she collapsed on to the floor.

"Somebody, call nine-one-one! She's pregnant!" The sound of Indie calling for help was the last thing she heard before the lights in her head went out.

Disaya woke up to an IV sticking from her arm, and Indie and his parents sitting in chairs around her hospital bed.

"Indie, baby, she's awake," Elaine said as she patted her son's shoulder.

Indie jumped up and rushed to her side. "Don't do that to me, ma." He kissed the back of her hand. "I thought I would lose you too."

If you knew what I did to your brother you wouldn't care. She began to cry.

"What happened up there?" he asked.

Disaya didn't know what to tell him. Thankfully, one of the doctors walked through the door and overheard the question.

"Stress, fatigue and pregnancy is not a good mix," the doctor said. "Her body is tired, and dealing with the death of a loved one can take its toll on you. You fainting is a sign that you need some rest."

"You don't have to worry about that, doc, because I'm not gon' let her lift a finger," Indie said. "You might have to flip a couple pages in magazines, though, so you can pick out your new furniture for our new home."

"I can do that," she replied with a weak smile.

"Well, now that I know that you're all right we can head home." Elaine stood up and kissed Disaya on her cheek. "Take care of my grandbaby, girlfriend, and call me if you need me," she said before kissing Indie and leaving the room.

"I've got a surprise for you," Indie said as he got up and walked to the door.

The doctor took her blood pressure as Indie left the room for a couple minutes.

When Indie walked back in, Mona was following him. She was in a wheelchair, and her movement was stiff, but she was still a sight for sore eyes.

"Hey, Mommy," Mona said as she reached up to hold her hand. "I hear I'm going to be an auntie."

Disaya started to cry.

"I'll give y'all some privacy." Indie walked out into the hallway.

"Why are you crying, girl? All of your dreams came true. Your Prada plan worked. You have a good man that is paid," Mona stated. "And you are having this nigga baby. That's child support like a mu'fucka, even if y'all don't stay together."

"Mo, something happened. I'm not gon' be able to keep this man," YaYa said.

The doctor left the room and then Disaya continued. She told Mona exactly what happened with Leah and Nanzi. Mona sat there in shock as she listened to her friend's story.

"I have to tell him," Disaya said as she cried. "I know that he is gon' leave me, but he deserves to know. He deserves better than me. I'm nothing but a girl from the hood, and that ain't what he wants. I've made a lot of bad choices, and now I've got to live with them."

"You can't tell him, YaYa. You better not tell him. You deserve everything that you have now. Yo, forget about Leah. You didn't kill his brother, she did. That bitch is psycho. You're lucky you cut her off when you did. Don't tell him, Disaya. Just be happy with him. Start over today. Don't think about yesterday. I wish I could start over," Mona said as she thought about the deadly disease plaguing her body.

"How are you feeling?" YaYa asked.

"I have good and bad days. Everybody here is real nice. I'm seeing a therapist trying to deal with all of this. I just wish I had been smarter, you know. I had sex with so many men after you left Elite, and I never once thought to make them wear a condom. I was popping ecstasy like it was candy, YaYa. I just lost control of my own hustle, you know. I was stupid, and blinded by the money. I didn't love myself enough to see I was hurting myself. See, YaYa, I'm just like you, a ghetto bitch from the neighborhood. I could have chosen to do something different with my life, but I didn't. I took the easy route. I chose to be promiscuous, and now I'm living with the consequences. I'm dying, YaYa. So, see, I'm not just telling you to live it up just for *you*. I have to live through you, because that's the only way that I can live. I want you to get married, have a bunch of big-head kids, and you know they gon' have some big-ass heads because Indie fine, but he got a dome."

Disaya wiped the tears from her face as she laughed.

"For real, girl, do all of the things that I can't do, YaYa. You deserve this life. Don't sell yourself short anymore. Don't ever let Indie find out about his brother because, if you do, he will never forgive you."

Disaya nodded and said, "I love you, Mo."

"I love you too, girl. Now get some rest so that your man can take you home."

It had been weeks, and Leah still hadn't heard from Disaya. She couldn't believe that she had played her the way that she did. *That bitch chose that hustling, backward-ass nigga over me.* She sealed the large envelope that she had in her hand. *As many times as I licked her pussy she had the nerve to give it to his ass. She think he love her. I bet you he won't love her after I'm through with her ass.*

Thinking about Disaya had Leah going crazy. She was furious. She had always gotten exactly what she wanted, from whomever she wanted. Rejection wasn't something she was used to. Disaya had dropped her like a bad habit and that pissed her off. *That bitch thinks she's better than me. She should've never let me taste the pussy if she wasn't gon' let me have it to myself.*

Leah stepped outside of her house and walked up the street. She turned many heads as she strutted up the block. On the outside she looked like the perfect woman, but on the inside she wasn't all there. She dropped her package in the mail and smiled as she thought about what she was about to do. *Karma's a bitch!*

Indie walked outside to the mailbox and retrieved the contents from it. He was shirtless and wore baggy sweat pants, causing the young girls on the block to gossip about his perfect physique. He walked back into the house as he flipped through the stacks of bills and opened up the Black Expressions package that Disaya had ordered. Her doctor had recommended that she read to keep her stress level low, so she'd joined several book clubs, like Coast 2 Coast Online and Black Expressions, and was into the street-fiction authors. Indie didn't tell her, but he was feeling the novels that she ordered.

He pulled out two books—*Diary of a Street Diva* and *Supreme Clientele* by Ashley JaQuavis. "Hell yeah, I can rock with these," Indie said as he put them on the counter top. He'd read their first joint, *Dirty Money*, and knew that they would bring the streets to life through their writing.

He continued to flip, until he came across a yellow package. He opened it up and pulled out a VCR tape. *What the hell is this?* He made his way to the basement and popped it into the player. He sat down in his leather La-Z-Boy and grabbed the remote to press play. His heart skipped a beat when he saw his brother's face pop up on the screen.

"I'm about to fuck tonight," Nanzi sang into the camera as he filmed himself.

"Fuck is this?" Indie sat up and leaned his elbows on his knees. He recognized his brother's bedroom. His brow creased in confusion when he saw Disaya appear on the tape.

"Dance for me, ma," his brother told her.

Indie's blood boiled as he watched her shake her ass for Nanzi. He clenched his fist and gritted his teeth as he watched her walk out of the room. He could hear his heartbeat in his ears as he waited to see what was going to happen next.

Minutes later he saw Disaya's ass cheeks appear back on the screen. He noticed the butterfly that was tattooed on her rear. His heart broke as he watched her get on top of Nanzi and ride him slowly. He lowered his head and closed his eyes as he heard the moans of his future wife. He took deep breaths. *Calm down,* he told himself. His heart ached at the pleasure on his brother's face. He couldn't see YaYa's face, so he didn't know if she was enjoying it or not. But it hurt him all the same. He squinted as he saw Disaya begin to reach for something. When she pulled out a gun and put the barrel to Nanzi's head, Indie's anger turned to blind rage.

"No!" he yelled when he saw the blood splatter on the tape as Disaya pulled the trigger. "Aghh!" he screamed in pain. He didn't want to believe what he'd just seen. "Aghh!" he cried as he fell to the floor and rocked back and forth, hitting himself in the chest, trying to stop his heart from hurting. He'd loved YaYa with all of his heart. "Aghh!" He cried like a baby because he thought Disaya's love for him was real. He knew she was a ghetto girl when he met her, but he looked past all the negative he saw in her and brought out the positive that he knew lived inside of her. Now, he didn't know if she was worth the time and energy. He felt as if he would die as he held his heart.

"Baby!" Disaya called out as she walked through the Harlem brownstone. The house had an old Harlem Renaissance flavor to it, and the deep shades of brown, orange, and cream complemented her style perfectly. She had always dreamed of owning something just like it, and her dreams became a reality when she received the keys to it the day her baby proposed to her. It had been completely renovated, and the house was exactly what she wanted it to be. Disaya was completely in love with her home and the man that she shared it with.

"Indie, baby, are you home?" she called out as she walked from room to room, unloading the many bags that she had purchased from her shopping trip earlier that day.

"Yo, I'm downstairs. Come here for a minute, ma. I got to holla at you about something," he yelled from the basement.

Disaya took off her Baby Phat thigh-high boots and eased herself out of her jeans. She hated wearing clothes, and when she was in her own home she seldom wore them. Her turquoise Victoria's Secret thong was swallowed by her voluptuous behind as she switched her hips, a habit she practiced even when she didn't have an audience.

"Here I come," she yelled back. She walked over to the refrigerator and grabbed a bottle of water and a Smirnoff. She also grabbed the Blockbuster tapes that she had gotten on her way home and then made her way to the fully furnished basement. She smiled as she descended the steps. "I picked up some movies on my way home. I've been shopping all day. I just want to sit back with you and chill." She approached him and kissed him lightly on the lips as she handed him the drink. She then walked over to the big screen and bent over seductively. She looked back at Indie as he stood and sipped at the Smirnoff.

He eyed her thick behind and the butterfly tattoo that was printed on it as she loaded the DVD into the player.

Disaya stood up and, before she could even turn around, felt the sting of the glass break against her face as Indie slammed his Smirnoff bottle into her head with full force.

"Aghh!" she cried out as her hands went up to protect her face. Blood seeped through her fingers and onto the white carpet.

"You fucking sheisty ho." Indie snatched her by the hair and pulled her back to her feet.

"Indie, stop it. Baby, you're hurting me," she screamed loudly as she clawed at his strong hands now wrapped around her delicate neck.

He held her away from his body with one arm and pointed his finger in her face with the other. "You dirty-ass bitch, I treat you good. I took your stanking ass out of the ghetto and you try to pull some okey-doke type shit on me!"

"What are you talking about?" Disaya asked in tears as she struggled to breathe.

"Don't fucking sit in my face and lie!" he yelled as he slammed her against the wall repeatedly. Tears built up in his eyes, and his stomach felt hollow from her deception. He looked at the engagement ring that he had given her and snatched it roughly from her finger, almost breaking it.

"Indie, no!" she cried as he took the most important thing in the world from her. "Baby, I don't know what you heard, but I haven't lied to you. I wouldn't lie to you. I've kept it real with you since the beginning. Baby, I love you."

She was pleading with him to believe her, and her eyes seemed sincere. He wanted to pull her into his arms and tell her that he could forgive her, that he could look past her disloyalty, but he knew that he couldn't. A major player in the drug game for years, he'd promised himself that he would never let a bitch knock him off his square, and this included her.

"YaYa, you could have had anything. I would've given you the world," he whispered as the pain of her actions set in.

"Baby, I didn't do anything," she cried as she struggled to breathe.

Indie's facial expression changed, and he loosened his grip on her neck. "YaYa," he said, calling her by her nickname, "I'm gon' ask you a question. I'm only gon' ask you this one time. I want you to think real hard before you answer me, okay?"

Disaya tried to think of what she could have done to deserve this treatment from him. "Okay," she whispered in reply.

"Have you ever done anything to hurt me? Have you ever lied to me?"

"I swear to God on our unborn child I haven't," she said convincingly as she touched her stomach.

Her words reminded Indie of the seed that she carried inside of her. They had just found out that she was six weeks pregnant. He remembered when she first told him that. He was the happiest man in the world. He had never felt more love for a person than he did that day, but now all of his love turned to hate as he stared at Disaya in contempt. Before he could think about his actions, he raised his foot and kicked her with all his might. His foot collided with her stomach, and she dropped to her knees in excruciating pain.

"Aghh!" she screamed in agony. *God, please let my baby be okay,* she thought. It was the first thing that crossed her mind. She was in disbelief. She would have never imagined that Indie would try to hurt her or do anything to hurt their child.

"Bitch, shut up! All this time, it was you. You sat back and watched me go through that shit, and all along you were behind it."

"What are you talking about? I didn't do shit!" she screamed. She held her stomach as she began to spit up blood.

"Oh, you didn't do shit, huh?" He grabbed her roughly and pulled her over to the wooden dinette set that occupied space in the basement. He sat her down forcefully and yelled, "Well, how do you explain this?" He stormed over to the entertainment center and pressed play on the VHS player. He had discovered the one thing that she had tried so hard to hide from him. "Explain it, YaYa," he repeated as he watched her betrayal on tape.

As soon as the tape began to play, tears filled her eyes. *Oh my God! Where did he get this from?* she thought to herself as she watched in horror. She was at a loss for words. She couldn't explain herself because in her heart she knew that there was no talking her way out of the situation. She closed her eyes as the hot tears streamed down her face.

"Uh-uh. Bitch, don't close your eyes. Watch it. I've already seen it from beginning to end. I've been watching the shit over and over again for the past five hours hoping my eyes were playing tricks on me."

Disaya couldn't bring herself to open her eyes but was forced to when Indie's fist collided with her face. She knew that the video only got worse, but she opened her eyes and watched it anyway to avoid him striking her again.

"I want you to watch this, so you'll know exactly why you are going to die," he whispered as his heart broke into two as he watched Disaya's triple-X performance.

I wish I could go back. I should have told him myself. It's not what it looks like. I could have explained to him how it really went down, she told herself as her mind wandered back to when it all began. *I should have just told him.*

Indie went into his waistline and pulled out his chrome 9 millimeter. He cocked the gun and pointed the pistol at her head as he closed his eyes.

"Indie, please listen to me!" she screamed.

"Shut up!"

"No, baby. Listen," she cried, "I love you. You're right, I lied to you about some things. I kept a lot of shit from you because I was afraid you would leave me if you knew the truth. That tape is not what it looks like. It doesn't show the truth. That's not me on that tape. Yes, I was there when Nanzi was killed, but I didn't know it was going to happen. I had nothing to do with it."

"The tape don't lie, Disaya," he said in a low whisper. He still had the gun pointed to her head.

"Indie, you know me," she begged.

"I thought I did," he said as he pulled the trigger.

Epilogue

Disaya didn't feel the bullet hit her because Indie turned the gun at the last minute, causing the bullet to become lodged in the bookshelf behind her. He couldn't bring himself to kill her. He hated her to the bottom of his soul, but the look in her eyes stopped him from taking her life. "If you want to keep your life, don't try to contact me," Indie said as he walked up the stairs and out of the house.

"Indie!" she cried for him. "It wasn't me!" she cried out loud. She felt blood leaking from her womb and feared for the life of her child. Her baby was all that she had left of Indie, and she wanted desperately to hold on to his seed. She hurt so badly that she couldn't stand up straight. When she heard footsteps come down the stairs, she hoped that Indie had come back for her.

"Indie?"

"No, YaYa. It's not Indie," Leah replied in a sinister tone. "Oh, look at you, YaYa. You chose this nigga." Leah peered closer at Disaya and noticed the slight bulge in her stomach. She bent down and touched the side of Disaya's face. She snickered at the sight of Disaya in pain. "You chose a nigga that would beat you like a dog while you carry his child."

"Bitch, you fucking set me up," Disaya screamed as she snatched her face away from Leah's hand.

"You set yourself up, YaYa. We could've been happy together. At first I came up with this whole plan so that I could get Indie out of your life. I contacted his brother and set up the hook-up. I got the same tattoo as you and styled my hair so that I'd look just like you. I made sure that the camera never caught my face. I knew that Indie would never be able to forgive you for killing his brother." Leah put her hands on her hips. She looked down and shook her head in disgust at YaYa.

"I didn't kill him, you did." YaYa held herself in pain.

"But it looks like you did. That's really all that matters, YaYa. At first I did this to get him out of the way so that I could be with you, but you played me, bitch. You tried to drop me, you fucking slut. You only think about yourself. You made love to me when you wanted to and then acted like it meant nothing."

"Made love to you? Bitch, it was sex. I got paid to fuck with you. Leah, it didn't mean anything. I did it for the money."

"Whatever, bitch." Leah pulled a gun from her purse. The same gun she used to kill Nanzi. "You remember this?"

Disaya's life flashed before her eyes as Leah pointed the gun at her. Indie's face popped into her thoughts, and the thought of losing her child caused her to beg for her life. "Leah, please . . . I'm pregnant. I'm sorry. I'll be with you. Just please get me to a hospital."

Leah laughed as she put the gun to Disaya's temple.

"Just fucking do it, Leah! What are you waiting for?" Disaya yelled as she closed her eyes and waited for the bullet to enter her dome.

"Bitch, please. I'm not gon' kill you. I'm going to hit your ass where it hurts. Indie is through with you, and he's hurting right now. I'll give him the time that he needs to grieve, and when he's vulnerable, we'll meet by chance. I know exactly what he wants in a woman. I learned that from you, so it will be easy to get him to fall in love with me. You told me everything, YaYa. I know how he likes to be fucked, what he likes to eat, how he likes to call you *ma*. Didn't your mama ever tell you not to tell your girls about your man? I'm going to take everything you ever had or wanted and make it mine, bitch. You'll never get out the hood. That little Prada plan of yours backfired. Indie was your only ticket out, and I made sure he'd never want to fuck with you again." She shook her head. "I wonder what the police would say if I sent them a copy of that tape."

Disaya watched as Leah climbed up the stairs and out the door. She felt a hatred for Leah that she didn't know existed. "Aghhhh!" She screamed, trying to release some of the pain she was feeling. Her body, mind, and heart were giving up on her. She crawled up the basement steps one by one and felt excruciating pain with each motion she made. She dragged her body across the hardwood floor and finally made it to the kitchen. She frantically grabbed her cell phone. *This bitch thinks it over. This shit has just begun.*

*   *   *

To be continued in *Prada Plan*, the novel, coming soon.

If you would like to contact Ashley to let her know what you think about her first solo venture, you can contact her at streetlitdiva@aol.com or go to <u>www.my space.com/streetlitdiva</u>.

"REAL BITCHES DO REAL THINGS"

By

JaQuavis Coleman

Prologue

"**Y**o, this is Wendy Wilson, and today in the studio we have the *New York Times* best-selling author, Jada Simone. She's here to talk about her controversial book, *The Duchess*. What's up, Jada?"

Jada leaned over the mic and spoke confidently, "What's good, Wendy? What's hood, New York City?"

"Glad to have you on the show. You know I'm going to get right to it. The streets is buzzing about your new book. It's a rumor that the book is about platinum-selling rapper, Young Money."

"Nah, it ain't even like that. It's just speculation. You know how the media blows everything out of proportion. It's just entertainment," Jada said, answering the same question she'd answered a million times before.

"Well, it seems that Young Money is getting quite a lot of heat from the feds from your novel. In your book, it describes a murder of a dirty cop in Brooklyn. The authorities say that your book tells the life of the girlfriend of an upcoming rap star and his connection to the drug game. To take things even further, your main character's name is the same as Young Money's government name, Braylon Nims. Girl, I have to keep it real. You have a lot of people upset with you right now."

Jada noticeably became uptight and responded, "Well, people are going to say what they want, but it's just a coincidence. I don't even know Young Money, and I didn't know that was his name that I used. It was an honest coincidence."

"I have a statement from a New York newspaper sitting in front of me and it states that"—Wendy looked down at the paper and began to read aloud—". . . Only a person responsible or affiliated with the murder would know the intimate specifics that Miss Simone's book tells."

Jada put her hand over the mic and looked at Wendy like she was crazy. She said in a low voice at Wendy, "What the fuck is yo' problem, bitch? You trying to get me murked? You said we were going to discuss my new book, not rumors."

Not covering her microphone, Wendy said loudly, "We are talking about your book. Let's see what New York has to say. We have a caller from the Bronx. Are you there?"

A female's voice from the phone line spoke. "Hello. What's up, Wendy? Jada, I loved your book and I can't wait until the follow-up to *The Duchess* comes out. Shake the haters off and keep doing ya thing, ma."

"Thanks, girl. I appreciate the support," Jada said, a wave of relief coming over her. The way Wendy was egging the beef on, Jada was damn sure that a hater would call and try to bash her.

Wendy quickly cut off the caller. "A'ight, thanks for calling in. We have another caller from Brooklyn on the line. Brooklyn, you there?"

"No doubt. What's good, Wendy?"

"Hey, baby. We have Jada Simone in the studio today."

"Yeah, I heard that *bleep* was in there," the man said in his low, raspy voice. "That's why I called up."

The room erupted in an instigating roar at the caller's harsh comments. "Ohhh!!"

Jada remained quiet and prepared to hear what the hater had to say.

"Yo, my fault, Wendy, but I don't know why this . . . this snitch is even getting attention and publicity for talking about stuff she knows nothing about. I'm telling you, she could end up getting hurt off of her book, fo' real, son. We don't play that in BK. She got my man Young Money under fire for something he has nothing to do with."

Jada tried to cut in, "Hold up, hold up!"

But the man kept talking over her. "People could end up getting rocked to sleep, nah mean?"

Wendy was smiling, loving every minute of this. Her lines began to light up with callers, and she loved all the drama. She knew that the caller was obviously a member of Young Money's camp.

"I'm out of here, *bleep* that. Let's bounce, Lou-Lou." Jada stood up and signaled for her bodyguard to follow her. She'd had enough when she saw the little smirk on Wendy's face. She knew that the host cared more about her ratings than the reputation of the guest. Jada was just there to promote her book, not violence.

She stormed out of the studio with her bodyguard

and, when she went past the host, thought about punching her dead in her face. But Jada decided to fall back and not react on her impulse. A girl from the hood all her life, now she wanted to get away from that, so she decided to just walk out like a lady.

"I can't believe this shit." Jada put on her $800 Christian Dior shades. She had another bodyguard waiting outside of the door for her. She, along with her protectors, made their way to the limo that waited for them outside of the studio.

Jada felt more comfortable with the guards. She'd hired them shortly after her book started to gain national attention. For months she had been receiving threats from anonymous callers, and hate mail. She honestly feared for her life. No matter how many times she changed her numbers, the calls still came. It even went as far as having security and metal detectors at her book signings.

In New York, she was extra careful. That was Young Money's hometown. While touring there, she would only have signings at closed areas, like Borders or Barnes & Noble. She refused to have them in open facilities such as malls. She had people at the front door with metal detectors for all people entering. It was crazy. Word on the street was that Young Money put a $100, 000 bounty on her head, so she was extra cautious and careful.

She stopped at the exit of the New York studio and waited for her bodyguard to secure the premises and make sure the limo was parked up front. She watched him call over the limo and scan the streets for anything suspicious. Once the coast was clear, he waved for them to approach the limo.

Jada's stilettos graced the pavement of the streets of New York and entered the vehicle. Her heart pounded erratically as she finally got in. She hated to admit it, but while in New York she always was uncomfortable. She'd been around the country promoting her new book for the last month and was ready to go back home to the Midwest, where she felt safe.

Her book had only been out for six months, but the success of it really surprised her. When word got out that the book was about hip-hop's king of rap, Young Money, it flew off the shelves. Shortly after, it was all over the news that Young Money was under investigation for racketeering and the murder of an undercover cop. Now, she was on the last stop of her book tour.

Everyone in the limo, Jada told the driver, "To La-Guardia, please." She looked at Lou-Lou and smiled. "I'm glad this shit is over. I can't wait to get the fuck out of New Yiddy. I hate it here."

Keyshia Cole lightly pumping out of the limo's speakers, Jada took off her shades and kicked off her shoes. "Turn that up please." She gently threw her head back and closed her eyes. She was ready to get out of the city that had no love for her.

Jada finally got a chance to rest as she quietly hummed the song's lyrics. She wanted to take a quick nap before reaching the airport.

The sounds of police sirens and flashing lights interrupted her brief rest. "What the fuck is going on?" Jada yelled as she sat up and watched as the cops jumped out of their squad cars with their guns drawn. Before she could even react, the cops had the limo's doors open, asking for everyone to step out.

One by one, with their hands up, Jada and her bodyguards exited the limo.

"What's the problem, officer?" Jada asked as she scooted out of the limo.

"Just get the fuck outta the car and keep your hands where I can see them, bitch!" The cop gripped his gun tightly.

Jada looked in the officer's eyes and knew that if she made the wrong move he would pop off. She decided to play it cool as she got out of the limo and was quickly handcuffed.

"You have the wrong person," Jada pleaded as she was face down on the limo's trunk.

"You have the right to remain silent. Anything you say can and will be used against you. If—"

"Wait, mu'fucka! What am I getting arrested for?" Jada screamed as the cop put the handcuffs on extra tight, intentionally trying to cause her pain.

"You are charged with murder in the first degree of a NYPD officer." The cop pulled Jada away and stuffed her in the back of his squad car.

Jada took a deep breath and knew that her past had finally caught up with her. She dropped her head in defeat, as in that single moment, her whole world came crumbling down.

The skinny man looked at the paper in front of him. "We, the jury find Jada Simone guilty of murder in the first degree."

"Fuck that!!! I am not Jada Simone. It's not me. You guys are charging the wrong person with murder." Spit flew out of her mouth as she yelled at the top of her lungs.

The judge banged his gavel, trying to calm down Jada, and her lawyer tried to restrain her.

It seemed as if Jada was going insane. She really believed in her heart that she was not Jada Simone. The look on her face was sincere as she professed her innocence. Everyone in the courtroom believed that the woman screaming at the judge had lost her mind.

Tears graced Jada's cheek as the realization of her fate set in. *Oh my God, this can't be happening. This can not be happening to me like this.* She closed her eyes and tasted the salty tears as they reached her mouth.

Jada's lawyer looked over at his client and thought to himself, *This bitch is either crazy as hell or a damn good actor.* He glanced over at the tattoo on her neck that had the initials *JS* on it. It was hard to try to convince a jury that she wasn't Jada Simone with that blatant tattoo. He'd advised her to plead insanity in the case, and after deep debate, that's exactly what they did. Now the only thing to do was wait for the sentencing.

The judge banged his gavel again to gain the court's attention. The court found Jada Simone guilty on all charges, sentencing to be administered after a mental evaluation.

The lawyer was upset that they'd lost the case, but he felt even more sorry for Jada Simone. She'd lost all grasp of reality and didn't believe that she was herself. The only bright side was that he'd convinced her to plead insanity, which would ultimately exonerate her from a heavy sentence. He knew that pleading insanity was the only way to avoid heavy time. If the evaluation proved that she was crazy, she would get a year in a mental hospital at the most. He believed she had a split personality, because Jada looked him in his eyes and told him that she wasn't the person that people thought she was.

Soon after the judge gave his verdict, the guards approached Jada and began to put her in handcuffs.

Jada became irate, screaming and kicking wildly, trying to escape their grasp. "It's not me. My name is not fuckin' Jada Simone!!!" she yelled while being restrained by three court marshals.

Flashing lights began to click away as every news reporter in the room tried to get a shot of the crazed best-selling author as she lost her mind. More spit flew out of Jada's mouth as she professed her innocence.

The guards eventually overpowered her, dragging her out of court and into custody.

Chapter One

"**D**amn, right there, daddy," Jada whispered as she rode Dr. Katz's thick chocolate pole.

Dr. Katz and Jada were in complete bliss on top of his cherry oak office desk. She still had on handcuffs, but it only aroused him even more. She grinded her hips in a circular motion as her juices dripped onto his lap. He couldn't believe that a mental evaluation session had become a sexual escapade. This was the first time he had been with a woman of such celebrity, and he loved every minute of it.

As soon as the security guard had escorted her into his office, he was overtaken by her beauty. He'd seen her on television, through her nationally publicized trial, but she was far more astonishing in person. As soon as the guard left them alone, Jada pounced on him, and he couldn't resist the temptation. He knew he was wrong for having sex with his patient, but he just couldn't bring himself to tell her to stop.

Jada put her finger in Dr. Katz's mouth as she rode

him. He circled his tongue around her finger and felt his manhood begin to pulsate. He was about to explode.

Jada, completely in sync with her shrink, hopped off his pole and caught all of him in her mouth. She continued to suck Dr. Katz until he was bone-dry. His legs shook. He'd just experienced the best sex he'd ever had.

Jada wasn't done with him yet. She took off her orange jail-issued top and bent over his couch, wanting him again.

For the first time, Dr. Katz was fully erect after busting a nut. He was eagerly ready for more. He walked up behind Jada as her juices dripped onto his hardwood floor, getting him even harder. He slid right into her and began to play with her hardened clitoris as he slowly went in and out of her.

Jada began to call out Dr. Katz's name, heightening his pleasure. The more she called his name, the harder and deeper he stroked. She threw her ass back, slamming against his balls, while sucking her own finger, completely turning the doctor out.

Dr. Katz's pole was throbbing and was hard as ever. He looked down at the veins that appeared on his manhood and let slob drip from his mouth, landing right onto Jada's other hole.

"Dr. Katz, Dr. Katz, Dr. Katz!" she yelled in pleasure.

"Dr. Katz, Dr. Katz, Dr. Katz!" Jada yelled as she sat in front of him.

Dr. Katz snapped out of his freaky daydream and sat upright in his chair. He stared at the beautiful woman fully clothed in a jail suit and was completely embarrassed. He cleared his throat and answered, "Yes, Miss Simone, you have to excuse me. I was reviewing your file." He looked down at the papers in front of his desk. Actually, he was trying to take a sneak peek at his crotch to ensure he hadn't become noticeably aroused. When he looked down, he noticed that he was standing at full attention and tried to think about baseball, to get himself off hard.

He focused back on Jada and began their session. "It says here that you don't believe that you are Jada Simone, but a girl from Flint, Michigan named"—Dr. Katz scanned her file—"Y'lesha Coleman."

"My name is Y'lesha Coleman," Jada said. "I am not crazy, and I didn't have anything to do with the murder of that cop. It's a big misunderstanding. You have to believe me. The real Jada Simone is dead, and I just made a big mistake." Tears began to fill her eyes. Her hands began to shake, and the sound of the handcuffs jingling filled the air.

Dr. Katz stared into Jada's eyes and thought to himself. *Either she is insane or a damn good actor.* The hurt was written all over her face, and Jada was very scared. She had a life sentence hanging over her head for a crime she didn't commit. Dr. Katz wanted to get inside the mind of Jada Simone, but knew he needed to gain her trust to get an accurate analysis. Jada had a raggedy book in her hand. He thought it would be the perfect opportunity to just break the ice.

Dr. Katz looked down at the book. "What is that you're reading?"

Jada looked down in confusion and noticed that she

had brought her book out from her jail cell without realizing it. "Oh this? This is an Ashley JaQuavis novel. It's the only thing that keeps me sane. Prison walls can drive you mad."

"What's it about?" Dr. Katz asked, pretending he was interested.

"I can't really get into it. It's kind of boring."

Dr. Katz rubbed his neatly trimmed goatee. "Do you believe that your name is Jada Simone?"

"I was born Y'lesha Coleman. I told you that before. You have to believe me."

"Tell me about Y'lesha, from the beginning." He jotted down on his pad: *Jada doesn't have a grasp on reality. She has created another persona named Y'lesha Coleman to cope with her harsh reality. I believe that she really believes that she is not herself. Her eyes show sincerity.*

Dr. Katz had been doing mental evaluations as a therapist for the correctional facility for ten years, but had never met a woman that matched Jada's beauty. He knew it was going to be a task to stay focused during his sessions, but he was determined. He was more than intrigued by Jada Simone. He sat back in his big chair and observed as Jada lay back on his leather chair and told him about Y'lesha.

Jada closed her eyes and relaxed as she prepared to give Dr. Katz the whole truth from the beginning. She thought back to the start and told him about Y'lesha, just a girl from the hood.

Chapter Two

"Damn!" Y'lesha yelled as the hot fish grease popped on her hand. It was two in the morning as she stood in front of the kitchen stove preparing a surprise for her boyfriend Petey, who stumbled in drunk thirty minutes earlier and passed out in their bed.

Y'lesha anxiously tapped her foot against the ground, waiting for the grease to get hot enough to fry some catfish. She walked over to the sink and let water trickle on her hand. She flicked the water in the grease, and it instantly began to pop. "Perfect!" she whispered as she looked at the catfish batter on the countertop.

The sound of a honking horn outside startled Y'lesha, and she went to the front window and took a peek outside. A cab was parked directly in front of the house. She grew agitated. She wanted to head outside to tell the cab driver about himself, but first she went to the bedroom to see if Petey was still 'sleep. She peeked in, and as she expected, he was still passed out, shirtless in the bed.

She headed for the front door and carefully un-locked it, trying not to awake him from his peaceful slumber. She walked to the passenger side of the cab as the driver rolled down the window.

"Someone called for a cab here, right?" the Hispanic driver said in broken English.

"Right, but I thought I told yo' ass not to blow the horn when you got here." She put both of her hands on her hips. She dug into her pockets and pulled out a crumbled twenty-dollar bill. "Keep the car running. I'll be back in a second."

Y'lesha returned to the house, grabbed the luggage that she had placed by the door, and headed back out to the cab. Once she put her bags in the car, she left the cab's door wide open and returned to the house. She tried to remain as quiet as she could, tiptoeing through the house, heading back to the kitchen. While in the hallway, she caught a glimpse of herself in the mirror and stopped in her tracks. What she saw brought tears to her eyes, and it only gave her motivation to go through with her plan. The sight of two black eyes and a swollen lip pained her heart. What once was a beauti-ful face was now a gruesome sight, and it was all at the hands of Petey.

It was definitely not the first time that Petey had beaten Y'lesha. She'd been hospitalized at least five times in the past year, and the mental abuse was far more degrading than the physical. With no family, Petey was the only person that Y'lesha had. She was half-Cuban, half-black. Her mother was of Cuban descent, and she had no knowledge of who her father was. Her mother was forced into prostitution and, in the midst, conceived Y'lesha. She couldn't tell Y'lesha exactly who her father was, but the thick hair and caramel skin indicated that Y'lesha's father was one of the black men that she had turned a trick with. She was illegally shipped to the States by her mother for a better life at the age of five.

By the time Y'lesha was 9, her mother was diagnosed with cancer and died a few years later. Petey met her when she was 14, and after the death of her mother, she moved in with him. She was now 19, and Petey was all she knew. Petey, ten years her senior, made her look at him like a father figure rather than a companion.

Y'lesha put her hand on her belly, and more tears began to fall as she thought about her miscarriage. She was used to Petey coming in drunk and putting his hands on her, but she honestly thought the news of her pregnancy would make the beatings stop, but it didn't.

Two nights before, she'd suffered a brutal thrashing from Petey for not having any dinner cooked. He came in yelling, screaming something about catfish. Y'lesha usually had his dinner done when he came home from work, but that day she went to the doctor to receive her pre-natal pills. It must have slipped Petey's mind, because that night, he beat her ass like a stranger on the street, causing her to miscarry the baby. That was the last straw for Y'lesha.

Y'lesha looked into her own eyes in the mirror and saw nothing. She had no soul because Petey had stripped it from her. *I can't take this anymore. I have to do what I got to do, and I refuse to be treated like a fuckin' slave. This nigga don't have any love for me, and I still sit here and let him degrade me. I can do bad by my damn self!* Y'lesha carefully walked into the kitchen. She reached for the cast-iron skillet but nearly burned her hand on the handle, it was so hot. She grabbed an oven mitt out of the drawer and attempted to pick the skillet up again.

She grabbed the skillet and slowly headed toward the bedroom where Petey was at. She carefully walked over to him, trying not to spill any of the scorching-hot grease, and stood over his snoring body. Almost in a whisper, she began to tell him how she really felt. "I hate you. I fuckin' hate you. You took the only thing that I had from me. My baby. Our baby. For years I let you beat my ass, and I stayed with your no-good ass. I was real to you." She closed her eyes and thought about reneging on her plan, but she remembered all of the mental anguish Petey put her through and whispered, "Real bitches do real things."

Petey sensed that someone was standing over him and, without opening his eyes, yelled drunkenly, "Bitch, where my damn food? Don't make me beat—aghhh!!!" Petey roared. Before he could even get out his threat, he felt the burning sensation of hot grease on his chest.

Y'lesha just stood there in shock, not believing what she just did, as the smell of burning flesh filled the air, along with Petey's cries. She watched as the smoke came off his body.

Y'lesha quickly came to her senses and knew she had better get the hell out of there. She took off and headed for the door. She rushed out of the house and jumped into the already open back seat of the cab. She looked back in time to see Petey running out of the house after her, holding his scorched chest. "Go! Go!" she told the cab driver. "Get the fuck outta here." And the cab driver pulled off before Petey could reach the car.

Y'lesha's adrenaline pumped as her heart raced at 100 miles per hour. She was terrified, but at the same time, she felt liberated. She threw her head back and began to cry hysterically, thinking about what she'd just done.

The cab driver looked at Y'lesha through his rearview mirror. "Where to?"

Staring out of her window and crying, Y'lesha whispered, "As far away from here as you can get."

An hour later she was at the doorstep of her best friend, Zya, her bags at her feet. She was in Detroit, an hour away from Petey in the next city. As she stood outside of her best friend's doorstep, the pouring rain, along with the tears, graced her face. Y'lesha was so ashamed, but she didn't know where to go. She didn't have any money for a hotel, she had no family, and the few friends she did have, Petey, being the jealous type, eventually tore her away from them.

Six months earlier, Petey had gotten a shop job in Flint and moved there, an hour away from Detroit, where they stayed. The beatings got worse once they moved.

Zya aka Lil' Bit was all she had, and Y'lesha hadn't seen her in about six months. Petey had managed to hamper their relationship too, and Y'lesha honestly didn't know how Lil' Bit was going to react when she saw her at her doorstep. *What if she closes the door in my face? I haven't seen Lil' Bit in months, and I don't know how she will respond. Fuck it. I don't have anywhere else to go.* Y'lesha cried a river and shamefully rang Lil' Bit's doorbell.

After a couple seconds of waiting and no response, Y'lesha's own reality sank in. She was all alone and had nowhere to go. She dropped to her knees and began to weep like a baby. Then she heard the door open and looked up to see Lil' Bit looking down at her.

"Y'lesha?" Lil' Bit said, as she looked at her friend in confusion. When she saw Y'lesha's battered face, her heart dropped. She already knew what had happened. "Oh my God," Lil' Bit whispered. She dropped to her knees and embraced her best friend.

Y'lesha tried to tell Lil' Bit what happened in between her cries, but she couldn't get it out.

Lil' Bit fully understood and tried to comfort her. "Shhh. It's okay. Girl, just let it out." Lil' Bit rocked her friend back and forth in her arms, both of the girls on their knees in the rain getting soaked.

After minutes of comforting Y'lesha, Lil' Bit grabbed her bags, helped Y'lesha up, and brought her into the house.

Lil' Bit comforted her friend all night, and Y'lesha told her about all the abuse she went through with Petey. By the end of the conversation, Lil' Bit was in tears, totally feeling Y'lesha's pain.

Y'lesha looked at her long-time friend and noticed that she still looked the same. Her petite body and her big mouth were just like she remembered it. Y'lesha was glad to be reunited with her. When the two of them got together, it was as if they hadn't been apart.

"Y'lesha, I never knew that he was putting you through all of this," Lil' Bit said as she sat across from her best friend, a small glass of Henny and Coke in hand.

"Nobody knew. When he beat my ass, he wouldn't let me leave the house until I healed up. Even then, I barely got out. He took my life away from me. I had no choice but to leave. He would've eventually killed me if I stayed there."

Lil' Bit dropped her head and shook it out of disgust. She had no idea that Y'lesha lived like that. Lil' Bit thought that Petey was a nice guy. She soon learned that he only treated Y'lesha good around others, but behind closed doors, it was a different story.

Soon, the sadness became happiness as the two old friends caught up on old times. Lil' Bit and Y'lesha stayed up all night as Lil' Bit put Y'lesha up on game about all the gossip and the haps of the neighborhood. "Yeah, girl," she said. "Keisha got a baby by fat-ass Jodi now."

"Fo' real?"

"Hell yeah. And you know Face doing it big now, right?"

Y'lesha scrunched her face up. "Face?"

"Yeah, you know Raymond from high school. They call him Face now. He's moving heavy coke. He got the hood on smash. He got about six cars, and he be stunting like a mu'fucka. He used to have a mad crush on you in high school."

"Yeah, I remember Raymond. His ass was ugly, though."

"Well, the nigga ain't ugly no more. I don't know if it's the money that makes him look good or what, but he got every chick in the *D* after him. Shit, he can get

some of this good shit if he wants it." Lil' Bit held her
hand up, laughing her ass off.

"You are so crazy, girl." Y'lesha playfully slapped her
friend's hand and joined her in laughter.

Lil' Bit told Y'lesha that she could stay with her until
she got back on her feet, and she humbly accepted the
offer, relieved to get the burden of Petey off her shoulders.

Dr. Katz rested his index finger on his temple as he
listened to Jada tell the life story of Y'lesha Coleman,
the woman she claimed to be. He looked at the clock
and noticed that they had two hours left in their first
session. In only three sessions, Dr. Katz had to decide if
the woman on his couch was really insane and had split
personalities. He picked up his pen and began to jot
down notes: *Her alter ego, Y'lesha, has a violent streak, and
she describes aggression in her past. Miss Simone has totally
lost all grasp of reality and has created a childhood scenario
for her "character."*

Dr. Katz put his pencil on his pad and slowly inter-
twined his hands. "Miss Simone, may I ask you a question?"

Jada smacked her lips. "My name is Y'lesha. Yes, you
may. Go 'head."

"Why aren't there any records of Y'lesha Coleman?
No birth certificate, no dental records, no anything?"

"You weren't listening. My mother and I illegally
moved here from Cuba. There wouldn't be any records
of me or of my mother."

Dr. Katz looked for signs of bullshit, but he couldn't

find any. *She really believes herself,* he thought. Intrigued by the tale, he wanted to hear more about Y'lesha before their session was over for the day. "Tell me more about this, this Y'lesha character."

Jada closed her eyes and went back into her story.

Chapter Three

It had been three weeks since Y'lesha moved in with Lil' Bit, and they were like teenagers again. They were both having the time of their life. Y'lesha managed to get an interview at Macy's in the mall and was finally getting her life together without Petey.

It was Saturday night, and they were on their way to the Zoo Bar in downtown Detroit, a popular hip-hop club. They rode down I-75 in Lil' Bit's '98 Honda Accord, bumping their heads to 50 Cent's CD. As they pulled up to the club, they noticed the line that wrapped around the corner.

"Damn, it's packed in there, Bit," Y'lesha said as she stared at the club's entrance.

"Yeah, I told you this was the spot. All the get-money niggas be in there," Lil' Bit said as she searched for a parking spot.

The girls exited the car and headed to the club. Lil' Bit knew the doorman, so they got straight in. When the girls entered the club, it was jumping. Everyone was bouncing to Young Money's new single and was having a good time.

Y'lesha felt kind of uncomfortable. She hadn't been in a club since she and Petey first began dating.

Lil' Bit noticed Y'lesha's mood. "Come on, girl. Let's show 'em how we do it."

The two girls began to dance with each other. At first, Y'lesha was stiff as a board, but after a while, she got her swagger back and was shaking that ass like a professional. Y'lesha seductively moved her ass in circles as a crowd began to watch her like a movie. Y'lesha was enjoying the attention, but when a guy tried to get behind her, she always turned him down.

Lil' Bit, on the other hand, shook her ass for whoever ran up on her. She even got on her knees and grinded a dude that was laying flat on his back. Bit was ghetto as hell and didn't have a problem letting the whole club know.

When the DJ put on Jeezy's record, the club went crazy. Everyone was bouncing with their hands in the air, and all the dope boys stood up as if it was an anthem. Lil' Bit was right in the mix. Her hands up in the air, she was reciting his lyrics.

For the next hour, they seductively danced and partied hard. Y'lesha became exhausted and took a break. "I'll be over at the bar," she said into Lil' Bit's ear as she grinded her ass in a dude's crotch. Y'lesha made her way over to the bar to get a drink. *It's hot as hell in this mu'fucka,* she thought. She waved at the bartender to get his attention. "Let me get bottled water," she yelled, trying to be heard over the loud speakers.

Y'lesha turned toward the dance floor and looked at Lil' Bit as she got sandwiched by two guys on the dance floor. Lil' Bit was holding her own with the two men as she began to attract a crowd. Everyone wanted to see the freaky petite girl work her magic.

"That's my girl." Y'lesha grabbed the water from the bartender and dropped a couple of dollars.

"That's all you drinking, ma?" a man's voice said from across the bar.

Y'lesha saw a familiar face when she looked over to see who was talking to her. She looked around and then pointed her index finger to her own chest. "Who me?" She noticed that the man was surrounded by other men, all of them wearing all-black with long platinum chains on.

"Yeah, you. What you drinking, ma?" The man stood up and emerged from the crew. He walked toward Y'lesha. When the man stood up, Y'lesha noticed that he stood about 6 foot 3, with a slim body. He had long braids and a neat goatee. The man approached Y'lesha with a Corona in his hand.

As the man got closer, Y'lesha began to put a name with the face. "Raymond?"

"What's good, Y'lesha? Long time no see." Raymond opened his arms, inviting Y'lesha.

Y'lesha embraced him. He'd changed a lot since high school. He had grown hair on his face and all the acne he used to have was gone. She also noticed that his gear had improved. He was fresh to death.

"Hey. How have you been, Raymond?"

"I'm good. I haven't seen you since high school, ma. What's been good?"

"Nothing. You got hair on your face now and shit. Look at you, growing up. You ain't lil' Raymond no more." Y'lesha playfully touched his chest, feeling his muscles.

"Yeah, a lot has changed. I go by Face now. Well, at least that's what everyone calls me."

"Face. I like that." Y'lesha smiled sexily. The more she looked at him, the more she remembered why she never gave him any play in high school. He had improved since school, but in Y'lesha's eyes he was still unattractive.

Face took a seat next to Y'lesha, and they began to catch up on old times. They ended up talking most of the night. Face saw that the night was coming to an end and decided to make his move. "Yo, who you come in here with?" he asked.

"Lil' Bit. She in here somewhere." Y'lesha looked around and saw Lil' Bit still shaking her ass on the dance floor.

Face had a look of disgust on his face when he heard Lil' Bit's name. He already knew how she got down. He frowned. "You still fuck with Lil' Bit?"

"Yeah, that's my best friend. Why you say it like that?"

"I just don't get along with her, that's all. But look, I'm about to bounce. I would like to take you out sometime, though. Can I get your number o' something?" Face displayed his gap-toothed smile.

Y'lesha had a good time talking to Face that night, but she wasn't trying to fuck with him like that. She was just fresh off a relationship, and on top of that, she wasn't really attracted to him. "You cool and all, but right now, I have to get myself together, you know, work on me. Maybe another time."

"Work on you? You look good to me. What you need? Maybe I can help you."

Y'lesha laughed at Face's persistence and jokingly said, "Nah, I don't think so. You can't get me a job." She hugged Face and began to walk off.

Face gently grabbed her hand. "Maybe I can give you a job. Let me leave my number with you, and we can work something out. As you can see, I'm doing good." He raised his wrist and showed his iced-out bracelet and shiny pinky ring.

Y'lesha hated a showboating-ass nigga, but she couldn't deny his shine. He was definitely getting it, by the looks of things.

Lil' Bit made her way over to them and immediately began sack-chasing. "Hey, Face. You looking good tonight." She stepped in between him and Y'lesha.

Face didn't even acknowledge her. He just gave her a nonchalant head nod. He wrote his number on a napkin and handed it to Y'lesha. "If you tryin'-a get paid, get at me. I got something for you." With that he headed for the door, and his crew, on cue, followed him out.

"That nigga so funny-acting." Lil' Bit rolled her eyes and sat down on the stool next to Y'lesha.

"Why you two don't get along?"

Lil' Bit grabbed a napkin and wiped the sweat on her forehead from dancing. "I used to fuck with his nigga Red, and he got robbed. Face swears up and down that I set him up, but it wasn't even like that. Even Red said

I wouldn't do that to him. But ever since that incident happened, Face has given me the cold shoulder. He needs to get over that shit."

Y'lesha looked at the number on the napkin and balled it up. She didn't want any parts of Face or his money. She already knew what type of trouble thugs brought. She'd learned her lesson from Petey. She didn't know what kind of job he was talking about, but she wasn't interested. "You ready to go, girl?" she said to Lil' Bit.

Lil' Bit nodded, and they headed out.

Before leaving though, Y'lesha sneakily scooped the napkin up and put it in her bra. She grabbed it just in case she changed her mind about Face. *Maybe I'll see what he's talking about. Maybe.*

The girls made it to the car, and Y'lesha remembered that she had an interview for the Macy's job the next day. "Shit!" she yelled as Lil' Bit started her car.

"What's wrong with you?" Lil' Bit asked in confusion.

"I forgot I got that interview tomorrow. I don't have anything to wear. You think you can get me some casual shit?"

"I got you," Lil' Bit said confidently as she pulled off. "I'll get something for you tomorrow morning."

"Bitch, start the car!!" Lil' Bit yelled as she ran out of the mall with her oversized purse.

Y'lesha looked in the rearview and saw Lil' Bit running full speed toward the car, two security guards on her ass, but Lil' Bit was too fast for them. Y'lesha fumbled with the keys and stuck it in the ignition. The window was down on the passenger side, so without even opening the door, Lil' Bit dove head first into the car. Her little body flew in, and Y'lesha pulled off full speed.

"Go, go!" Lil' Bit screamed, her ass in the air and her face buried in the seat.

"Damn, Bit!" Y'lesha said while maneuvering the Honda through the parking lot.

Lil' Bit began to laugh hysterically as she looked at her nervous friend zoom out of the mall's parking lot.

Y'lesha kept her eyes on the road. "What the hell is so funny?"

"I'm laughing at yo' scary ass," Lil' Bit managed to say between laughs.

Y'lesha reluctantly let out a chuckle. She knew that she was a nervous wreck. "They were on ya ass. I thought you were about to get caught. What the fuck happened anyway?"

"I had the suit in my bag after I came out of the bathroom. So I shopped around a little bit, tryin'-a play it off. I noticed that two securities were following me. They were waiting for me to leave with the shit. It was too late to put the shit back, so when I hit the door, I took off."

"You crazy."

"I got your outfit, didn't I?"

Lil' Bit pulled a spliff out of her purse. She scraped the guts out of the Dutch and began to fill it with the goods. After rolling up, she put her bag on her lap and pulled out a black two-piece business suit. "You're going to get that job wearing this."

Y'lesha looked over at the two pieces. "Yeah, that shit is fly. Thanks, girl. How much I owe you?"

"You my girl. Don't worry about it," Lil' Bit said, firing up and leaning back in the seat.

Y'lesha looked at the tag and frowned up. "You boosted this shit from Macy's," Y'lesha yelled as she stopped at a red light.

"Yeah. Why?" Lil' Bit asked, the weed smoke still in her lungs.

"Because that's where my interview is, Bit." Y'lesha shook her head from side to side in disbelief. *How am I supposed to show up to an interview with an outfit on that was stole from there six hours ago? I don't have any choice. Fuck it.*

"So you have no work experience at all?" the Caucasian lady asked from behind her wooden desk.

"No, but I am really good with people and. . . ." Y'lesha tried to explain as she twiddled her fingers nervously.

"We will give you a call, Ms. Coleman." The lady stood up and extended her hand.

No, this bitch didn't cut me off like that. Y'lesha plastered a phony smile on her face. She already knew that her lack of work experience shrunk her chances of getting the job. Petey had taken care of her financially for as long as she could remember. She came to the realization that she had to really start all over. Y'lesha stood up and shook the woman's hand.

The woman looked Y'lesha up and down with a huge smile. "That is a pretty outfit," she said.

Y'lesha instantly became nervous. She didn't know if the woman knew how she got it or if she just really liked it, but Y'lesha wasn't going to wait and find out. She gave her a quick, "Thank you," and headed out.

Y'lesha went to the bus stop to catch the next bus back to Lil' Bit's house. *This is some bull. That bitch talking about 'We'll give you a call.' I just can not catch a break.* Y'lesha sat on the bench and pulled off the shoes from her aching feet.

What Y'lesha saw next nearly made her heart skip a beat. She felt her breaths begin to get shallow as she watched Petey's all-black Dodge Charger slowly roll up and stop right in front of her. Y'lesha froze up, not knowing what to do. Her mind told her to take off running, but she was stuck. Her body did not move.

The tinted windows rolled down, and a familiar face emerged from the car. The face wasn't Petey's. It was Raymond's aka Face. "Yo, what's good, ma?" Face smiled at her.

Y'lesha tried to speak, but she had a lump in her throat. She thought for sure that it was Petey in the car. They had identical cars. She put her hand on her chest and then let out a sigh of relief. "Hey, Raymond," she managed to let out.

"You okay? You don't look so good," he said, noticing how uptight she was.

"Yeah, I'm good. I thought that you were someone else."

Face maneuvered his hand so that it was on top of the steering wheel, to show off his diamond bezel. It was a different one from what Y'lesha had seen last night. This one was gold and full of diamonds. He then looked at Y'lesha and tried to spit game. "Want a ride, ma?"

Y'lesha peeked at Face's arm and then looked at his

24-inch tires on the whip. She wanted to accept the offer because she hated catching the bus, but when she looked at him in the face, she remembered why she never gave him any play. He just wasn't her type. "Nah, I'm good, but thanks anyway." Y'lesha smiled and crossed her legs.

Face wasn't going to give up that easy. He was going to get at Y'lesha one way or another. "Why yo' man got you catching a bus? You supposed to be sitting behind something new, nah mean?" He picked up his ringing BlackBerry to see who was calling. He ignored the call and looked at Y'lesha's clothes. "What you all dressed up for? You work out here?"

"I wish. I had a job interview here today." Y'lesha un-loosened her hair and let if fall onto her shoulders and slowly shook her head.

"Fuck a job out here. If you want to make some real money, you should come and see me."

"Oh really? Work for you? Doing what, exactly?"

"Well, I need a chick to make runs for me. The chick that used to do it for me moved out of town."

Y'lesha was from the hood, and she already knew what type of runs Face was talking about. She normally wouldn't consider doing anything like that, but her current situation had her contemplating taking Face up on his offer. She just remained silent.

Face continued, "Look, I'm in the hood. Lil' Bit know where my spot at. If you change your mind, come and see me, or call."

"I'll do that," Y'lesha said as she saw the bus coming up the street.

Face slowly pulled off and left Y'lesha alone to tend to her thoughts.

Maybe I might see what he talking about. If he's getting it like Bit said he is, it might be a good idea. I can't live with Lil' Bit forever, and mu'fuckas ain't trying to hire me. I just might holla at his ugly ass.

The bus pulled up, and Y'lesha hopped on and headed home.

Chapter Four

Lil' Bit pulled up to Face's auto shop, Y'lesha on the passenger side. "This is his spot right here." Lil' Bit threw the car in park.

Y'lesha saw a group of men standing outside the auto shop.

The men began to look at the car, to see who was in front of their spot. One man even reached under his shirt as if he was reaching for a gun.

Y'lesha looked over at Lil' Bit and bit her bottom lip, something she always did when she was nervous. "Bit, please come in here with me. Those grimy-ass niggas looking at me all crazy and shit."

"Girl, they ain't going to do nothing. Just go up there and say you are there to see Face. And you know Face don't like me like that. I can't just go up in there."

Y'lesha took a deep breath and slowly got out of the car.

It had been a week since she'd seen Face at the mall. She thought hard about taking him up on his offer all week then decided to give him a call to see what was good. Earlier that day, he'd told her to meet him at the spot, so they could go over the logistics.

Y'lesha began to walk up to the front entrance. Now, all the frowns on the men's faces became envious stares and stupid grins.

"I'm here to see Face," she said in a slightly shaken voice.

They all just stared at her like she was an art exhibit.

Y'lesha became irritated and smacked her lips. "Well, is he here or not?" she asked as she put both of her hands on her hips.

One of the men finally spoke. "He is in a meeting right now. You can wait for him in the waiting room." He pointed inside the shop.

Y'lesha brushed past the men and headed toward the waiting room. She took a look around the body shop and noticed that no cars were being worked on. There were no mechanics anywhere, just cars lined up. By the way the men were dressed, Y'lesha knew that they weren't fixing any cars in that attire.

She looked on as the men took duffle bags out of a car trunk and walked into the back room with them in their hands. It was like an assembly line. As soon as the cars were emptied, they pulled it out and pulled another one in.

Y'lesha reached the waiting room and entered. She took a seat and waited to see Face. She was impressed. It was by far the best auto shop she'd ever seen. The waiting room had a large flat-screen television and was well decorated. She glanced around and knew that this was more than a car repair shop. This had to be Face's factory.

Y'lesha heard a muffled scream come from the back room, and she quickly glanced at the closed door. Then she heard a loud thud and Face's voice yell, "Mu'fuckas think it's a game. Where is my money?"

Y'lesha quickly became nervous and started listening closely. She realized Face was talking to another man.

"Face, I'll get you your money," he said. "It's just—"

Face said, "Put your hand on the table."

A moment of silence filled the air.

Face repeated himself, yelling, "Put yo' mu'fuckin' hand on the table!"

Moments later Y'lesha heard the sound of wood being chopped and soon after the sound of a man's scream. Y'lesha had heard enough. She quickly got up and headed toward the exit, but before she could reach the door, the office entrance opened.

Y'lesha quickly turned around, and there stood Face, a machete in his left hand. He had his shirt off, displaying his tattooed body, and there was blood on his face.

She tried to act as if she didn't overhear what was going on and pretended she was entering the waiting room, rather than trying to get the fuck up out of there. "Hey, Raymond. They told me to come in here and wait for you." She glanced behind Face and saw the man rocking back and forth with a bloody hand. She looked closer and noticed that the man's finger was cut off. *Oh my God!* She grimaced and put her hand over her mouth.

Face smiled and slowly closed the door. "Don't worry

about that, ma," he said, as if everything was all good. "How you doing?" He put down the machete and walked over to Y'lesha, sweat dripping from his ripped body as he approached her.

Y'lesha didn't have any idea what Face was going to do to her for witnessing his malicious act. As he approached, she tensed up and closed her eyes, but to her surprise, he walked right past her and headed to the water dispenser in the corner. She opened one eye and watched as he drank the water up and then turned toward her.

"You ready to start working, ma?" Face asked as he stood before her.

Before today Y'lesha was really considering working for Face, but after she saw what he did to the man, she began to have second thoughts. *Hell nah. I ain't trying to work for your crazy ass.* She gave him a fake smile.

Face read right through her. He continued, "If you worried about what happened to him, it's simple—He broke the rules, so he had to pay, nah mean? If you ain't planning on doing nothing sheisty, you have nothing to worry about."

Y'lesha still wasn't buying it. She was trying to get out of that shop as fast as she could, but she didn't want to upset him, so she just listened.

Face walked up toe to toe with her. "I can trust you, right?"

Y'lesha looked down at his hands and became uneasy at all the blood. She didn't want to say the wrong thing to Face, knowing what he was capable of. "Y-yeah, y-you can trust me," she stuttered.

Face walked to the door and waved for one of his workers in the office. He threw his head in the direction of the backroom where the man was, and his worker headed back there and dragged the crying man out.

Face taunted the man while his worker was dragging him out. "Next time you come short, it's going to be the whole hand, *B.*"

He calmly focused his attention back on Y'lesha. He reached in his pocket and pulled out a rubber band full of money. He tossed it to her and said, "Once a week, I need you to take trips for me. It's easy. Drop off my package in Flint and pick up my money. Everybody you deal with is close to me, so you have nothing to worry about. I just need to know if I can trust you. Can I?" Face grabbed a towel and wiped the blood off his hands.

Y'lesha, without thinking, nodded her head in agreement, letting him know he could trust her.

"You need a driver's license, and if you smoke trees, you don't anymore. I need you to be completely focused while getting this money. You can't be high on the job. I need you to dress in church clothes while making the runs and always ride solo. This way you lower your chances of drawing attention to yourself. You got all of this?"

Face was hitting Y'lesha with so much, she was overwhelmed. He was talking so fast, she didn't have time to think it out. She wanted to decline the job, but when she took a look at the knot in her hand, it was hard to pass it up. She began to flip through the bills, noticing that they were all hundreds and fifties. *Damn, it's about five thousand right here. I could use this right here. But this nigga is crazier than a mu'fucka. I don't know,* Y'lesha thought.

"That's a two-week advance." Face looked at the wad of money in her hand.

Y'lesha did the math in her head and figured that meant she'd be making about $2500 a week. That was enough for her to get on her feet. Since no one was trying to hire her, she thought, *Fuck it.* "You can trust me, Face," she said in a shaky voice. "When do I start?"

Chapter Five

6 Months Later

The cold steel of the knife sliced across Y'lesha's cheek, rudely awakening her. She screamed in pain as she opened her eyes to see Petey standing over her with an unbuttoned shirt, exposing his bandaged chest. She tried to scream for help, but he put his hand over her mouth, muffling her. He put the knife to her neck and just barely pierced her skin, causing a drip of blood to trickle down her neck. Y'lesha knew that Petey came to kill her.

He had a crazed look on his face as he straddled her body. "If you scream, I will jam this knife through your throat." Petey's bloodshot-red eyes stared into hers. He slowly removed his hand from her mouth.

Tears began to fall from Y'lesha's eyes, and she began to apologize. "Petey, I'm sorry. I'm so sorry. I didn't mean to hurt you," she pleaded, looking into the eyes of the crazy man on top of her.

Without even responding, Petey stabbed her in the chest with the knife repeatedly. The unbearable pain shot through her body as she lay there helplessly and Petey stabbed her for the tenth time.

"Wake up, bitch! Bitch, wake up!"

Y'lesha didn't understand what Petey meant as she felt her life begin to slip away.

Lil' Bit nudged Y'lesha from her nightmare. "Wake up, bitch!"

Y'lesha woke up in a frenzy, not knowing what was going on. She felt her chest and breathed a sigh of relief when she realized it was just a bad dream. Sweat dripped from her forehead as she sat upright, breathing heavily.

"Are you all right, girl? I came in here when I heard you screaming. You were having another one of those nightmares, weren't you?"

"Yeah." Y'lesha began to wipe the light sweat that formed on her neck.

Away from Petey for six months, Y'lesha had still been having frequent nightmares about him finding her and killing her. Sometimes she regretted what she'd done to him, but a woman scorned is a woman scorned.

"Okay, I have to get back in here with these bitches before they try to steal my shit," Lil' Bit said, referring to the girls in her living room looking through her rack of boosted clothes.

"Go 'head, girl. I'm all right," Y'lesha said as she got out of the bed.

Lil' Bit headed back into the living room, leaving Y'lesha in the room by herself.

Y'lesha went to the bathroom that was connected to

the guestroom and stood over the sink. She splashed water on her face and rose up and looked at herself in the mirror. She was happy with her situation.

At first she made runs for Face all the time, but after he found out she was staying with Lil' Bit, the jobs slowed up. He always told Y'lesha that Lil' Bit was bad luck, and he didn't want anything to do with her or anybody who deals with her. But Y'lesha had made so much money from it, she wasn't tripping. She'd saved up a nice piece of change.

She jumped in the shower and prepared for her day. She clicked on her radio, and the sounds of Young Money pumped out of the stereo. She began to sing along to the popular rap song, closing her eyes and letting the water cascade down her naked body. Her big brown nipples began to get erect and stood at attention. She was definitely past due for some pipe to get laid down.

The last time she'd had some was with Petey, and that wasn't exactly what she called sex. He was so drunk when they sexed, it always was horrible. He prematurely ejaculated every time; he never failed.

Y'lesha let the water hit her face, and her hand caressed her own breast. Her hands never felt so good on her body. Her hands eventually made it down to her lil' mama, and her two middle fingers reached her clitoris. She began to massage herself in slow circular motions and couldn't control herself. The slow motions quickly sped up, and her knees began to shake as her love came down.

Thirty minutes later, she entered the living room, where three girls were flipping through Lil' Bit's clothes rack. If you didn't know, you could mistake Lil' Bit's living room for a small clothing store.

Lil' Bit was sitting at the table eating breakfast, keeping an eye on her customers. She looked at Y'lesha as she entered the front room and said to her, "Hey, girl. I left you some breakfast in the oven."

"Thanks." Y'lesha made her way to the stove to get some food.

One of the girls yelled out, "Lil' Bit, how much you want for this coat?"

Lil' Bit thought for a second. "Give me a hundred for it."

"Damn! A hundred, Bit?"

"A hundred? It's three hundred twenty-nine dollars on the tag. I'm giving you a deal."

"How about I give you twenty and two tickets to the Young Money concert. You know I work at the Joe Louis Arena, and I get free tickets."

"Young Money? Stop bullshitting."

"For real, girl. I got 'em right here. I got VIP passes too. I would have gone myself, but I have to work that night."

Lil' Bit got up from the table and went over to the girl as she dug through her purse, searching for the tickets. She dug them out and handed them to Lil' Bit.

Lil' Bit examined them, and just like she said, there were two tickets and two VIP passes to the concert. "Bet!" Lil' Bit smiled and began to think about what she would wear to the concert. She glanced over at Y'lesha and held the tickets over her head and shouted, "Girl, we going to the Young Money concert."

* * *

It was the night of the concert, and people filed in the arena, trying to get a glimpse of the star. Y'lesha and Lil' Bit were right there in the midst as they stood in line. The girls were definitely dressed to impress. Y'lesha had her hair pulled back in a tight ponytail, letting her baby hair rest on the edges. She wore tight, low-riding Apple Bottoms jeans and a black halter-top. Her stilettos were just the cherry on top. Lil' Bit had on denim Daisy Dukes that exposed just barely the lower portion of her butt cheeks. She had on a cherry-red belly shirt that displayed her flat stomach and diamond belly ring.

All eyes were on them as they made their way into the arena. Niggas were definitely checking for them. By them having VIP passes, they got right in and headed backstage. Lil' Bit was searching for one thing and one thing only—a hood-rich nigga with major dough.

"It's really packed in here tonight," Lil' Bit said as they made their way to the backstage entrance.

"Hell yeah. Everybody and their momma are in this joint tonight." Y'lesha applied her lip gloss.

Once they entered the back, they noticed that it wasn't nearly as packed as the main floor.

Lil' Bit smiled, knowing that her chances of catching a baller just multiplied. She scanned the whole scene. "I'm trying to meet Young Money tonight so I can give him some pussy. I need a nigga to take care of me, feel me?"

"You lil' whore," Y'lesha joked, laughing at her ghetto-ass friend. Even though Lil' Bit said it as a joke, Y'lesha knew she was dead serious. Lil' Bit got down for hers, and it wasn't any shame in her game. She was always looking for the next nigga to pamper her, and because of her looks, usually got what she wanted.

Y'lesha and Lil' Bit approached a group of men standing by the curtains to the front stage. Y'lesha noticed that some of them had microphones in their hands and were waiting for the show to start. Lil' Bit made an effort to switch her ass even harder as she walked past the group of men, who all wore YM shirts with blinged-out pieces around their necks, letting the girls know that they were a part of Young Money's entourage.

Lil' Bit crossed her fingers as she began to work her magic. She shifted her ass from left to right, right to left and walked with a model's precision as she threw out the bait for one of the men to bite.

Y'lesha wasn't trying to gain any attention. She was just there to enjoy the show, but she was the one getting all of the attention.

As soon as the girls walked by, all eyes were on Y'lesha's ass. She had some junk in the trunk, and her small waist made it seem even bigger.

"Yo, ma!" a man with a New York accent barked out.

Both girls turned their heads to see who was calling them.

"Yeah, y'all two." The man stepped to the forefront. "Can I talk to you for a minute?"

"Bingo," Lil' Bit said to Y'lesha, hardly opening her mouth.

The two girls sashayed over to the men, all of the men's eyes on them.

"Hey, shorty. I'm Jus." The man extended his hand to Y'lesha.

"Hey. I'm Y'lesha." Y'lesha shook his hand. "And this is my girl, Lil' Bit," she added, looking over at her. Y'lesha looked the man up and down and definitely was impressed.

"I was wondering if you two wanted to chill with Young Money after the show. He likes for me to select a few ladies to chill with him after the show. Y'all game?"

Y'lesha looked at Lil' Bit to see what she was going to say, and Lil' Bit had the biggest smile spread across her face. Y'lesha knew what Jus really meant. She wanted to decline the offer right then and there, but she fell back. She wasn't a groupie by far, but at the same time, she didn't want to go against the grain and step on Lil' Bit's toes.

"We game!" Lil' Bit sexily licked her lips, showing Jus the length of her tongue.

Before Jus could even respond, the music stopped on the main stage, and the DJ announced that it was time for Young Money to come on the stage. The dressing room door opened, and there he was in the flesh. With his shirt completely off, revealing his tattooed body, Young Money walked out and headed toward the curtains.

Jus quickly looked at Young Money and then back at the girls. "All right," he said, "meet us in the green room right after the show." He gave Y'lesha two gold passes and joined his crew as they prepared to go on stage.

"There go Young Money!" Lil' Bit said, practically drooling over the rap star. Lil' Bit's pussy got wet at the sight of the rapper. She didn't know if it was him or the money she was attracted to, but she was attracted. "That

nigga is sexy as hell. He looks even better in person."
Lil' Bit was staring a hole in him.

"Damn, girl. You all on that nigga dick and ain't
never met him. He a'ight." Y'lesha tried to be discreet.
Damn, that nigga is fine as hell, Y'lesha thought to herself
as she checked him out.

"You see how he was looking at us. I'm about to show
Young Money the time of his life tonight. These other
bitches in here ain't fucking with us. That's why they
picked us to get down. You betta get with the program,
Y'lesha."

Young Money and his crew entered the stage and
began the show. Y'lesha and Lil' Bit walked to the side
of the stage, where they joined a group of about ten
girls, to get a better view of the show. Y'lesha noticed
that all the girls that crowded around were talking
about how they were going to fuck and suck whoever,
and they had the same gold tickets in their hands that
she got from Jus.

Lil' Bit tried to pretend she didn't notice it. It was her
way of convincing herself that she wasn't just another
groupie, but Y'lesha had already decided that if they
wanted more than conversation from her, she wasn't
fucking with them.

Two hours later the same group of women that were
on the side of the stage were in the green room waiting
for the superstar and his crew to arrive. Almost every
girl in the room was looking in the mirrors, trying to
look as perfect as she could, hoping to be the lucky girl
to get picked by Young Money.

Y'lesha and Lil' Bit were on the sofa talking about the

show. "He was rocking it out there," Lil' Bit said, staring in her personal mirror.

"It was hot. His live show is crazy," Y'lesha responded.

Before Lil' Bit could even say anything back, the doors opened and the room's noise suddenly ceased. Jus and the other entourage entered the room without Young Money. Jus stood in the middle of the floor and said, "Young Money wants four girls to come to the room with him, so could everyone line up, so we can pick who rolling out with us."

All twelve of the girls lined up and put in their bid to get picked. Jus walked up and down the line, staring at each girl's body individually. He stopped at a heavy-set chick and began to chuckle. He looked back at a member and stated loudly, "Rico, you must've gave her a gold pass. Lord knows, you love them big bitches."

The men bust out into laughter. They knew Jus was telling the truth.

"Shorty fly, though. Look at that ass." Rico pointed to the girl's backside.

Jus shook his head. Then he put his hands in the air. "Okay, if yo' ass weigh over a hundred and sixty pounds, bounce!"

Y'lesha thought to herself, *Shit, I weigh one seventy-two. I ain't tripping, though. If he says something to me I'm-a cuss his ass out.* Y'lesha's weight was well distributed, and even though she was well over 160 pounds, it looked good on her. She didn't look to be her actual weight.

None of the girls budged after the comment, and Y'lesha and Lil' Bit looked around to peep the competition. Lil' Bit looked at the slightly heavy girl next to her and decided to take matters into her own hands. *Shit,*

I'm trying to see Young Money. I need some of these bitches to go. She cleared her throat to get attention. When the men looked in her direction, she threw her head in the girl's direction.

Jus looked at the girl and walked over to her. He smiled to himself. He almost let a lard ass get through. "Yo, ma, it's been real, but you gotta bounce. You got rolls hanging out of yo' joint. Money ain't tryin'-a see that," Jus said in a kind voice. "Feel me?" He wasn't trying to hurt her feelings, but at the same time he had to keep it real with her.

The chubby girl smacked her lips and stormed out of the room with a major attitude.

The guys in the room bust into laughter the way Lil' Bit put her on front street.

Jus managed to weed out four more girls because something was wrong with them—their weave, their face, or their butt wasn't big enough. Only seven girls remained, and Y'lesha and Lil' Bit were still in it.

"All right, ladies, we want all of y'all to come back to the hotel with us to meet Young Money. But I'm going to tell you now—We are trying to have a good time. We need bad girls that ain't scared to put it on the floor. Anybody have any objections can leave now."

" 'Put it on the floor'?" Y'lesha put both of her hands on her hips.

"Yeah, bitch." One of the men grabbed his dick. "Put it on the floor!"

Y'lesha already knew what the deal was. She rolled her eyes at the man and headed toward the door. "C'mon, Bit," she said as she reached the door. "Let's bounce."

Already, the men began to mingle with the girls, and a man was already in Lil' Bit's face.

"Girl, I'm-a catch up with you," Lil' Bit said. "I'll be okay." She took the bottle of champagne from one of the dudes and took a large swig.

Y'lesha wasn't about to get treated like some little whore, so she was out. She headed out of the door.

Lil' Bit followed seconds behind her. "Y'lesha, hold up," she said, bottle still in her hand.

"What?"

Lil' Bit stared at Y'lesha, and Y'lesha returned the harsh gaze.

Lil' Bit made her eyes cross and stuck out her tongue. It worked like a charm every time.

Y'lesha began to lighten up. She laughed.

"Girl, I'm trying to meet Young Money. Come with me on this one."

"Nah, girl, that ain't my type of party. I'm just going to go home. Are you going to be okay?"

"Yeah, I'm good. Here are my car keys. I'll have one of them take me home." Lil' Bit dug into her bra and grabbed her keys.

"Nah, girl, go 'head. I'll catch a cab. I don't want you to be stranded nowhere. I love you, girl, and be careful."

"Love you too, girl. Bye. Gotta go." Lil' Bit danced back into the green room, where everyone was at.

Y'lesha couldn't believe how ho'ish her girl could be sometimes, but that still was her best friend, and she took the good with the bad. Y'lesha's feet were killing her. She took off her heels and began to walk toward the exit. She was just ready to go home and take a hot bath.

A distant voice yelled, "Yo, ma!"

Y'lesha turned around and saw Jus heading her way. She ignored him and continued to walk. *What the fuck does he want?* She sped up, hoping he would get the picture.

"Hey, wait up," Jus said as he finally reached Y'lesha. He gently touched her elbow, trying to get her attention.

Y'lesha stopped and turned around. "What!"

"Whoa, whoa, ma. I just want to talk to you for a minute," Jus said, showing his gorgeous white teeth.

"You don't need to talk to me about anything. I'm not like them other girls. I don't get down like that. You're barking up the wrong tree." Y'lesha folded her arms and shook her head from side to side.

"I know you're not like them other girls. That's why I ran after you. I just want to talk to you for a minute."

Y'lesha looked Jus up and down and noticed that he wasn't half-stepping. He had on crispy Tims and Evisu jeans. The iced-out watch on his wrist matched his platinum bezel chain. She tried to resist, but a slight smile formed on her face. It was something about a thug that turned her on. And even though she didn't want to admit it, she was attracted to him. "What you want to talk to me about? We ain't got shit to talk about."

"Look, let's start over. Hello, my name is Justin." Jus extended his hand to her.

He is fine as hell. Maybe I'll see what this nigga is all about. "Hi, my name is Y'lesha." She shook his hand and stared at him. That's when she noticed his big, pretty brown eyes.

The two of them bust out into laughter as they realized how corny they were acting. Jus was the first to speak. "Y'lesha, let me take you out to eat. I promise I will show you a good time. You down?"

"I'll take a rain check, but you can give me your number." Y'lesha licked her lips and sexily grinned.

Jus pulled out a hundred-dollar bill and wrote his number on it. "I'll be waiting for that call, ma." He handed her the money.

Y'lesha grabbed the bill and stuffed it in her cleavage. "I'll talk to you later, Jus." Then she turned around and headed toward the back exit, switching her ass even harder, knowing that Jus was staring at her behind as she walked away. Just to make sure, she took a glance back, and like she thought, his eyes were glued on her.

Y'lesha was tempted to take him up on his offer, but Petey had left a sour taste in her mouth. She didn't want to get involved with anyone. She ran down a cab and headed home, where she could relax, calling it a night.

Chapter Six

The cab arrived at Lil' Bit's house, and Y'lesha was ready to take a hot bath and relax. The whole cab ride home Y'lesha couldn't stop thinking about Jus. She kept looking at his number and was eager to call him. It was something about his eyes that turned her on and had her interested. *He didn't seem like a bad guy. I'm-a call him up and see what he's about.*

Y'lesha entered the house and immediately took off her heels. Her feet were killing her, and that bathtub was calling for her. She'd just bought a new book and decided she would start it tonight in a hot bubble bath. She then flicked on the light switch and realized that the bulb had gone out again. "Damn," she whispered as she entered the dark living room. She knocked over the vase that was on the floor and nearly tripped. She headed toward the hallway closet to grab a bulb but stopped in her tracks when she smelled smoke. "What the—!" She jumped when she saw the silhouette of a person on the living room couch, puffing a cigarette. "Bit, is that you?"

She squinted her eyes to get a better look. *I know she didn't make it home that quick.* "Bit?" she yelled as she made her way over to the corner and flicked on the light. When she saw the man that sat on the couch, fear overcame her whole body. She was speechless, and her legs began to shake. Petey was on the couch with a gun in one hand and a cigarette in the other.

"It's been a long time, bitch. You thought I wouldn't find you, didn't you?" Petey calmly took another puff of his cigarette.

Y'lesha looked at the door and thought about making a run for it.

Petey saw that she was contemplating an escape and pointed his gun at her. "Do not even fuckin' think about it. I'll blow yo' mu'fuckin' head off, bitch."

Y'lesha began to cry. She put both of her hands in front of herself, trying to block the gun. The look in Petey's eyes was that of a madman.

"Petey, I-I-I—" Y'lesha stuttered as she tried to find the words to say. But what could she say to a man she'd tortured months back?

Petey, with the gun still pointed in her direction, walked toward her. "Shut up, bitch!" he yelled as sweat formed on his forehead. He struck her across the temple with the butt of his gun, and Y'lesha's head instantly began to bleed as she hit the floor. Then he followed up the blow with a kick to her mid-section.

"Aghhh!" Y'lesha screamed in agony as she folded up in a fetal position.

Petey ripped open his button-up shirt, revealing his burnt chest. "Look at me, bitch!" he yelled as he began to slob in complete madness. "Look!" he screamed.

Y'lesha spat up blood and began to beg Petey to stop. "Please, Petey, please."

Petey kicked her in the head before the words could come out of her mouth.

Y'lesha's head began to throb unbearably as her vision became blurred.

Petey dropped to his knees, grabbed her by the hair, and made her look at his chest. "Look what you did to me," he screamed. "Look, Y'lesha." Spit flew out of his mouth and onto her face.

Y'lesha looked at his deformed chest, and the sight of his scalded, hairless skin almost made her vomit. She cried even harder when she saw what she had done to him. She knew that Petey had found her to make her suffer.

Petey ripped off his shirt completely and hovered over her. With all of his might, he punched her in the head as he remembered the night that she'd caused him so much pain.

Y'lesha's ear began to bleed. "Please stop, Petey." She held her throbbing head.

Petey smiled at the sight of Y'lesha suffering and began to laugh. "Bitch, you are about to feel what I felt. I have been waiting for this day for a while. You're going to die tonight," he said, right before he stomped on her head again, causing her to lose consciousness.

The liquid splashing on Y'lesha's face woke her. She was butt-naked in the middle of the living room floor in a puddle, Petey standing above her with a deranged smile on his face. Y'lesha thought Petey was urinating on her as she slowly regained her consciousness. She quickly turned, trying to guard her face. Her eyes began to burn. That's when she discovered that it wasn't urine. Petey was pouring gasoline on her body. She instantly tried to scream, but Petey had duct taped her mouth. Her hands were also taped together. Y'lesha began to blink vigorously, trying to get the gasoline out of her eyes. Her eyes felt like they were on fire, and her body ached all over as she squirmed, desperately trying to free herself.

Petey pulled out a book of matches from his pants pockets. "See you in hell."

Y'lesha cried, knowing that she was about to die an excruciating death.

The sound of Lil' Bit's voice and a man could be heard from outside the door, as well as the sound of keys jangling. That got Petey's attention.

He nervously tried to strike a match but accidentally dropped the book. "Fuck!" he yelled as the matches fell in the gasoline. He picked them up and knew that he couldn't light it now. He put both of his hands on his head in a blind rage. "No, no, no!' he yelled as he realized that he had fucked up. Out of frustration, he kicked Y'lesha in her mid-section.

As the front door opened, he took off for the back door.

Lil' Bit stumbled in drunk, followed by one of the men who was at the concert. They were so busy kissing and feeling each other up, they didn't even see Y'lesha lying on the floor.

The man sniffed the air. "Is that gas?"

Lil' Bit noticed the smell of gas inside the house. She pulled from the guy and scanned the room. She saw her best friend naked and tied up on the floor. "Y'lesha!" she screamed as she ran over to a squirming Y'lesha. She dropped to her knees right next to Y'lesha, landing in the puddle of gasoline, and slowly peeled the duct tape off Y'lesha's face. Blood instantly poured out of her mouth.

"Oh my God! Y'lesha?" Lil' Bit said as she stroked Y'lesha's soaked hair and looked at her battered face. She was barely recognizable, her face swollen three times its original size. The sight brought tears to Lil' Bit's eyes. Y'lesha was barely breathing and was slipping in and out of consciousness. She grabbed Y'lesha in her arms and screamed for her guy friend to call 911.

"C'mon, Y'lesha, stay with me," Lil' Bit said as she held Y'lesha in her arms.

The last thing Y'lesha saw before she totally fainted was Lil' Bit's teary eyes.

Chapter Seven

Y'lesha woke up in the hospital bed and immediately became terrified. She had no idea where she was at, and when she tried to get out of the bed, the pains of the beating said hello. Her whole body was sore, and she yelled in pain. A movement from the corner of the room startled her, and she quickly looked over in the direction where it came from. She saw Lil' Bit sleeping in the chair. Y'lesha called for her, but her swollen mouth prevented her from being coherent. She felt her face, and it was tender and swollen at the touch.

She tried to call for Lil' Bit again, this time managing to get a sound out. "Lil' Bit," she said in a raspy whisper.

Lil' Bit vaguely heard her, but woke up out of her sleep. "Y'lesha, don't try to get up." Lil' Bit hopped up and hurried over to the bed and gently made her lay back down. "Y'lesha, you need to relax. I was worried about you."

"I need to get out of here before Petey comes for me," she said, just before breaking down and crying.

"He's not going to hurt you. Face has one of his goons outside of the room. I called him a couple of days ago and told him what happened." Lil' Bit rubbed Y'lesha's hand.

"A couple of days ago? How long has it been?"

"You've been in a coma for five days." Lil' Bit pushed the red button to alert the nurses that Y'lesha had woken up.

"In a coma? I have to get out of here before Petey comes back for me." Y'lesha's paranoia was written all over her face. "I have to get the fuck up out of here," she said in a slurred tone.

Before Bit could even respond to Y'lesha, Face walked into the room, a necklace dangling from his hand. He got Y'lesha's attention. He approached the bed, a concerned look on his face, and looked at her bruised face. "I see you finally woke up. Here, I got something to make you feel better." Face dropped the chain on her stomach.

She slowly grabbed the chain and held it up. A diamond cross hung from the necklace. She knew exactly where it had come from. It was Petey's. "What?" Y'lesha whispered.

Face rested his hand on her leg. "Shhh. Just get some rest. Let's just say that you don't have to worry about that nigga anymore."

A feeling of relief overcame Y'lesha as she dropped tears. She once loved Petey, but now he was the cause of her pain. She didn't know if she was crying because of the news of his death or crying tears of joy. She closed her eyes, trying not to envision what he'd done to her or what she'd done to him. She whispered, "I'm just glad this is over," and turned her body away from her guest.

Chapter Eight

Two months Later

Y'lesha was on her way to Face's shop to pick up the product. She was anxious to get the run over with so she could have some major cash in her pocket. Face hadn't given her a job in a couple of weeks, so she really needed some money. She had butterflies in her stomach as she flew through the Detroit streets. *New York is far as hell to be driving, especially with dope in the car. I hate dealing with Face crazy ass, but fuck it, I got to do what I got to do. After he breaks me off with the cash, Detroit won't see my ass anymore. I'm gone!*

She pulled up to the shop and blew her horn at the gate.

Seconds later, Face pulled up the gate and appeared in front of her car. He waved her in. Face's Charger was parked inside, and Y'lesha pulled right behind it. She got out and headed into his back office.

"This is a big job, ma," he said as he filled the duffle bag with cocaine bricks.

Y'lesha sat in his office and watched as he stuffed the bag to capacity. This was by far the biggest job she'd be doing for him. He wanted her to drive to New York with 10 kilos of cocaine and bring back $150,000 in cash.

Face went over the logistics again with Y'lesha as he zipped up the duffle bag. "It's very simple, ma," he said, as he sat on the passenger side. He pointed to the On-Star system. "You have a navigational system on the dash that will direct you straight to New York. My man Cease will meet you at this address." He gave her a piece of paper with an address on it, along with a printout of MapQuest directions. He wanted to make sure she got there without getting lost. "He's going to give you a duffle bag containing the cash and you bring it back home. Easy as one, two, three." Face clapped his hands together to emphasize his point. "I booked you a hotel at the halfway mark in Philly. I know it's almost impossible for you to drive straight down there with no sleep and be on point. Remember, you roll dolo—by yourself—feel me?"

"I got it." Y'lesha fixed the rearview mirror to her height. "How do I know this nigga won't try to rob me? What about me?"

"You don't have to worry about anything. Dean is my first cousin and we have been doing it like this for years. It's easy as hell. You just have to follow directions and be cool, feel me?"

"Why me? Who used to do it for you?" Y'lesha asked, trying to cover all bases.

"The chick I had moving the weight got a fucked-up driving record. I had to cut that bitch off. She accumulated so many tickets and thought I wouldn't find out. I can't take the risk of having someone on the highway with my shit with a bad record. Cops like to fuck with niggas, and it wouldn't be smart for me. Your shit is clean, and I know I can trust you, right?"

"Yeah, you can trust me, Face. Since I been working for you, I never tried anything grimy."

"You never rode with this much, though. Think you can handle it?"

She thought long and hard about the $15,000 Face promised her after she returned and knew that she couldn't turn this job down. "I got it. You are going to hit me with fifteen stacks when I get back, right?"

"I got you. You just make sure you do your part." Face loaded up the trunk of the two-door Benz with the bricks.

Y'lesha walked over to the car and jumped in. Her adrenaline began to pump as she got in the car. She wasn't anxious about the trip to New York, but the $15,000 she would make was enough for her to stop dealing with Face and get a start on a new life. She hated what she did, but it paid the bills.

Face stared at her scrumptious ass, and his dick began to rise in his Sean Jean jeans. He walked over to the window and bent down to be eye level with her. "You know you could make an extra five thousand if you . . ." He leaned forward, licked his lips, and looked at Y'lesha's thick thighs.

"No, Face, I'm good," Y'lesha said bluntly, turning

down Face for the hundredth time. She started up the car.

Face pushed the button on the wall, to let the garage door open, and Y'lesha pulled out.

Just as she exited the garage, her cell phone rang. She looked at the caller ID. "Bit, what's up, girl?" she said, merging into traffic.

"Have you left yet?"

"Nah, girl. I'm about to jump on the highway as we speak."

"I left my ID in your purse when I borrowed it. Can you bring it to me before you leave?"

"Can't you just wait until I get back?"

"C'mon, Y'lesha. I'm trying to go to the club tonight. Pretty please?"

"All right, Bit. You know how Face is. He doesn't like me to make any pit stops. I'm about to pull up in five minutes. Be looking for me."

"Thanks," Bit said before she hung up the phone.

Y'lesha made a big U-turn and headed to the house, which was a couple of blocks away. *That girl is always forgetting something. I'm on a time schedule. She betta have her lil' ass on the porch when I pull up,* Y'lesha thought to herself as she cruised down Detroit's streets.

Five minutes later, Y'lesha was in front of Bit's house, blowing her horn.

Bit came running out of the house with a Baby Phat mini-skirt and an overnight bag in her hand. She locked the door behind her and jogged to the car. She jumped in the car and threw on her knock-off Gucci shades. Bit looked forward and leaned her seat back, trying to get comfortable.

Y'lesha looked at her like she was half-crazy. "What the hell do you think you are doing?" Y'lesha dug in her purse and held Bit's ID in the air.

"I'm rolling out with you, girl. You gon' need some company," Bit said, a big smile plastered on her face.

"Uh-uh. Girl, you know Face ain't trying to hear that shit. He don't play that shit, Bit. When I make runs, I have to be solo. You know that." Y'lesha hit the unlock button on the car, signaling Bit to bounce.

Bit turned her body toward Y'lesha and raised her shades to the top of her head. "C'mon, Y'lesha, it will be fun. It can be a little road trip, like a girls' night out."

"No. Hell no. This is a big job. I told yo' ass last night you couldn't go. I bet that's why you called me back here. You ain't slick."

Bit had begged Y'lesha all week to go on this trip with her, telling her that she needed to get away for a minute because she was tired of looking at Detroit's raggedy setting, but Y'lesha told her repeatedly that this run had to be solo.

See, Y'lesha had made the mistake of making runs with Bit before. Face never found out, but if he did, Y'lesha didn't want to see the repercussions.

Bit puckered her lips, knowing how to persuade her best friend to see things her way. "C'mon, Y'lesha, stop acting like that. You're going to be bored riding all the way to New York by yourself."

Y'lesha thought to herself, *This is a long trip to be taking all by myself. Maybe I should let her roll.* But the image of Face and the man's bloody hand popped in her head. Pissing Face off was the last thing she wanted to do. If she was considering letting Bit go with her, that definitely killed the notion. "Nah, Bit, I can't do it."

Bit began to dig in her bag and began searching for something. She smiled when she found what she was looking for. "I know what will get you." She pulled out a CD and slipped it in the DVD player. She put in their theme song, knowing it would sway Y'lesha's decision. She turned up the volume on the radio, and Beyoncé began to blare out of the speakers.

"Everything you own, in the box to the left!" Bit sang as she threw her hands in the air to the song, knowing Y'lesha couldn't resist her favorite song. She nudged her arm and stuck out her tongue.

Y'lesha smiled and couldn't help herself.

"To the left, to the left." Bit sang, hoping to soften up her friend.

"You must not know 'bout me, you must not know 'bout me," they both said in unison.

Bit smiled, knowing that she had just broken Y'lesha down.

"A'ight, Bit, just this one time." Y'lesha threw the car in drive and pulled off.

Lil' Bit threw her hands around Y'lesha and gave her a hug, causing her to swerve a little. The girls busted out in laughter and were on their way to the Big Apple, New York City.

Chapter Nine

The girls had been on the road for six hours straight and were beginning to get sleepy. The sun was going down, and the highway was semi-clear. Lil' Bit pulled a blunt and a bag of weed out of her purse. Y'lesha was so busy singing along to the Lauryn Hill CD, she didn't even notice Lil' Bit roll up the spliff. Lil' Bit sparked up.

"What you doing, Bit? Put that shit out!" Y'lesha looked back and forth at the road and Lil' Bit.

"Just let me get a couple of puffs, girl." Lil' Bit took a deep pull.

Y'lesha smacked her lips and grabbed the blunt directly out of Bit's mouth. She rolled down her window and tossed it out.

"Damn, Y'lesha!" Bit yelled, trying to keep the weed smoke in her lungs. "That was some hydro, girl. I paid thirty dollars for that bag."

"That's why I didn't want yo' ass to come. You always on that ol' bulllshit. You must want us to go to jail. Do I have to remind you that I have ten bricks in the trunk, bitch?" Y'lesha shook her head from side to side, regretting that she'd let Bit come.

"Damn, girl! It was just a lil' blunt." Lil' Bit blew the smoke out and tried to change the subject. "We should hit a club in New York when we get there." She sat upright.

"Nah, Bit. We have to stay on task. Face has me on schedule, and I don't want to fuck up this job." Y'lesha pointed to the navigational system on the dash.

"You're boring."

"No, I'm smart." Y'lesha yawned. She noticed on the navigational system that they were five miles away from her checkpoint in Philly, where Face had booked her at a hotel. She was ready to hit the sack.

Lil' Bit knew that Y'lesha was becoming agitated with her and tried to lighten the mood. "How many bricks you say you had?"

"It's not any of your business—but ten."

"How much does that make?"

"I am supposed to bring back one hundred fifty thousand dollars to Face from his man."

"Damn! That's a lot of money." Lil' Bit's eyes shot wide open. Just the sound of that much cash got her excited. "You know how much I could do with that money?"

"Yeah, that could change a lot of shit for me. I wouldn't have to be taking penitentiary chances on the highway like this." Y'lesha smiled, imagining life $150,000 dollars richer.

Lil' Bit began to smile and stare in space as if she was contemplating hard about something.

Y'lesha already knew what Bit's sheisty ass was thinking. "Don't even think about it."

Lil' Bit bust out into laughter, knowing that Y'lesha
knew exactly what she was thinking.

"I'm just saying, that is a lot of money." Bit flipped up
her Sidekick and began texting.

"Too bad it's not ours."

Y'lesha pulled into the Holiday Inn right off the highway. It was nearly midnight, and both of the girls were
exhausted. Y'lesha parked and popped the trunk. She
grabbed the bag out of the trunk, and they headed into
the hotel.

As the girls walked into the lobby, they noticed that
the hotel was far from luxurious.

"Face sure does take care of his girls," Bit said sarcastically, scanning the rinky-dink hotel.

Y'lesha smacked her lips and toted the bag to the
front desk. She began to check in and was ready to get a
good night's rest.

Bit noticed that the hotel had a small bar and grill in
the corner. She took a look at the small bar and then
back at the front desk's clerk. "Does the bar serve
drinks?" she asked the clerk.

"Yes, it does, ma'am. The last call for alcohol is at
two A.M."

Lil' Bit flipped up her Sidekick and checked the
time, noticing that it was just after midnight. She smiled
and looked at Y'lesha. "Girl, I'm about to get a drink before it closes. Are you coming with me?"

"Nah, Bit. I got to get up and drive in the morning. I
think I'm going to call it a night." Y'lesha grabbed the

two room keys from the clerk. She gave one to Lil' Bit and headed to the elevator to get to the room.

"I'll be up in a minute," Lil' Bit yelled as she made her way over to the bar.

Y'lesha made her way up to the room and was ready to relax. She went into the two-bedroom suite and headed directly to the closet to stash the drugs.

After that, she took off all her clothes and went into the shower. Y'lesha began to think about what she would do with the $15,000 she would make after the run. *Maybe I'll move to New York and turn over a new leaf. I always wanted to live in the Big Apple. Maybe I could go to a small community college and get a degree. Yeah, that sounds like a plan.*

Y'lesha finished up her shower and headed into the room. She noticed that Lil' Bit hadn't yet come up. She looked at the clock and noticed it was 1:30, thirty minutes before the bar would close. She wanted to go to sleep but decided she would have a drink to relax her. She slipped on a comfortable Rocawear jogging suit and pulled her hair into a ponytail. She left the room and headed down to the lobby.

When Y'lesha reached the lobby and walked into the bar, Lil' Bit was nowhere in sight. "Where is this lil' heiffa at?" Y'lesha whispered playfully. She scanned the room and saw her friend over in a booth, engaged in deep conversation with a man. Y'lesha smiled as she looked at how fine the man was. *That's my girl.* Y'lesha took a seat over at the bar. "Let me get a Long Island iced tea," she said as she laid a twenty-dollar bill on the bar.

Lil' Bit noticed Y'lesha and excused herself from the

booth. She approached her almost staggering. "Y'lesha, what took you so long, girl?" Lil' Bit sat on the stool next to her. "That nigga finer than a mu'fucka. You see him over there?" Bit threw her head in the dude's direction.

Y'lesha nonchalantly glanced in his direction. "I can't really see him from here," she lied.

"Well, he says he's got a presidential suite on the top floor, and he wants me to come up for drinks."

"Damn! You about to give him the coochie already?" Y'lesha took another sip of her drink.

"It ain't even like that. He seems to be a nice guy. I'm just going to go up and talk with him for a minute."

"Do you even know his name?" Y'lesha turned up her nose and looked over at Lil' Bit's male friend typing in his BlackBerry.

"Jodi." Lil' Bit snapped her head. She'd heard enough of Y'lesha's hating and rose up from her seat. She hugged her girl and whispered to her in her ear, "I'll be in the room in a minute."

"All right, girl, be careful. Do you have your room key?"

"Yeah, I got it." Bit walked back over to the man, trying to poke out what little ass she had, to make it seem bigger than it was.

Y'lesha seemed to notice and got a little chuckle out of Lil' Bit trying to make a mountain out of a mole hill. Y'lesha was ready to go to sleep and finished up her drink and headed back to the room.

As soon as she hit the room, she started to feel the effects of the liquor. She didn't even take off her clothes before she was sound asleep in the bed.

* * *

"Bitch, wake up!" a man's voice yelled, awakening Y'lesha out of her sleep.

Y'lesha jumped up, not knowing what was going on. All the lights in the hotel room were on. She saw two people standing over her bed and squinted her eyes to see what exactly was going on. She rubbed her eyes, and what she saw made her heart begin to pump. The man that Lil' Bit was talking to earlier was holding a big chrome gun to her head. He had a handful of her hair as he pressed the gun to Bit's temple.

The man clenched Bit's hair even tighter. "Rise and shine, sleeping beauty."

Y'lesha looked at Lil' Bit's face. It was full of sheer fear as tears streamed down her face. Y'lesha, caught totally off guard, froze in terror.

The man pulled the gun from Bit's temple and pointed it at Y'lesha. "Where the bricks at?"

Y'lesha immediately put both of her hands in front of her and began pleading for her life. "What are you talking about?" she said, trying to appear clueless.

"Oh, you think I'm playing, huh?" The man rushed over to her and backhanded her.

As blood began to drip from Y'lesha's lip, Lil' Bit tried to help her friend by jumping on the man's back and began to bite him on his neck. But he flung her like a rag doll against the wall, causing her to become dizzy.

Y'lesha began to cry and yelled, "What are you talking about? I don't have anything."

"Your friend already spilled the beans. You betta come off them bricks, or I'm going to shoot your girl in the head." The man pointed the pistol over at Bit in the corner.

"Okay, okay!" Y'lesha screamed. "It's in the closet, in the duffle bag. Just take it and leave." She wiped the blood from her mouth.

The man rushed over to the closet and lit up when he saw the duffle bag sitting on the floor. He opened the bag up and smiled. He'd just stumbled upon his biggest lick ever. The sight of all the coke gave him an ultimate adrenaline rush. He looked back at the girls to make sure they didn't try anything and then took the bag out.

"You got what you wanted, so just leave!" Y'lesha rushed over to her friend in the corner.

The man didn't like Y'lesha's tone of voice, so he decided he didn't want the robbery to stop there. When he saw Lil' Bit's small breasts hanging out of her halter-top, his manhood began to harden. He had more than the dope on his mind at that point. He walked over to the girls as they shook in fear. He pointed the gun at Y'lesha's head and . . .

Boom! Boom! The sound of heavy hands knocking on Dr. Katz's door filled the office, interrupting Jada's story.

The office doors opened, and two prison guards walked in. "Dr. Katz, your time is up," one of them said as they stood behind Jada, preparing to return her to the west wing, where her cell was.

Jada picked her book up off the floor and stood up with her hands behind her back.

Dr. Katz locked eyes with her and couldn't help feeling sorry for her. By listening to her talk, he knew she was very intelligent. He couldn't believe a beautiful girl like her had gone through so much. He watched as her eyes began to water and the guards carried her away. Dr. Katz dropped his pen on his desk and took a frustrated deep breath. Tomorrow, during their session, he would dig deeper into her thoughts to find out more about Y'lesha Coleman.

Chapter Ten

Jada shuffled into Dr. Katz's office, her hands and feet handcuffed. The guards were right behind her, obviously enjoying the rear view. Actually, every male guard in the facility tried to get a peek at the infamous author.

He watched closely as she walked into the room. Even though she was dressed in prison clothes, she still had a sophisticated swagger about her. She had her long hair pulled into a tight ponytail, and her big brown eyes locked onto Dr. Katz's. He could tell that she'd been crying all night because of the puffiness around her eyes. Dr. Katz noticed that the guards' eyes were fixated on Jada's body. He decided to break up their parade. "Thank you, gentlemen. You can leave now." He unbuttoned his cufflinks and picked up his pen so he could start day two of his mental evaluation.

Dr. Katz was so intrigued by Jada's/Y'lesha's story, he had been thinking about it all night. He was dying to find out what happened next to Y'lesha. Dr. Katz didn't want to admit it, but for some reason, he believed that Jada was sane, and maybe she was telling the truth. *Her story is too detailed, and I see the pain in her eyes when she tells me about her past. This woman is not insane.*

Just before the guards exited the room, Dr. Katz called for them. "Excuse me!" He looked at Jada's hands and then back at the guards. "Please uncuff her."

One guard grew a skeptical look on his face. He grabbed his belt buckle and pulled up his pants. "I can't do that, Doc. It's against procedure."

Dr. Katz knew that he wouldn't be able to get a good read on Jada, with her being shackled. He wanted her to be as comfortable as possible when evaluating her. He squinted his eyes and looked directly in the guard's eyes. "It's against procedure? Maybe I need to call down the warden and let him know how Jon Love on cell block six gets his drugs in. What do you think?" Dr. Katz dropped his pen and folded his hands.

The guard quickly changed his whole attitude. "No, that wouldn't be necessary, Doc." He quickly walked back over to Jada, took off the handcuffs, and hurried out with a dumbfounded look on his face.

As soon as the door closed, Jada and Dr. Katz began to laugh at the situation.

Jada put down her book and began to rub her chafed wrists. "Thanks, Dr. Katz. Those cuffs do get uncomfortable at times." She smiled innocently at Dr. Katz.

"Don't mention it." Dr. Katz looked down at the floor and noticed that Jada had a different book than she had the previous day. "I see you like to read. Did you finish the other book you had?"

"Yeah, I finished it. This is their next book."

"Did the book get better? You called it boring yester-day."

"Not really. Their books are the only street books in the library. Prison doesn't have an extensive collection, you know." Jada sat back on the couch and closed her eyes.

Dr. Katz smiled, knowing that she was comfortable, and decided now would be the perfect time to ask her to continue from where she left off.

"So, Jada—"

"Please call me by my name, Y'lesha," she said in a sincere tone.

"Okay, Y'lesha, can you take me back to the time you were at the hotel room with Lil' Bit?"

She closed her eyes and took Dr. Katz back to the horrific night.

The man pointed the gun at Y'lesha's head, a crazed look on his face. He talked slowly and precisely as he looked into Y'lesha pupils. "Go over to the bed, and you better not move." He pointed to the twin bed closest to the door.

Scared to death, Y'lesha slowly got up and followed his instructions. She glanced down at his crotch and no-ticed the growing bulge in his sweatpants. Tears began to form as she wondered what he was about to do to her. "Please, just leave. Please . . . you have what you want." Y'lesha kept her hands up and shuffled to the bed.

The man used his free hand to reach in his pants and pulled out his 10-inch hammer. He focused his attention on Lil' Bit as he stood over her. He began to stroke his dick and lick his lips.

Lil' Bit's hands began to shake as she covered herself up, trying to look as unattractive as possible.

The man used the barrel of the gun to brush Lil' Bit's hair from her face.

She cringed at the touch of the cold gun and yelled while crying, "Please, don't hurt me."

Y'lesha watched as the crazed man masturbated right over Lil' Bit. The man had no regard for the women's cries as he continued to please himself. When he was fully erect, he made Lil' Bit give him oral sex. Y'lesha cried like a baby as she witnessed her friend's rape.

"If your teeth touch my joint, I'm rocking you to sleep." He pointed the gun at Lil' Bit's temple.

After what seemed like forever, the man climaxed and released his fluids on top of Lil' Bit's head, totally degrading her. Lil' Bit just cried like a baby as the man skeeted on her.

Y'lesha felt so helpless. She knew that she would be next, and her heart crumbled at the thought of her being raped or killed. To her surprise, after the man climaxed and shook off the remaining juices from his penis onto Lil' Bit, he picked up the bag and hurried out of the room.

As soon as the man left the room, Y'lesha rushed over to the door and locked both locks. She then went to her friend's side and held her. Y'lesha yanked the sheet off the bed and began to wipe the semen off Lil' Bit's face and head. The musty smell nearly made her gag as she tried to comfort her girl. "Oh my God, Bit. Oh my God, are you okay?" she asked as she cried along with her.

"I thought we were dead. It's all my fault. I'm so sorry. I'm so sorry, Y'lesha," Lil' Bit said, crying uncontrollably.

"You didn't know, Bit. It wasn't your fault."

But Lil' Bit knew it was all her fault. She ran her mouth and caused the whole fiasco.

Y'lesha got up and walked over to the phone.

"What are you doing?" Lil' Bit asked.

"I'm calling the police."

Lil' Bit hung up the phone and shook her head from side to side, totally not agreeing with Y'lesha. "No, you can't call the cops." Lil' Bit sat on the bed and began to wipe her tears away. "What are you going to tell them? A man just robbed you for a bag full of cocaine? You have to call Face."

Y'lesha flopped down on the bed and placed both of her hands on her head, contemplating her next move. "I can't call Face. He will fuckin' kill me."

"It's my entire fault. Just tell him it was all on me," Lil' Bit said in almost a whisper. She felt so bad about what she'd caused.

"No, you don't understand. Face specifically told me to ride alone. If he found out you came with me, that would only make him want to kill both of us rather than just me. I'm fucked!" She took a deep breath and tapped her foot rapidly against the floor. She shot up and began to pace the room.

"Damn! Lil' Bit what were you thinking telling him about the drugs? You are always running your damn mouth. I knew I shouldn't have let you come. This would've never happened if it wasn't for you. Do you know what you running your mouth got me? I'm dead."

Y'lesha remembered how Face dealt with that man that owed him money. She couldn't even imagine what he would do when he found out that she had just lost ten bricks of his cocaine.

Lil' Bit buried her head in her hands and wept as guilt overcame her. "I'm sorry."

Y'lesha's mind was in overdrive as she paced the room, debating whether or not she should call Face. She blocked out all of Lil' Bit's apologies and didn't even hear her repeatedly asking for forgiveness as she thought, *What am I going to do? He's going to kill me. I know it. I can't go back to Detroit empty-handed. If I hadn't brought this heiffa with me, this would have never happened. She almost got us killed. Now I have to answer to Face.* She dropped her to knees and began to cry, knowing that she was in some deep shit.

Chapter Eleven

Dr. Katz listened closely as Jada Simone told him her story. The more she talked, the more he was convinced she was sane. Her pain almost brought tears to his eyes. The strong, confident woman that he'd seen on television was nothing more than a young black girl lost. Jada's eyes were watery as she explained the vivid scenes to the doctor, and Dr. Katz wondered how she got wrapped up in this mess.

"So what happened after the man stole the bag from you? Did Face ever catch up to you?" he asked, totally engrossed in her story. He wanted to know what she did to get out of the situation. From the way she'd described Face, he knew that she would have hell to pay.

Jada sat up from the leather couch and wiped her teary eyes. Just the thoughts alone of that night made her quiver in her skin. She paused before she answered, and she managed to smile. "Well, I couldn't go back to Detroit because I knew Face would kill me. So I knew I had to lay low for a minute, just until I figured out how to get him his money. I only had five hundred dollars in my pocket, so I went to the bus station and bought a ticket to New York. I was so angry with Lil' Bit at that point. I just gave her a hundred dollars and told her she was on her own. I loved my girl, but she was the one who'd caused all of the shit. I let her have the car and told her to drop me off at the bus station."

"So, just like that, you gave her the car and fled?"

"Yeah, pretty much. I knew that it wasn't safe to keep the car. I didn't know if Face could've traced it because of the navigational system or what. He was stone-cold crazy, and I didn't want any part of it."

"What about Lil' Bit?"

"I had to separate myself from her. I worried for her, but I had to take care of self first, feel me? She'd caused too much already. I didn't even tell her where I was going. I didn't want her to know anything more than what she already did. I just her told I was going away for a while. She pleaded with me, telling me that she would go with me and tell Face that it was all her fault. But I knew it would all lead to the same fate, Face killing me, so I left. I caught a bus to New York. That's when I met Jada Simone."

Dr. Katz was befuddled. He thought that the woman in front of him was Jada Simone. He grew a confused look on his face. "Jada Simone?"

"Yeah, Jada Simone, the realest bitch I've ever met."

"Is that right? How did you meet her?"

"Well, I had been in New York for about eight months. I hadn't heard from Lil' Bit since we got jacked. I tried to call, but her phone was disconnected. I got a job at a hospice as a nurse's aide and had been working there for a couple of months before I met Jada. I could never forget the day I first saw her." She closed her eyes and lay back on the couch, thinking back to that day.

"What are you staring at? I don't bite," the woman said as she sat in the hospice bed, writing in a notebook.

Y'lesha was staring at the woman from the doorway and didn't realize she was being rude. On that day, she had gotten switched to the east wing of the hospice, which was where the AIDS patients stayed. She was very uncomfortable about dealing with infected patients and was noticeably shaken up. "I'm sorry." She looked down at her clipboard, trying to find the patient's name. "Miss. Simone."

There was an awkward silence in the room as Y'lesha stood in the doorway, not wanting to approach the lady. Jada Simone was a beautiful woman and looked to be in her late twenties. She had long, jet-black hair and dark skin that seemed to glow. Y'lesha couldn't believe that the gorgeous woman was an AIDS patient and expected her to be sickly-looking.

"I'm here to take your vitals and check your blood pressure, Miss Simone," Y'lesha said as she looked down at her chart.

"Well, what the hell you just standing there for?" Jada said playfully. She continued to write in her thick notebook.

Y'lesha hesitantly walked over and began to take Jada's blood pressure. She glanced down at her pad. Trying to lighten the mood, she said, "So what are you writing about?" Y'lesha took a peek at her notebook and noticed "Chapter Ten" scribbled at the top of the paper. "Are you writing a book or something?" Y'lesha asked as she took her pulse.

Jada hurried and closed the notebook. "No, just my journal. It helps to write things down sometimes."

Y'lesha didn't want to stare, but Jada's beauty captured her attention. Her silky, wavy hair and dark skin were breathtaking. "I love your hair," Y'lesha said as she continued to check her vitals.

"Thanks."

Y'lesha looked at the pictures that sat on Jada's stand and noticed that she had a picture with Young Money. They were posing on the sands of a beach with the ocean as a backdrop. She looked closer to see if her eyes were deceiving her but realized that they weren't. The way that he held her in his arms, she could tell that they were romantically involved.

She finished up with Jada before asking her about the picture. "You know Young Money?"

Jada looked at the picture of her and the rapper and slightly smiled. She put the picture face down and said, "No, I just took a picture with him. I ran into him in the Bahamas a couple of years back."

Y'lesha kind of felt that she was lying, but she just smiled and began to fill out Jada's health chart.

After weeks of caring for Jada Simone, Y'lesha grew close to her. They would have long conversations about life. Y'lesha was surprised to find out that Jada Simone had lived a hell of a life. Jada would tell her stories about some of the most infamous players in the dope game that she'd encountered. Y'lesha learned that Jada Simone was the daughter of well-known kingpin and had inherited his street fame.

Y'lesha would sit up for hours talking with Jada as she reminisced about her past. That's why it hurt even more when Jada's disease began to take a toll on her body. In the short time that they knew each other, they'd established a tight bond. It hurt Y'lesha's heart to see the deadly disease run its course on Jada.

Y'lesha had taken some vacation time-off and hadn't seen her in a week. She was excited to see her because she'd bought them some Keyshia Cole concert tickets. She had just started her shift when she walked into Jada's room. "Hey, sis."

Jada was writing in her notebook and smiled when she heard Y'lesha's voice.

Y'lesha began to take off her jacket. "I know the doctor said that you should get bed rest, but I have a surprise for you." She hung up her coat and grabbed the tickets out of her pocket. She walked over to the bed, and her smiled quickly disappeared when she saw how Jada looked. "Oh my God!" Y'lesha put her hand over her mouth. Jada had lost about ten pounds since she'd last seen her, and around her eyes were red. She looked real bad.

Jada tried to ease the tension. "What are you staring at, girl? Don't make me feel any worse than I already do," she said in a low, raspy voice.

"Jada, I-I-I—"

"I'm dying, Y'lesha. It's nothing either of us can do about that. Don't feel sorry for me. I've lived life to the fullest and have no regrets. You reap what you sow. My fast lifestyle made me contract this disease, and now I'm paying for it. Smile, baby." Jada began to cough violently. "You've made these last three months heaven for me. You are a real bitch."

"Real bitches do real things," they said in unison, mimicking their motto. They both began to laugh.

But the laughs quickly turned into cries as tears flowed down Y'lesha's face. She knew her friend was about to die soon, but she remained silent.

Jada looked at Y'lesha's hands. "What do you have there?"

"I was going to surprise you with Keyshia Cole tickets for tomorrow. I was going to sneak you out so we could see her perform. I know you love her music, but you need to get some rest. Never mind these." Y'lesha put the tickets on Jada's nightstand.

"Bitch, is you crazy? I love me some Keyshia. I might be dying, but I ain't dead yet." Jada slowly picked up the tickets and examined them.

Jada sat in a wheelchair in the front row. She clapped as Keyshia Cole took her final bows.

Y'lesha stood behind her and watched as Jada enjoyed herself. Throughout the concert, Y'lesha dropped a couple of tears, knowing that Jada's life was on a countdown. She stood behind her so that Jada wouldn't see her crying.

Jada was too weak to even walk, so Y'lesha snuck her and the wheelchair out of the hospital for the night.

Y'lesha clapped along with the crowd. But what she saw next made her heart skip a beat. She saw Lil' Bit on the side of the stage with a man. It wasn't seeing Lil' Bit

that surprised her, it was the man that she was with. Lil'
Bit was smiling and talking to the man, holding his
hands and acting all lovey-dovey. She prayed that her
eyes were deceiving her, but she could never forget the
man's face. It was the same man who'd robbed them in
the hotel room.

It all made sense to Y'lesha now. Lil' Bit had set her
up. *That bitch set me up. She was behind the whole thing.*

Jada looked back at Y'lesha and saw the look in her
eyes. "Are you okay, Y'lesha?"

Y'lesha was speechless and didn't know what to say.
She was more hurt than anything. She just stared at
them as they stood on the side of the stage chatting.

Jada followed her eyes and noticed that she was looking at the couple. She looked at the man and then back
at Y'lesha. "You know Dino?"

"What?"

"Dino. You know that nigga?"

Y'lesha bent down to get ear level with Jada, telling
her that he was the one who'd robbed her in the room.
Y'lesha had told Jada about her and her best friend getting robbed months ago.

Jada was shocked at the coincidence. She knew who
Dino was. Actually she knew him well. He was one of
her father's workers years back. Her father had dropped
him from the squad after he got word that he was a
stick-up kid. Her father believed in karma and didn't
want any negative attention around him. Dino also was
her old boyfriend's bodyguard—Young Money, that is.
Jada quickly tried to diffuse the situation, telling Y'lesha
she was ready to go.

"I'm about to go back there and beat the brakes off that bitch!" Y'lesha said, her fists clenched.

Jada grabbed Y'lesha's hand. "Do you trust me?"

Y'lesha remained silent and just stared at Lil' Bit and Dino.

"Do you trust me?" she asked again, this time raising her voice.

"Yeah, you know I do," Y'lesha told her.

"Well, let's go."

"But—"

"Let's go!"

They exited the coliseum without saying a word. Y'lesha's heart was broken. Her best friend had pulled grimy on her, and she was boggled. *Why would she do that to me? I was nothing but good to her. She put my life in danger with no remorse. I can't believe her. I can't.*

One week later

The hip-hop world mourns the loss of Tony "Dino" Jones, Young Money's friend and bodyguard. His body was one of two dead bodies found in a Dumpster last night. The other was that of a woman thought to be between the ages of eighteen and twenty-five. Her identity is not yet known. More on this story after the weather.

Y'lesha turned off the television and sat on her couch in her small apartment in awe. She knew that the news reporter was talking about Lil' Bit. She didn't want her to be killed. Her stomach began to knot up as sadness overcame her. She fell to her knees and wept like a baby, calling out Lil' Bit's name. Her sadness quickly transformed into anger as she knew how this had all come about. She knew that Jada was behind it somehow. Jada had told her that she could have anyone touched at any time because of her father.

Thirty minutes later, Y'lesha was already in the hospital, storming into Jada's room, to ask her why. She went into the room yelling, "Why did you do—" She stopped mid-sentence when she saw no one in the bed and all of Jada's pictures gone.

A nurse making up the bed was startled by Y'lesha.

"Where is Jada?" Y'lesha looked around the room in confusion.

"Oh, Miss Simone passed this morning," the nurse said.

"What?" Y'lesha had just seen her a couple of days ago and couldn't believe it.

"She died around noon." The nurse walked up to Y'lesha and placed a hand on her shoulder. "I know you two were close," she said. "She's in a better place now." The nurse walked out and left Y'lesha in the room alone.

Y'lesha had just lost the two best friends she ever had on the same day. A single tear slid down her cheek. She quickly wiped it away, knowing that if Jada was there she wouldn't want her to cry for her. She was in a total daze as she walked around the room. She remembered the good times they'd shared in the short time they'd spent together.

She noticed a small box sticking out from under the bed. She slowly walked over to the bed and knelt down to pick it up. She opened it and saw a stack of notebooks. When Y'lesha saw the books, she knew exactly

what they were. She opened the first book and read—
The Duchess: The Life and Times of Jada Simone.

Dr. Katz sat at his desk with the evaluation sheet in front
of him. He remained silent, soaking up what she'd just
told him. When Y'lesha broke the story down for Dr. Katz,
it all made sense to him.

His job was to inform the court of Jada Simone's
mental state. The only problem was, Y'lesha Coleman
wasn't Jada Simone. He thought to himself, *Her being
an illegal immigrant explains why she has no birth certificate
or records of her existence. She told her life story and cried
when she explained the harsh times and smiled at the good
times. I could tell in her eyes that she had been through so
much. I can't let an innocent woman go to jail for the rest of
her life.*

Dr. Katz picked up his pen and began to write on Y'lesha's evaluation sheet. He was about to give a false diag-
nosis to the courts, a violation of the ethics of his
profession. But he knew that the courts had convicted
the wrong woman, and this was his way to make it right.
His heart wouldn't let him tell the court the truth—that
Jada/Y'lesha was sane and very intelligent.

He wrote: *Jada Simone is mentally ill and has no grasp of
reality. She has created an alter ego to suppress her memory
and to deal with traumatic experiences. She is insane, and I
believe that if she goes under intensive psychiatric treatment
she could be helped. I recommend 12 to 16 months.*

All of Dr. Katz's attention was on Y'lesha as she told
her life story. Throughout his evaluation, he'd felt a
bond with her. He couldn't imagine how hard it was for

her. Her story was saddening, and her overcoming all of those obstacles only made him admire her.

To him, the woman that the judge called insane was a survivor, not crazy. Her fate rested in his hands, and if he didn't say she was crazy, she would go to jail for the rest of her life. On the other hand, if he lied and diagnosed her as insane, the most she would do is one year in a mental institution. He was between a woman and a hard place and he was torn. Her story was so vivid and too in-depth not to be true. He was a master of the human mind and knew when someone was being sincere. As far as he was concerned, Y'lesha was speaking the truth.

Chapter Twelve

Jada kneeled in her cell and prayed to God. She cried tears as she confessed her innocence. She knew she was in a bad situation. Today was the day she'd know her fate. She hated the fact that she had to plead insanity for a crime she didn't do, but her lawyer had informed her that it was the only way to avoid jail time. She was far from insane and didn't want to be labeled that.

As she told the doctor her story, it was like a burden was being lifted off her shoulders. She hated living the life of Jada Simone. She just wanted to be Y'lesha, a girl from the hood, but without all of the pain that the ghetto had to offer.

The guard yelled as he opened her cell, "Miss Simone, it's time to go to your session. Assume the position."

Jada stood up and placed both of her hands in front of her as the guard handcuffed her and escorted her out of the cell. She knew that her future rested in the hands of Dr.Katz. She believed deep in her heart that if she told Dr. Katz the truth about her past, then somehow she would be okay. The cold air in the jail sent chills through Jada's body as she took the long walk through the corridor. She knew that if the doctor diagnosed her as insane, she would get off.

But she had to tell him her story, the story of Y'lesha Coleman. She felt in her heart that maybe, just maybe, if he heard her life story, then he would know that she didn't deserve to go to jail and would falsely diagnose her as insane.

Jada sat in front of Dr. Katz's desk as the security guard unleashed her from the handcuffs. When the guard left the room, an uncomfortable silence filled the air.

Dr. Katz stared at his client. He wanted to give an accurate analysis of the woman that sat in front of him, but doing that would send her to jail for life. In the very short time that he'd been around, he'd become attached to her. He felt like he knew everything about her. "Y'lesha, how are you today?" Dr. Katz said.

She smiled from ear to ear. "You don't know how good it feels to be called Y'lesha again," she said, adjusting herself in the chair.

"Today's our last session. I know you've been through hell and back throughout your life. I don't care what the court says. I know you're not insane. Actually, I believe you are very intelligent. A woman that has endured what you had to has my respect. We will go before the judge tomorrow and—" Dr. Katz stood up and looked out of his window that overlooked the jail yard. He knew that he would regret what he was about to do but felt it was morally right. "I'm going to diagnose you as insane . . . so that you won't have to serve jail time. The chances of you telling the judge your real story and him granting you an appeal is slim. So I feel this is the only way for justice. You are a strong woman, Y'lesha Coleman, and I wish the best for you," Dr. Katz said as he stared out of the window.

When he turned around, Y'lesha was approaching him with tears in her eyes.

"Nobody has ever treated me nice. It feels so good to finally get my secret life off my chest. You helped me do that." Jada dropped to her knees in front of Dr. Katz and began to unbuckle his belt buckle, to show her appreciation.

As much as he wanted her to pleasure him, his conscience wouldn't allow it. His erect penis sticking out of his boxers as she was about to put it in her mouth, Dr. Katz pulled back. He grabbed her by her shoulders and gently pulled her to her feet. "You don't have to do that. You are a strong, intelligent woman, and I want you to remember that." He buttoned his pants back up.

Jada fell in his arms and cried like a baby.

Dr. Katz felt good, knowing that he'd just made things right for her. He felt that he was her savior, and that was enough gratification for him.

After a few minutes crying in the doctor's arms, she felt embarrassed and headed toward the door. Just before knocking on the door to signal to the guards that her session was over, she turned to Dr. Katz. "Thank you." She knew he had just saved her life.

"You're welcome, Y'lesha." Dr. Katz watched the guards handcuff her and take her away.

He noticed that she'd left behind one of her books. "Hey, you forgot . . ." But the guards had already taken her out. He went over and picked up the book off the floor and took a look at it. It was another Ashley JaQuavis novel. He flipped it over and noticed a picture of a man and woman on the back. As he looked at the book closer, he realized that Ashley JaQuavis were two authors writing under one name. "That's different." He tossed the book onto his desk and planned to give it to a guard later to return to her.

Chapter Thirteen

Two years later

Dr. Katz sat at his desk reading the *New York Times*. The picture he saw on the front page grabbed his full, undivided attention. The headline read: BEST-SELL-ING AUTHOR JADA SIMONE RELEASED FROM MENTAL HOSPI-TAL. SHE SAYS NEW NOVEL IS ON THE WAY. Dr. Katz smiled. He thought about the brief time he spent with the author. He was glad he had helped her get a new start on life. Dr. Katz whispered to himself, "I'll never forget you, Y'lesha Coleman."

Just as he finished his sentence, he heard a knock on the door. "Come in," he said, focusing his attention on his office door.

A stocky delivery man wearing his brown uniform stepped in, package in hand. He looked down at the package to make sure he pronounced the name right. "Dr. Peter Katz?"

"Yeah, that's me."

"I have a package here for you." The delivery man held out a pen for the doctor to sign off.

Dr. Katz rose up and walked toward the man. He signed off for the package and looked at the sender's name. He smiled when he saw Y'lesha Coleman's name written at the top of the package. He opened up the package, wondering what the thick envelope contained. He was surprised when he saw the contents—two of Ashley JaQuavis's novels with a handwritten note that read:

> *You helped me more than you will ever know.*
> —*Jada Simone*

Dr. Katz smiled and walked over to his desk. *Maybe I'll take a look at these books.* He felt good knowing that Y'lesha was still thinking about him after two years. He opened up the novel and began to read the acknowledgments. To his surprise, he saw that both authors thanked Jada Simone:

> *I want to thank my fellow author, Jada Simone, for all the support.*
> —*JaQuavis Coleman*

I didn't know she actually knew the authors, he thought to himself. But when he looked closer, his heart dropped as he discovered something. Under Ashley's acknowledgments it read:

Thanks for the support, Jada Simone. Good luck to you in your writing ventures.

—*Ashley*

Dr. Katz couldn't believe what he was reading. He grabbed a pen and a sheet of paper to see if what he saw was correct. He began to write: *Ashley . . . Y'lesha . . . A-s-h-l-e-y . . . Y-l-e-s-h-a.* "Oh my God," he whispered, when he discovered that if you unscrambled *Y'lesha* you could spell *Ashley.* He then looked at the other author's name and noticed that Coleman was his last name, which was also Y'lesha's last name.

"JaQuavis Coleman?" he whispered in disbelief. He didn't want to believe the obvious. He immediately began to read one of the novels.

As I threw the blistering hot grease onto my boyfriend's chest while he was asleep, I felt a gigantic burden being lifted off my chest. I hurried out to the cab and left him yelling in pain in the house, feeling guilty yet liberated at the same moment.

Dr. Katz threw the Ashley JaQuavis book across the room as he realized what had happened. He was mentally manipulated and outsmarted by Jada Simone.

During the next three days, Dr. Katz had read all five of Ashley Jaquavis's novels. He noticed that Jada had taken pieces from every story and told them to him as if it was her life story, cleverly combining different scenarios from the books. "She made up the whole fucking story. She killed the cop. She did it and got off scot-free."

Dr. Katz couldn't believe how he had been totally bested by a woman. He stood from his desk and flopped on the very couch where Jada had made up the whole story of Y'lesha Coleman. He took a glance at his desk and stared at his master's degree from Stanford and chuckled to himself

At that moment, it all began to make sense to him— Jada was an author, so it was easy for her to make up a fake life. She'd created a story right before his eyes, and he fell for it. Dr. Katz's first name was Peter. Jada told him that her abusive boyfriend's name was Petey. Dr. Katz was totally shocked by how he was fooled and all the evidence was in his face. Jada had played a mind game with him, using things around her to tell her story. She even carried Ashley JaQuavis's books to their sessions, and Dr. Katz didn't think anything of it. It was all a game to her, and he was her toy.

"I can't believe it," he whispered as he sat there in total disbelief.

Jada lay in her two-piece Burberry swimsuit on the luxurious beach, writing her next best-seller. She smiled as she thought about how she'd just gotten away with murder. To her, it was a big game, and she was the star player. She had manipulated her way out of a murder charge and, in the process, became a world-famous author. Being a hustler's wife really paid off.

In her book, *The Duchess*, she told a no-holds-barred tale of the life of a drug dealer's woman. She even described how Young Money ordered her to seduce an undercover cop, who she eventually killed with his dick in his hands and got away with it.

She sipped on her Long Island iced tea and smiled as she thought about how she cleverly admitted to involvement in a cop's murder and got off. She smiled as she finished up her drink and signaled for the Jamaican waiter to bring her over another drink.

Her Chloe shades covering her eyes, she continued to type in the laptop as she lay in the sun. "Maybe I'll make this book about how a crazy bitch got away with murder and wrote a book about it," she said to herself as the waiter approached her and handed her a drink. She was so into her novel, she didn't even acknowledge the waiter as he handed her the drink.

Pop! Pop!

The muffled sounds of two hollow-tip bullets from a silenced 9 millimeter filled the air, bullets flying through her skull, and blood splattering all over her laptop as she stared into space with dead eyes.

The waiter, Young Money aka Braylon Nims, quickly put the gun in his pants and took off his fake dreadlock wig. "You dirty bitch," he said. "I used to love you. You thought that I'd never find you. Look at yourself now. Look at yourself, snitch. Now write a book about that." Young Money nonchalantly walked away, leaving her corpse lying on the sands of the beach in Puerto Rico.

The Duchess: The Life and Times of Jada Simone . . . com-ing soon

"The Last Woman Standing"

By

Ayana Ellis

Carl Thomas's "I Wish" came through the speakers as Londa and Yazmine came back from shopping at Long Island's Tanger Outlet. Londa had more than enough clothes, and she damn sure set Yazmine out enough. She just wanted to catch a few sales, and things for her mother. But she ended up spending $600 on her mother and another $900 on herself. Yazmine walked alongside her holding her $400 worth of merchandise.

Picking up a few things to send to her boy Blake, Londa called it a day with the shopping. "I am tired as hell!"

Yazmine yawned as she got in the passenger side.

"You need to be driving. I am so tired of playing Mr. Bentley. Every time we go someplace, I can't enjoy myself because I have to drive, while you on the side fucked-up, drinking and shit."

"I'm afraid of the road," Yazmine said.

Londa sucked her teeth and backed out of the parking lot. Soon they were on the expressway in their own thoughts, Yazmine thinking about why Mo hadn't called her phone all day, and Londa about her money.

When the girls pulled up in the hood around Yazmine's way, the block was crowded. It wasn't even a good month out of winter, but the weather was nice and the hood was open off of it, dudes walking around in their fresh kicks and flight jackets, girls in their tiny leathers and fresh wraps. Not one to hang around, Londa relented today and decided to hang out with the peoples for a little while, nothing much to do at home anyway.

A neighborhood shorty named Sy said, "Londa, let me get twenty for this bottle of Henny."

Londa peeled off forty. "Bring me back my change, boy."

"Yeah, a'ight" he said, deading her, knowing Londa didn't care.

Yazmine was off with her hand on her hips, talking to a few guys that worked for Mo, probably grilling them about where he was. Londa rolled her eyes and put on a mix CD with the latest hip-hop on it and turned her stereo up.

Soon the block was crowded, and a few guys sat in Londa's car to roll up their weed and drink their shit without getting a ticket. Londa, as cool as ever, just leaned against the front of her car with her arms folded, observing everyone.

Mo appeared from out of nowhere. When he saw Yazmine, he rolled his eyes and walked up to Londa and gave her a big hug. "'Sup, small wonder?"

"Hey, Mo, ya big self, you think you gon' stop blowing up, nigga? Soon it ain't gon' be cute."

"My lady loves it." He laughed and rubbed his stomach.

"Who? Yaz?" Londa laughed.

"Man, she better go 'head. Wifey out here, so . . ."

"Oh Lord," Londa said, knowing all too well about Yaz's and Nuny's confrontations.

"So whaddup? Where you live at now, Londa?"

"Fort Greene. Like Clinton Hills-*ish*."

"You thinking of buying a house? I got a good realtor. Man, she is the shit. She can get you some good prices. She my lil' shorty on the low, you know. I know you got that house money stashed up, right? You ain't all fly but broke, right?"

Londa opened her Chanel fanny pack. "Look in there. What that look like to you, son?" Londa joked.

Mo gave her a pound. "Do that shit, shorty." He turned his head as he heard a commotion.

Mo's baby mother, Nuny, was on top of Yazmine, fucking her up something terrible. Londa ran over and pulled Nuny off of her, and Mo pulled Yazmine away.

"Tired of you calling my man, bitch!" Nuny yelled. "Londa, get off me!"

"No. Nuny, enough is enough, no!" Londa said, holding her wrists.

"That fucking friend of yours? I'm telling you, Londa, I'm-a kill that bitch. Look how many times she called my man today!" Nuny showed Londa the caller ID.

"Why not be mad at Mo too, though, Nuny? Why keep fucking Yaz up? I mean, she only fuck with him 'cause he fucks with her, right?"

"Fuck that. That bitch disrespecting me by fucking my man and she know he got a family, fucking bum bitch."

Londa peeped Yazmine off to the side, wrapping up her hair and fixing her clothes. She had no idea why Yazmine continued to fight this 4 foot 11 powerhouse that didn't give a shit.

While Nuny rambled on, Yazmine ran up on her and punched her in the back of the head. Nuny, a short girl with a big ass, turned around, picked Yazmine up and body slammed her on the hood of someone's hooptie.

The guys in the neighborhood screamed and got hype, surrounding the two women and screaming, "Ooh," and "Aah." Soon breasts were coming up out of shirts, and blood was flying.

Someone said, "Yo, Mo, break that shit up."

Mo coolly walked over and pulled the girls apart, his big 6 foot 4, 290-pound frame towering over the two women, who fought over him at least twice every summer for the past three years. He stepped in her face. "Nuny, go home!"

She wasn't scared of Mo at all, no matter what his rep was on the streets. She knew he wouldn't lift a finger to her. "Nigga, you coming with me. I'm not leaving here without you, so get your shit and let's go."

Mo turned to one of his workers and said something, then threw up the peace sign.

"You out, son?" someone shouted.

"Yeah. Let me take wifey home and cool her off. I'll be back. Londa, take your girl upstairs or out the hood, man. I can't deal with this shit, you heard?"

Yazmine, seeing Mo leaving, walked to him. "Mo, it's

like that? Huh? You was just with me last night and you was just fucking me last night. Now you acting like I'm nobody? Huh?"

Londa hated when Yazmine humiliated herself like this. "Yaz, come on. Let's be out, come on," Londa said, standing between her and Mo.

"No, fuck this shit, Londa. This nigga be fucking me every day and all that, and when this bitch come around he can't even speak? This nigga ain't gon' just treat me like a piece of pussy. Fuck that!"

Nuny jumped back out of her coupe and started yelling from behind Mo. "You are just a piece of pussy—don't you get it by now? I got his kids, a coupe, a house, the bank—Every fucking thing, bitch!"

"Yeah? Well, he's fucking me every day, so I guess we sharing then, huh?"

"Sharing? You know what, when I catch you without Mo around, bitch, I'm-a tear your ass up something awful. Watch."

"Do that shit now. Fuck Mo. Do that shit now!" Yazmine yelled back.

Nuny bust through Mo and landed on top of Yazmine, this time knocking her to the floor, straddling her and punching her in the face back to back.

Londa got on top of Nuny again and threw her off of her friend. This time Londa and Nuny were face to face, toe to toe.

"What, Londa, what? You want some of this too?"

"Man, Nuny go 'head, all right. I ain't with that shit. You need to go home," Londa said as Mo dragged Yazmine away from Nuny and picked her up, and Nuny backed up from Londa.

"You need to get rid of this bitch!" Yazmine cried.

Londa turned around and yelled at her friend, "Yo, you need to chill, Yaz. You know that's wifey. She ain't going nowhere. I told you this shit from day one."

Yazmine continued to yell. "Well then, I tell you what—Stay the fuck out my pussy then, Mo!"

"Yaz, shut up, a'ight. You embarrassing yourself. Come on, let's be out." Londa walked toward her friend.

"No, fuck this shit!" Yaz yelled. "I can't deal with her coming to my hood disrespecting me, Mo, and you defending her."

Nuny was on mark, ready to pounce on Yazmine again.

This time Londa wasn't going for it. "Nuny, don't do it."

"Or what, Londa?"

"Or it's gonna be some unfair shit happening, and I don't want to do it. You need to get in your car and go home. Just go."

"Man, fuck that. This bitch still talking to my man?" Nuny hauled off and smacked Mo and pulled him away by the back of his shirt. She then ran after Yazmine, who covered her face and cowered in the corner as Nuny rained on her ass before the summer even started. Then she jumped in her red Lexus coupe after Mo sweet-talked her and made her go home.

Yazmine's mother called her upstairs angrily, and Londa decided to take her ass home for a much-needed nap.

It was a beautiful spring day, and that only let Londa know one thing. The weather was going to start getting nice, and so the need to floss was urgent. She had

$80,000 sitting in her house, from a few jobs that she'd pulled off, and the only people who knew about it were Blake and Yazmine. She had to take money and stash it soon. She hated to keep anything over $6,000 in her house at a time, but she had been so busy that the money just accumulated.

Yazmine didn't really know the ins and outs of what Londa did. All she cared about was accompanying her to the mall when she was bussin' up thousands, knowing Londa would take care of her too. Yazmine was her best friend, who she kept fly because she was her homie, and Londa felt that she couldn't be fly and Yaz not.

Blake was Londa's partner, but they'd called it quits after he got locked up for two years. She found it easier to do her jobs without him once he was gone, because he was too "strategic" and not spontaneous enough. And he was bossy, so when he got locked up for two years, Londa had no choice but to strike out on her own—which meant more money for her. He was against Londa using sex to get money, but at the end of the day, she felt that if she could get big money from a few minutes of pleasure, she would do it. Blake would try to talk her out of it, but she did what she had to do.

Londa was thinking extra hard on what she wanted to buy as she made her way to the corner store, waving to a few people along the way, making small talk. Finally reaching the store, she picked up a few groceries for her mother.

Londa decided that she'd upgrade her Camry to an Infiniti, not wanting to draw any attention to herself, and give her mother some money. She never asked where Londa got it from and just assumed some dude was taking care of her. Lord knows, Londa never worked a day in her life, even though she'd graduated high school and wasn't a dummy. She was 22, had her own place, her own car, and was the flyest girl in Bed-Stuy.

Londa lugged her bags back up the ramp and got on the elevator of her mother's project building. She wasn't home, so Londa left her a note and an envelope with $3,000 in it and told her to call.

Doing 60, she then left Bushwick, headed home to count her money, get on the computer, and go crazy on the Chanel website. She had her heart set on this beige-and-brown hobo bag that cost $2,300, and she planned on getting the shoes and sneakers to match.

As a habit, she held her keys in her hand so that she could have it ready, in case some pervert was chasing her. Then, she could easily run in the house. When she inserted her key, a dirty high-yellow girl came out from the staircase right next to her door. Londa looked at her and opened her door anyway, thinking she might be looking for the young knucklehead that lived down the hall with his grandmother.

"Aye, girl," she said.

Londa held the knob and looked at her. "Yeah?" Londa asked sarcastically.

"You Londa?"

"Who wanna know?"

She stopped and said, "You ain't tired of fuckin' people man?"

Londa had no idea what she was talking about. "What? Who's your man?" Londa said, not wanting to entertain this girl at all. She wasn't really messing with anyone like that, because she didn't trust anyone in the line of work she did.

While in thought, three other girls appeared, all dirty, all looking like they wanted to rob her or something. She thought about what she had on. She never left the house without her huge diamond earrings and her Chanel fanny pack.

Damn! Before she knew it, the girls charged her, and she fell into her apartment. These bitches were in her house, stomping her out. She had no time to swing or do anything, so she just protected her face and balled up. They had to have come in through the back of the building.

Somebody knew something, Londa thought. She was mad as she felt foot after foot stomp and kick her. They were pulling her hair, making her braids tight, and it hurt like hell. She felt someone snatch her earrings out of her ears—$8000 gone just like that. She just prayed no one had a blade. She kept thinking of what she could've done wrong to receive this karma, but at the time, nothing came to mind.

Londa grabbed someone's foot and began biting, anything to get herself out the corner so she could see some faces and identify these bitches. She grabbed the one that initially stepped to her and started fighting with her. She was a little weak, but her energy quickly picked up the angrier she got. They all backed up as Londa stood there disheveled, in pain, and breathing heavily.

"What? What y'all bitches want? Who the fuck is ya man?"

"Stay the fuck away from people's man," one of them said.

A tall girl walked up to Londa and punched her dead in the face, knocking her against the wall, and the rest of the girls were running through the apartment, tearing shit up. They appeared to be looking for something.

As Londa stood there yelling for them to get the fuck out of her house, a short black one with a little bit of hair ran up on her and snuffed her. Londa and the girl started to fight. The bitch knew how to throw down. Londa couldn't concentrate on winning this fight because she was too busy looking at the tall, light-skinned girl that was getting way too close to the stash in the large Japanese vase.

Nobody but Londa's mother knew where the stash was. She didn't trust anybody. She wanted her mother to know where it was, in case anything happened to her. Her mother was her best friend, and Londa would give her her last, just as she'd sacrificed and did for her as a single mother. That's why she hadn't worked in a year. Londa told her to take a break.

They were tearing up the house and snatching up any valuables they could find, bum bitches that they were. Then a light bulb went off in Londa's head. She remembered the burner that was in the top junk drawer. She'd tried her best to forget it was there. She was just holding it for Blake until he got home. The tall, light-skinned girl made her way to Londa. She had to think fast to get these bitches out of her house before they caused some major damage. Londa then turned and ran toward her bedroom, the light-skinned girl running behind her. She wasn't sure if the other girls followed. She just knew she had to get to her piece so she could clear this apartment.

Londa opened the drawer as the light-skinned girl entered the room. Frantically, she pushed the papers and an old T-shirt to the side and retrieved her piece just as the girl ran up on her. She had no idea what she was going to do, but as mad as she was, anything was possible.

"What's your name? Who sent you here?" Londa was shaking. She was hoping this girl couldn't see how nervous she was.

Before she could answer, her friends appeared in the doorway, all backing away slowly upon seeing Londa brandishing iron.

"Get the fuck outta my house now!" Londa yelled angrily.

The girls ran out of the house screaming and scampering down different staircases. Londa ran down the closest staircase, leaping down flights, hot on the trail of the tall one that punched her in her face. She was on her, all the way down to the second floor, where she was sure they were all going to be because it led to the iron staircase that let you out the back.

A big part of Londa wanted the girls to get away. She didn't want to kill anyone; she just wanted to send a message. She couldn't run as fast as she wanted to because she was sore, but she kept on pushing. She heard her run through the second floor. She caught up to her, but the girl jumped into the iron staircase. Londa let off a shot that echoed loudly. Then she heard a scream. The more she thought about them violating her in her house, the angrier she got. She let off a shot for GP and ran through the iron staircase, where she saw the four of them loading up in the car.

She stopped, aimed, and let off the last three shots, breaking the car windows. She heard the bitches scream, but she knew no one was hit. She was out of bullets. *Fuck!* she said, as they pulled off doing about 70.

Londa walked back upstairs to the fourth floor slowly, in pain. She was tired and her shoulder hurt from using this gun that Blake left in her house before he got locked up. He was the only man she trusted, because they did so much dirt together, and she knew him most of her life.

When she got to her apartment, the door was still open. She closed it and sat down on the sofa and started crying out of anger, trying to think about who these chicks were. They never said who this so-called nigga was. Londa figured it was just some jealous girls that hated on her. She knew she wasn't messing with nobody's man. Blake lived on the other side of Brooklyn, and he was locked up. She couldn't even see him messing with girls that looked like that, as fine and fly as he was, and the few dudes that she had in her life were sprinkled all over, from Maryland to Harlem, and they never saw her that much, let alone some chick they knew trying to get at her.

Londa took a shower and put Nas's *God's Son* CD. She lotioned her aching body slowly and started to cry angry tears. She couldn't wait for Blake to call. If he didn't, she vowed to visit him upstate. She then called Yazmine and told her to come over. She needed to vent and pop shit about the day's events. Yaz told Londa that she was of course sitting in the car talking to Mo and that he'd have him drop her off.

Yazmine showed up an hour later dressed in True Religion jeans, a fitted Brooklyn T-shirt, Prada sneakers, and her hair in two corn rows. Yazmine was pretty, but she was one of those girls that just knew a nigga would take care of her forever because of her looks. How wrong was she?

"Got that nigga to up some dollars!" she sang, counting the three hundred Mo gave her.

Londa was too mad to be disgusted with her and her chump change. Mo was playing her. Yazmine finally got off Mo's dick long enough to notice the situation.

"What happened to you?" she asked, noticing the black and blues forming on Londa's face and body.

Londa stared in her eyes and found sincerity and shock, so she immediately crossed her out as a suspect. But she and Blake were the only two that knew how she got down. She sat down and poured a glass of champagne. "You want one?"

"Yeah, sure. What happened, Londa?"

Londa began to tell Yazmine the story as she sipped and touched her bruises.

"Who you think would want to rob you?"

Londa shrugged. "You could tell they were looking for something. They ransacked my crib, was turning over pillows and shit."

"Well, did they find anything? I mean, you do have your stash in here, right?"

Too sharp for the rhetorical questions, Londa simply said, "Nah."

"Hmph. Well, those bitches wasted their time then. You got a bank account? You gotta be careful, because you know the feds start investigating after you put more that ten thousand in your account."

"Nah, I don't put my money in no bank. I keeps my bank. I just wanna know where these broads came from. How do they know where I live?"

"You ain't tell none of those dudes you fuck with about, you know, how you get money, right?"

"No, I don't tell nobody shit. The only people that know are you and Blake."

"Well, you know I ain't set you up. Shit, that wouldn't even make sense, when you always holding me down, regardless. You spoke to Blake? When is he calling you?"

Londa shrugged.

"He short now, huh? I can't wait for my baby boy to come home his crazy-ass self."

Londa quietly wondered why all of a sudden Blake was Yazmine's boy.

Yeah, sure, they all were cool, but Blake was Londa's people, and he knew Yazmine on the strength of Londa, but not enough for Yaz to be on some I-can't-wait-for-him-to-come-home shit. "Your boy? From where?"

"Don't trip. Me and Blakey is cool."

Blakey? "He'll be home in a few months."

Londa wanted to change the subject, but Yazmine wanted to keep on talking about Blake.

"You gon' set him out, or he got dough?"

"He should be a'ight. I'm sure he got a stash some-where. I mean, if he needs something, I got him though, but he should be okay."

"Damn! Them bitches did a number on you, Londa. That shit is fucked-up."

"I'm so mad. I wish I didn't miss any of them when I started shootin'."

"You was bussin' ya gun, girl?" Yazmine asked, wide-eyed. "Are you nuts?" She sipped her champagne.

"Are *they* fucking nuts?"

Yazmine leaned back and looked at Londa. "Girl, you are losing your mind."

"No, baby. I'm protecting what is mine."

"Well, let's get out of this house and go do something. Sitting in here, you just gon' get tight thinking about those girls that jumped you. Did they take any jewelry or anything?"

"Yeah, the bum bitches took my Chanel fanny pack, and it had a few hundred in there, my earrings I had on, and one of them even took a shoe. One fucking shoe."

"Shut up, Londa. You serious?" Yazmine laughed.

"Yes! I had a pair of Pradas right there, and they took one shoe. I mean, is it that serious?"

"Apparently, it is." Yazmine got up. "Come on, get dressed. Let's go riding around or something." She threw back her second flute of champagne, counting her three hundred dollars in singles again.

Yazmine and Londa decided to go get massages at Body by Brooklyn on Park Place in Brooklyn. Londa got the hot stone massage for $190 an hour, and Yazmin got aromatherapy. The girls lay side by side, moaning in pleasure, especially Londa, who took a real ass-whuppin' this afternoon. *Who would want to rob me? I mean, I'm cool with everybody. I can't begin to think of who had the balls to run up in my house.* Londa was still pissed, thinking about the one girl that snatched her studs out of her ears and swiped up her fanny pack. She sucked her teeth out of frustration.

"You okay over there, girl?"

"Yeah, I'm fine. Just thinking. How's that massage going down over there?"

"Tell Flex to drop a bomb on this shit. Oh my God, we need to go sit down someplace, eat and get fucked up after this. Maybe catch a comedy show or something. We haven't been to Caroline's in forever."

"Oh, word. Mo gave you money, so you can treat me for a change," Londa said matter-of-factly.

"Shut up. Three hundred dollars ain't nothing, and you know it."

"Is that right?"

"Girl, stop tripping. So can we go on a date, please?" Yazmine joked.

"You think I'm your fucking man or your mother— That's your damn problem. When are *you* going to take me out?"

"Your birthday is coming up soon, right?"

"Yeah."

"Okay, for your birthday, even if I gotta give Mo a private dance to get the money, I'm going to take care of you. How's that?"

"You know I'm not tripping over that shit. Just once in a while it would be nice for you to treat. I mean, damn."

"Shut up. I'll leave the tip." Yazmine laughed.

When the girls left the massage parlor, they hopped in Londa's Camry and headed to Fifth Avenue and

Twenty-first, to a seafood restaurant that played music and normally had white-collar men in attendance. Feeling relaxed and actually looking it, the women sat at a table for two and ordered a bottle of champagne to start.

"I don't want any hard liquor today," Yazmine said. "Just straight champagne and flying high. That massage was the shit."

"Yeah, it was. It got the knots and kinks out of my back. Is my eye still dark?"

"A little. You look fine, though."

"I need to find out who set me up, Yazmine."

"I know you do, and when you do, holla at me so I can be there to help you set it."

"Hmph. If I can. I might not have time to get off that bitch ass and make no phone calls. I will call you from jail, though."

"I hear you." Yazmine laughed.

"Okay, so what you ordering?"

"Scampi in wine sauce."

"I think I'll have some clams, some lobster tail in butter sauce, oh yes, and some garlic bread." Londa licked her lips.

"Damn, bitch, that's a lot of shit you're ordering."

"Yup, that's how I roll—Fuck asking for the price, just order that shit." Londa laughed. "Life is good, ain't it?"

"Sure is, with friends like you, girl. Can I order some lobster too?"

"Of course. We're just going to sit back here, drink fine champagne, eat fine food, and laugh our asses off," Londa said, knowing she had $1,000 in her small Gucci clutch wrapped tight in a rubber band.

"I hear that. So what's going on? What happened to that dude from Long Island you was fucking with?"

"What dude?" Londa said, sipping.

"The half-white guy with the Astor Martin."

"Oh, water boy." Londa laughed.

"Why you call him water boy?"

Yazmine laughed, not knowing why, but Londa was a funny bitch when she was ready, so she knew it was a reason for it.

"Don't he look like one of the lil' water boys and shit that be in the locker rooms and shit?"

"He looked corny as hell."

"Yeah, but he had gwop. A lot of it."

"He spent any dough on you?" Yazmine inquired, wondering how Londa got the men to take notice. She always figured she was prettier than Londa, because she had the good hair, was light-skinned, had a nice shape, and she was fly. Londa was cute, brown, kept her hair in tiny corn rows that hung down her back, and had a cute shape. She was more breasts than ass, but she was fly as hell. Londa wore shit that nobody Yazmine knew could afford, not unless you were an entertainer of some sort. And Londa wasn't out there like that. She knew a lot of guys, and they respected her swagger. But it was Yazmine who was out there doing all the fucking and getting a rep. Everybody knew Yazmine on the strength of her pussy, getting beat up by Mo's baby mother, or rolling with the flyest bitch in Brooklyn, Londa.

"Yeah, he was giving me cash." Londa sipped her champagne. She thought about the night she put a gun to Dorian's head and made him withdraw $60,000 from his bank account.

As far as he knew, Londa's name was Jennifer, she was visiting from Georgia, and was a sweet girl. Dorian had jungle fever, and got caught up in the jungle, for real.

"He is the one that copped me that diamond necklace with the rubies in it," Londa said, thinking of the $20,000 necklace she got with the money she'd jooked from him.

"That necklace is hot." Yazmine wondered where the fuck Londa kept all of that expensive jewelry she rocked. "What did he do for a living?"

"His family had old money. I had to drop him, though. He had a small dick."

"Oh my God. You ain't know? You could tell his geeky ass. Ugh! Why you even fucked wit' him in the first place?"

Londa shrugged and sipped.

"Where you keep all that shit at? You better not keep it in your house." Yazmine took her plate from the waiter.

Londa simply replied, "I don't. So, girlie, what is up with you and big worm?"

Yazmine fell out laughing. "Who? Mo?"

Londa laughed too. It was just like old times.

"He a'ight, you know. Still not shaking that bitch of his, but whatever, man, as long as he keep them dollars coming."

"I know that's right, but on some real shit, you should get a little job just to, you know, keep your ass covered."

There was no way Yazmine was going to get a job, not with Londa balling out of control and not working. She could not fall down the nine-to-five path while her best friend led the life of a superstar. "Job? Bitch, you get a job." Yazmine laughed.

"Shiiit, not the kid. Not me. Nah, soon I plan on getting a job, in like six months. My mother's starting to beef," she lied.

"How is your mother anyway? I haven't seen her in a while. She doesn't question where you get money from?"

"She thinks I got men tricking on me, that's all. So now she is on me like, girl, you can't be out there like that, you gotta get your own shit. So to appease her I'm going to get a little job and even go back to school. I need to anyway. My money isn't long like that."

"I hear that. Well, when you go get a job, I'll go. Until then—"

"Just freeload off me, bitch, right?" Londa laughed. Yazmine didn't.

Blake and Londa had been friends for a long time but began fooling around about two years ago off and on mainly because they spent so much time together and got caught up. But a lot of the time they argued because he wanted her out of the game—the game that he'd turned her on to. A lot of times she took it as him hating because she was flourishing in a game that he put her on to, and since he was behind bars helpless, he didn't want her to make a name for herself in the streets and take his shine. Londa felt that Blake was afraid that one day she wouldn't need him anymore.

The truth was, she never did. She was his silent partner, but after a while, the streets took notice and realized that she was up to no good running with him. No one was really sure. Listening to Blake and thinking about the dough she could get out of this thing here turned her on more so than him.

She was a woman, so she didn't have to rob drug dealers and do wild shit unless she was with him. She just scoped out the suckers and put that thing to them and made them ante up. There was no better high than sitting her pretty ass on her king-size canopy bed, counting stacks and paying rent off for the year. She even had a spot out of town that nobody knew about, not even Blake or Yazmine. Only her mother knew about it.

Blake said the only way he would get back in the game was if he came up with a big fish. He said he wasn't coming home to be doing any minor bullshit. The last time Londa spoke to him, she'd told him she wasn't visiting him upstate anymore, that she'd see him when he got home. But after those girls ran up in her house, she had to go talk to him and find out what was going on. He said he'd been hearing things about a guy named Val, who supposedly was hood-rich and kept all his money and guns at his girlfriend's house. He said once he came home he'd look more into it, but in the meantime advised Londa to lay low.

When Londa reached Downstate Correctional Facility, she felt bad for her friend and hoped that she never had to spend a day in jail. She hadn't killed anyone, thank God, so the money she had was untraceable because it was dirty. Blake came out from behind the gate looking around for Londa. When he spotted her, he didn't smile. His eyes didn't warm up to her or welcome her. Londa could see the jealousy in his eyes as he looked her up and down on the visit, but she knew it was only because he was locked up and frustrated.

"You fly as usual," he greeted her.

Londa hugged him warmly.

"Come on, you know me. So what's going on with you, playboy? You'll be home soon. You excited?"

"Yeah, and I appreciate the things you been doing for me since I been down, Londa. I miss your punk ass."

"I bet you do." She winked.

"So who you fucking with? What's been going on out there? How you holding up?"

Londa contemplated telling Blake about the jobs she'd pulled off, but she couldn't tell him everything. Nor could she hide things from him. However, she decided not to tell him who or what she stuck or just how much she got from it. Well, not all of it. "Blake"—She leaned in closer and looked around—"I got a big fish by myself."

"Word? Who? How big?"

"I was messing with a dude and pretty much found out he had more than what he was presenting to me. Anyway, fuck him. This nigga was holding cash, had shit in his glove compartment and all kinds of shit, Blake. Anyway, he was so open off of the sex that he wasn't even realizing that whenever he'd leave me alone in his house, I'd be robbing his ass for a few G's here or there. See, I never told him my real name or where I was from. I made a copy of his keys. I knew where he kept his stash and all that, frontin' nigga, letting me push his *V* and all that. He came home one day and—"

"Realized he been had, huh? So how much was it about?"

She wasn't about to tell him that it was $64,000 in cash and jewelry. "A lil' over thirty G's."

"Word?" Blake eyed Londa. He'd taught her well. He knew she skimmed a good ten to fifteen off the top, but he was cool with that.

"Yeah, Blake, but I'm about to wrap it up soon and get my shit get together. I got enough money to live comfortably. I mean, I can get a little job and buy a car, you know, and just chill and not have to live check to check. I can buy a house somewhere and rent it out."

Blake's eyes widened. "You holding like that?"

"Yeah, I can stand to get one more big one then lay low."

"You should, Londa. You don't wanna get caught up in this shit. So where you keeping ya stash at? You know you can't keep everything in one place."

Instantly Londa was reminded of the reason she came to see him in the first place.

"You know the rules—Never tell anybody where you got ya dough spread at. You got money stashed for you when you come home, right?" Londa asked, knowing Blake should have at least $70,000.

"A lil' something. Yeah, I'm good, but I want one big job and I'm done too." He looked at her. He'd heard about her in the streets, how she was rocking different minks every Saturday, and although she was low-key, people took notice of her. They woke up in the morning just to see what Londa would have on that day. Blake foolishly spent his money flossing on bitches, losing it in dice, and buying material things. He barely had $15,000.

"Blake, someone ran up in my crib the other day. You heard about it?"

"Yeah, I heard something about that. Some chicks, right?"

"Yeah, how you knew about that?"

"Yaz told me."

"Yaz, huh. You been talking to Yaz?"

"Come on, man. You know it ain't nothing. When I can't find you, I just call Yaz. It ain't nothing, right? We peoples."

"Visitors, five more minutes!" the C.O. shouted out.

Blake and Londa stood up to embrace. This time Londa didn't feel the need to hug him warmly, yet he hugged her tight then kissed her forehead.

"Your time is real short. I won't be back up here, but I'll see you when you get home, okay?"

"Can I hit that when I come home?" He smiled that handsome smile.

"Call Yaz if you can't find me." Londa laughed and switched out the door in her skintight Seven jeans.

Blake watched Londa walk out, unsure if he really knew the woman that just left him.

Straight from the facility, Londa took a cab to Nate's Car Show in Queens. Her mind was foggy. She couldn't understand this relationship between Yaz and Blake. Not that it was out of the ordinary, but it seemed to have bloomed after he got locked up. And Londa couldn't recall Blake or Yaz ever telling her about them sparring on any level without her.

Her paranoia was erased as she saw Fats approach her. He smiled when he saw her walk in. "Hey, sunshine," the short, fat, balding white man said to her.

"Fats. Hey, how you doing?"

"I'm fine, baby girl," he said, kissing her cheek. "What can I do for you, doll face?"

"You can just hand me the keys to my baby. Is she ready?"

Fats's face lit up. "You know she is. I hooked her up nice for you."

"Nice, nice." Londa rubbed her hands together eagerly.

Londa pulled out of the car dealership in a brand-new 2007 silver Infiniti truck. She turned her radio on and blasted Fabulous's "Brooklyn" song, featuring Jay-Z and Uncle Murder. *I gotta call my girl Yaz, take her for a spin. Fuck it. Let her have my Camry, with her no-car-having ass.*

She laughed at Yazmine's fear of driving but figured once a car was handed to her, she'd have no choice but to drive it. Her mother already had a car, a cute black 2006 Mountaineer. With her funny suspicions of Blake and Yaz, she still found a soft spot in her heart to look out for her home girl, who was fiending to live the good life but didn't know how to go about it. Yaz balled on a much smaller level, fucking niggas to get outfits and pocket money. She wasn't ready for the big world, but she'd take whatever scraps she could.

For some strange reason, on her way to see Yaz, Londa decided not to drive her truck. She parked it by her house and took her Camry instead. Feeling good on this warm day, she pulled out her Razor phone and dialed Yazmine's mother's house.

"Hi, Ms. Bailey. How are you? . . . I'm good. Where's your daughter? Is she home? . . . She's outside someplace? Okay . . . No, don't tell her I called. I'll drive through and find her. Thank you." Londa hung up and hit the BQE. She stopped at Sapolo's on Myrtle Avenue and got two mai tai's, one each for her and Yazmine.

Londa was feeling really good about the purchase of her truck. She couldn't wait to tell her girl about it . . . one day. She didn't want anyone to know she bought a new car yet. Sipping on her mai tai and listening to Mary J. sing "Take Me as I Am," Londa drove slowly down Marcus Garvey looking for her friend. Slowly she drove, knowing Yazmine was around someplace. She honked the horn in the front of Yazmine's building, and a few guys from the courtyard came out.

A neighborhood slinger by the name of John-John approached Londa. "Let me hold suttin'." He smirked.

Londa laughed. "Have you seen Yazmine?"

"Yeah. She on the other side with Mo and them."

"Good looking, babe."

"You looking good, Londa. Do ya thing, girl. Don't let them haters stop you!" he shouted out.

Londa honked her horn in acknowledgment and headed around the corner to snatch up Yazmine, who was probably up in Mo's face about his baby mother as usual.

Londa pulled up slowly alongside the curb as she spotted Yazmine in a navy blue Juicy Couture sweat suit, her wavy hair pulled back in a bun. She didn't recognize the girls that Yazmine was talking to, so she reclined her seat back and watched as Yazmine animatedly told a story about something, punching her fist into her open hand and rocking from side to side in ghetto-girl fashion. Then a tall, light-skinned girl came from out the courtyard, laughing with Mo and smoking a cigarette. Mo seemed annoyed by her presence as he got on his cell phone.

Londa immediately recognized her as the girl that came to her house, and the pieces all started falling into place. The rest of the girls were the girls that jumped her and tried to rob her. *What the fuck is Yazmine doing with them?* Londa fumed as she sat back sipping her mai tai till it was gone and started sipping on the one she had for Yazmine. *How does this bitch know them?*

Through her rearview mirror, she saw John-John walking up, so she pulled off slowly, not wanting her cover to be blown.

Driving home steamed, Londa called Mo's cell phone. She knew now that Yazmine was a snake.

"Yo," he answered.

"Mo, whaddup. It's Londa. What you doing, boy?"

"Hey, Londa. What's good? What you been up to?"

"I'm chilling. Just looking for my partner in crime. Is Yaz outside?"

"Yeah, she over there talking shit. How you been, baller?"

"I ain't no baller. I'm struggling like everybody else. Who she talking to?"

"I don't know. Some chicks she been sparring with lately. Some bum bitches. I thought you and her wasn't talking, but apparently you are so. Anyway, bullshit, shorty. You doing it bigger than most dudes I know." He laughed.

"Whatever, Mo. Let me hold suttin'."

"Let *me* hold suttin'. I'm dead-ass."

Mo was a big-time hustler with workers all up and

through Bed-Stuy with a crazy baby mother that constantly whooped Yazmine's pretty little ass for hanging around him. Londa never understood why Yazmine acted as if she didn't know that Mo was still seeing his baby mother. Everybody knew that Yazmine was the chick on the side. But he bought Yazmine gear and put money in her pocket, so sadly, that was enough for her. Yazmine was too silly and didn't have the heart to run with Londa on any jobs. She'd fold quick, that Londa knew for sure. Under all that tough talk, Yazmine didn't have what it took to do illegal shit, so Londa never told her anything. Yazmine never knew what Londa was into or when she was going to handle anything. For some reason, though Yazmine was her girl, she never trusted her, and now she had a reason why.

"Yo, Londa, you there?" Mo lowered his voice.

"Yeah, baby. What's up?"

"Listen, don't fuck with that nigga Blake when he come home, you hear me? He ain't right. He's a grimy nigga, and I don't want anything to happen to you."

"What you heard, Mo?" Londa's heart dropped. She knew that whatever Mo was saying had to be true because he wasn't the catty type of dude that would just make up things. Mo only knew Blake because Blake's grandmother lived next door to Mo's baby mother. They knew each other and respected one another's street rep but never did things together.

"I'm just hearing things through the wire, Londa, like he hatin' on you and all that. I know y'all got y'all thing, nah mean, but don't trust him. When a nigga is fucked-up in the game, he will turn on his peoples, and you know he got a rep to be a slimy nigga. I ain't heard nothing concrete, but he ain't to be trusted. Just watch him, a'ight."

"I got you, Mo. Thanks for the heads-up."

"Yeah. Now that'll be five thousand for my services, baller."

"Whatever, man. You see that lil' chickenhead, Yaz?"

"Yaz is right here, though. Good talking to you. Hold on."

Londa took a deep breath and put on her best voice.

"Hello?" Yazmine got on.

" 'Sup, girl? You on the ave?" Londa asked, trying her best to sound civilized.

"Yeah. Where you been all day? Your phone kept going straight to voice mail."

"I had some things to do. You want me to come scoop you? I'll be around your way soon."

"Yeah. Meet me by my mother's, okay?"

"Okay, I'll be there in a few."

"Okay, cool."

Londa started driving, wondering why Yazmine would do this to her, as much as she looked out for her.

When Blake came home, the first thing he did was go to his grandmother's house in Bed-Stuy, where he didn't talk to anybody. The only person he did talk to was Mo and a few other dudes that he knew was well-respected and got money. Since Yazmine was fucking Mo and was up his ass, he knew that she wouldn't be too far. He needed to talk to her anyway, so he chatted up Mo, although he really didn't want to. He wasn't in the mood for any flashy dudes being in his face, considering all he had was $15,000 in his stash, though he'd told Londa that he had more than that.

"You home, yo?" Mo gave Blake dap as he came down the block.

"Yeah, man, out the pokey. You going to visit the kids and all that?"

"Yeah, more or less, then I'm out of here for like a month. Time to hit the freeway."

"I hear you, man," Blake said, stuffing his hands in his pockets.

"I saw your girl come through in some silver Infiniti or some shit the other day. She doing it big, huh. I'm sure she held you down and got a stash for you."

"Nah, I was straight before I went in, so I got a lil' suttin'."

Mo knew Blake was broke. "You good? You need me to put you on?"

"Nah, I'm good, man. Thanks. Where Yaz?"

"Oh, she around." Mo laughed. "Yaz is crazy. That's my lil' shorty, though. She good people."

"Yeah. Tell her to holla at me when you see her."

"No doubt." Mo gave Blake dap again then headed up the block.

Blake ran into the house and found his grandmother's once-decrepit furniture replaced with new suede sofas and more up-to-date furniture. "Nana!" Blake called out and found her in her new bedroom.

"Hey, baby. You home?" She sat up and smiled.

Blake hugged his grandmother and looked around. He smiled. "What you do to the place?"

"Oh, I just figured, let me just hook my house up, you

know. I'm not moving, so I might as well make it look good in here, you know. So how you been?"

"I'm good, lil' lady. I'm fine. Just came to get some things that I left in the attic then I'm heading over to the other side."

"I hope you plan on staying out of the clink, son."

"I do, Grandma, I do," Blake said sincerely. Then he got up and jogged upstairs. Blake moved the boxes and pictures and didn't find the rusty keepsake box that he put the cash in. He looked around for a while and pondered. "I know I left it right here." He ran back downstairs.

Nana was in the kitchen cooking and humming Minnie Ripperton's "Loving You."

"Nana, what you do with the rest of my money?"

"What money?"

"Nana, the money I left up here. Where you put it?"

"Oh, son, bills had to be paid. I gave that little gal you sent over here the two thousand dollars you told me to give her, and that's that."

Blake sucked his teeth. "Nana, that money wasn't yours. Did you even save me anything and you know I was coming home? I gave you some money for yourself. Why you had to take mine?"

Nana instructed him to pass her the big black pocketbook on the sofa. She opened it and took a few hundred out of her wallet. "This can buy you a few outfits, some money in your pocket. That's all I got."

Blake threw the money on the table and walked out.

Luckily he ran into Mo again as he was about to go into his kids' mother's house. "Yo, Mo!" Blake shouted out. "Come here."

" 'Sup?"

"I'm-a need to take you up on that offer, man. How much I'm good for?"

"You? I can spot you ten to get on. Then, you know, you can get at me when you get at me."

"Good looking, man. I'll be back through here tonight. I gotta go to the 'Ville, to my sister house and see her. I'll be back around eleven. Let me get your numbers."

"Fo' sho," Mo said, jotting his number down. *I ain't giving that nigga shit.*

When Blake reached his sister's house, the first person he called was his man Peedi. Peedi was his friend since childhood and his getaway driver for everything he did.

Peedi came to the house with a gallon of Hennessy and two girls. "You home?" He gave Blake dap. "'Sup? You a'ight?"

"Nana spent my paper, son. I have nothing."

"Yo, so call up Londa. You know she sitting on some paper. I know she got a twenty spot for you."

"I don't want to ask her for anything right now. I can't, you know. My man from the Stuy is supposed to hit me off tonight, though. We gon' hit up Val, and then I can pay him back and keep going from there, build up my paper. I'm not asking Londa for shit."

"I saw her the other day. She ain't see me, though. She stylin', son."

"Yeah, I know. I heard. Good for her."

"You saw her yet?"

"Nah, not yet. I spoke to her, though, as soon as I got

to Nana crib. I'll get up with her. I gotta get up with Yazmine first, though."

"Yaz? Who that? Her home girl, right?"

"Yeah, she was supposed to be handling some shit for me while I was away."

"You got that bitch on the ho stroll or suttin'?" Peedi laughed as he poured Henny in a plastic cup.

Blake took a long swig of his Henny and laughed off his response, changing the subject. "Whaddup, Selena, Lecia!" Blake shouted out to the two girls that came in with Peedi. They were on the sofa giggling and rolling a blunt.

"We see you, baby. Whaddup?"

"Y'all ready to go get some dough?"

"Always. We just hope you know what the fuck you talking about next time. That silly bitch, Yaz, wastin' time," Selena said. She was one of the girls that jumped Londa.

"I'm-a talk to Yaz tonight about it," Blake said. "Don't worry."

"Welcome home, my nig," Peedi said, in a toast.

Yazmine was in her bedroom trying on different outfits for when she saw Blake tonight. She never fucked with him like that, but planned on doing so. They'd sent one another dirty letters and talked sex on the phone when he was away. He even gave her money to set Londa up and promised her an even bigger payday when he got home. She knew he had to be sitting on more cash than Londa, so with a little bit of sex, she was sure to get him hooked and have him and Mo tricking on her in no time.

She decided on short dungaree shorts, a tube top, and a pair of Gucci mules that Mo bought her for her birthday last year. Satisfied, she wet her curly hair and let it air-dry into a pretty, curly mane.

When the phone rang it came up private. Hesitantly, she picked it up. "Hello."

"Hey, you. It's Londa. What you doing?"

Yazmine rolled her eyes in annoyance, but her voice said otherwise. "Oh, hey, you. Nothing. Just chillin', getting dressed. Well, I'm dressed but—"

"You going out? Where you going?"

"Nowhere, but I figured I'd come out, walk the ave, get into something. I know Mo is out here somewhere. I figured we could go eat, or I was gonna call this next cat I met the other day when I was with my mother downtown. What's up? Where are you?" Yazmine was hoping Londa didn't want to hang out.

"In front of your house. Come outside. Let's hang out for a while."

Fuck! "Oh, okay. I'm coming out now." She flipped her phone shut. She looked in the mirror, admiring herself for a minute. "Ma!" she yelled out and walked into the kitchen.

"What?" Yazmine's mother looked her up and down. "You going out to run the streets again, huh? You need to get a damn job, Yazmine."

"Mommy, please . . . okay? Can I have fifty dollars?"

"Hell no. You know better. Get a damn job, and don't come in my house after two either."

Yazmine had already sucked her teeth and hit the staircase mad because she was broke.

Londa sat in her truck hurt and frustrated about what was happening around her. Yazmine had set her up to get robbed. She would no longer be her friend. There was nothing that Yazmine could say to her to make her change her mind or convince her otherwise. Londa even changed her cell phone number and everything, so Yazmine wouldn't be able to contact her after today.

Her heart was beating fast, thinking about fucking Yazmine up. She could barely hold herself together as Yaz came out the building stuntin' in Chanel shades, probably looking for Londa's Camry. Londa sat back smirking, her hair in tiny neat corn rows that hung long and loose down her back, her wild eyes hiding behind vintage Versace shades.

Yazmine was sick to her stomach when Londa bust a U-turn and pulled up in front of her building. Smiling and hiding her envy behind shades, Yazmine smiled and walked up to the passenger side.

Londa rolled down the window and had her right hand gripping the steering wheel tight, showing off a bulky diamond bracelet that Yazmine didn't comment on but had to have seen. *Good thing you got on them shades, bitch.*

" 'Sup, girl? You creeping or what? What you doing over here in the hood?" Yazmine laughed.

"Creepin'. 'Sup? Get in," Londa said, unlocking the door.

When Yazmine hopped in, Londa honked the horn at the fellas outside and began to drive, going nowhere in particular. "You want some mai tai's?" Londa offered.

"Oh yes, and let me tell you about this nigga Mo and that fucking baby mama of his. I'm about to stop fucking with him. Watch."

Yeah right. How you gon' eat? Londa noticed that Yazmine said nothing about the new truck with its TVs and navigation system inside. *Damn! This bitch is a hater.*

"Do you know that he came over here with that bitch and his kids and had a fucking cookout? A cookout?"

"Where was I? Why didn't you call me?" Londa said dryly.

"I was just mad as hell. Besides, I wasn't alone. Some of my neighborhood friends were out and about. I was so fucking mad, I just went in the house and went to sleep to stop me from playing myself." Yazmine shook her head.

"You wanna watch a movie or something? I got mad shit. I got *Menace, Madea's Family Reunion, Raw.* Open the glove compartment," Londa said, ignoring Yazmine's bullshit story about Mo. She was tired of her hood-rat ways.

"This is nice," Yazmine finally forced out. "When you copped this?"

"Some weeks back."

"And you just now saying something? Why you ain't tell me you copped this? You are the number one stunner, you know that?" Yazmine rolled her eyes.

"For what? I figured you'd see it. I gotta announce when I buy shit? You know how much stuff I have that you have no idea about? Shit, I *was* gonna give you my Camry."

Yazmine said nothing. She sat quiet, waiting to hear why Londa decided not to give her the car.

"I said fuck it. Might as well hold on to it. You never know, right?"

"True, true," was all Yazmine could come up with. *Bitch gotta be the only one driving.*

Sometimes it was so hard for Yazmine to hide the jealousy she felt for Londa. She babbled on for close to a half-hour about herself, Mo, and his baby mama drama. They were damn near in Long Island, and she still didn't shut up.

"So how long you gon' fuck with Mo before you realize he's just beatin' ya shit up and giving you chump change?"

"He ain't hardly giving me chump change, Londa," Yazmine said, hurt. "You know that."

"Come on, his baby mom's got a house out of him. Bitch push a Lexus coupe, she stay fly, the kids be fresh, going on vacations, and all that. Girl, please . . . You ain't getting shit for being his mistress. Them lil' bags and shit he buy you ain't nothing to him. Nigga live in a mansion in Long Island or some shit. The mistress of a ballin'-ass nigga like Mo, shit, you supposed to be one step under his wife. You ain't been on vacation or nothing. You ever been to his mansion?"

"No. I never asked to go!" Yazmine snapped.

"You shouldn't have to ask, Yazmine. If he feeling you like that, that's where you'd be, not in the hood fighting Nuny and shit every summer. I heard he fuck with that girl that be driving the Tahoe now too; that brown-skin girl with the hazel eyes . . . um, um, Charlotte."

"He don't fuck with her. She got a man."

"Nah. I heard he's sweet on her, for real. She's into

real estate and got a house in Queens, but her mother lives around the way."

Yazmine was hot. She was pissed off and ready to slap the shit out Londa. "Why you hating on me, Londa? No, for real, why the fuck you telling me now about the bitch Charlotte? How long you knew?"

"He got a baby mother that fucks you up on call. What the fuck you worrying about some next bitch for, like he is your man? He's not your man, and drink that mai tai before it gets watered down." Londa chuckled. She looked in her rearview mirror and made an illegal U-turn.

"You need some dick, and you need to worry about who Blake fucking now that he's home."

"Blake is the least of my concerns, baby. He's not my man."

"Yeah? Well, your fucking ass need to stay out of my business with Mo, and stop hatin'."

Londa quietly made her turn before answering Yazmine.

"Hate on you for what, Yaz . . . really?" She laughed.

"I mean, you don't get no dick, you don't have a man. Girly, you need some," Yazmine said, trying to make light of the convo.

But it was too late. Londa was ready to go in. "Dick? What's dick? Come on, Yaz, you and I both know, if I put my pussy on the line like most bitches, I'll have all y'all hoes mad at me, like, 'Why all the dudes want her?' I get mine. 'Cause I don't bring niggas through the hood and talk about my pussy every ten seconds I ain't getting none?"

"So you hiding shit from me?"

"Hiding what? I don't have to announce every dick I suck, Yaz. That's childish. Besides, none of these dudes are my man, so they ain't worth talking about. And they damn sure can't do shit for me that I can't do for myself, so they ain't worth bragging about. And hate on you? Yaz, please . . . I put you on."

That statement made Yazmine hot. Even in the middle of a beef, Mo would throw that in Yazmine's face. Daily, she had to hear the hot boys talking about how fly Londa was, how she got money like a dude, and how they respected her hustle, and all of this bullshit, and now Londa was saying it for herself.

"How you put me on? Bitch, please."

"Yaz, let's be real. You a'ight, but I'm stepping out in Jimmy Choo, Prada, House of Deréon, and you rocking regular shit. Who else was taking you shopping? Shit, you say I ain't getting any. I need to be getting some from you, with all the money I spend on your silly ass. You know deep down your yellow ass is jealous of me. It's okay, though. Just don't ever cross me, yo."

Yazmine was fuming on the side but said nothing. "Londa, I will give you back anything you got for me and be a'ight. You ain't spend that much on me. And if you did it out of love, why you throwin' it back in my face?"

Londa sucked her teeth. "Bitch, who bought you your first Gucci bag? Me, not some nigga you were fucking. Who took you to your first five-star hotel and restaurant? Me, not some nigga. First shopping spree, first vacation, gave you your first grand. Me, not some nigga you was fucking. So let me say it again bitch, *I put you on.* You give me back everything I bought you and you'd be finished, bitch. You think Mo gon' trick on you hard? Doubt it. After three years, you ain't get your own crib out that nigga, and Mo is holding."

Yazmine was pissed at this point. She didn't know who the fuck Londa thought she was, trying to air her out. She had no idea why Londa was going so hard on her, and she was hurt.

"You ain't gotta give me back nothing. That shit is nothing to me. I bought you all of that shit out of love, Yaz, bet that. I can wipe my ass with the money I spent on you, sis. It ain't nothing. But for you to bite the hand that fed you, man, that's some grimy fuckin' shit, yo. Anyway, have you seen your boy Blakey yet?"

Yazmine sat there with her arms folded.

"You heard me, Yaz? You talked to Blakey boy yet?"

Not wanting to show her pain or weakness, Yazmine mustered up all she could to answer Londa without shade. "No, but I spoke to him once or twice. He got things to do, but we gon' get up. So, 'sup with you, Londa? You seem a little uptight. I mean, you got anything you want to tell me?"

"Nope. You? Drink that mai tai, girl." Londa laughed wickedly.

Yazmine sat back. "Londa, we got beef or something?"

"You got something you want to tell me?" Londa said, gunning the engine.

"Other than the fact that I had an abortion two weeks ago by that nigga Mo, and he gave me a thousand dollars to do it, no."

Londa was so disgusted with Yazmine, she didn't know what to do. She kept driving and sipping her drink. Normally Yaz would entertain her, but right now she wasn't in the mood.

Yazmine noticed how quiet Londa was, so she asked her what was wrong again.

"I can't trust you—That's what the fuck is wrong," Londa blurted as she pulled over.

"Me? What I do?" Yazmine snatched her shades off and looked Londa square in the face.

"The fact that you can look me in my eyes right now scares me, Yaz, you know that?"

"Londa, what the fuck are you talking about, girl? Why are you so paranoid?"

"You set me up, bitch, and I want to know why."

"Set you up? What you talking about?" Yazmine leaned back toward the window and folded her arms.

"You knew those girls that ran up in my house a while back, Yaz. And don't lie to me and say you don't."

"What girls? No, I didn't."

"I was too mad to even say shit to you. What the fuck you set me up for? I do everything for you, Yaz. Shit, I kept you fly enough to make a baller like Mo take notice of your bum ass, and this is how you thank me?" Londa screamed.

"Bum ass? Bitch, you ain't all that, and I did not set you up. You fuckin' buggin', Londa. You paranoid. You need to chill the fuck out and stop doing so much dirt, and maybe you won't be feeling like niggas is setting you up."

"Bitch, I saw you by the courtyard with the same bitches that ran up in my house. Explain that shit to me, Yaz."

Yazmine sat there stuck, wondering how Londa could

keep this in. For a split second, she worried what Londa dragged her out here for.

"I don't know them. They been coming around the way to chill with some peoples they know. I just kick it with them because I be out there with Mo."

"You didn't hear about them robbing me?"

"Yeah, I heard a little something, but I didn't want you to get all amped about it and get caught up in some shit, so I didn't say shit."

"Like what? They know where I live, and they could come back at any time to do me dirty, and you ain't tell me? You hanging in the hood with these bitches? You think I'm stupid, Yaz? You think I believe that you didn't set me up? Huh? You fucking bum bitch, get out my fucking truck. I can't stand the sight of you." Londa turned her engine back on.

"Get out? No. You drove me all the way out here, you better take me back to the hood."

"I better do what, Yaz? I said, 'Get the fuck out,' . . . before I drag yo' ass out. You know you can't beat me, Yaz. I'll have Nuny come up here and fuck you up real bad. You know she up in Mo's mansion not too far away."

"It's like that, Londa?" Yazmine asked, holding on the door. She tried to give Londa the sympathy face, but Londa felt nothing.

"The fuck out."

As Yazmine jumped out, Londa pulled off, causing Yazmine to stumble and fall a little bit, kicking up dust in Yazmine's face, not giving a damn how she got home. She got on her phone and started making calls to find out where Blake was. Unbeknownst to Londa, Blake

---

knew just what a snake Yazmine was. Yet, naïve Londa called Blake. She had to tell him not to trust Yazmine.

Mad and feeling vindictive, Yazmine cried into the phone as she told Mo everything that went down, asking, could he come get her, and making it seem as if Londa was on some fly shit. Either way, Mo told her he was caught up and couldn't come get her.

She called Blake next. She had a hard time finding him for a while, until she called his sister's house in Brownsville and caught up with him.

"Yo, Blake, some girl on the phone for you sounding all frantic and whatnot," Chello yelled out.

Blake jogged to the phone and snatched it playfully from his big sister. "Yo."

"Blake, this is Yazmine. That bitch Londa is out of control. She gotta get dealt with."

"Why? What happened?"

"She drove me out to Long Island and left me out here. She is on to me setting her up and all that, but she doesn't know you're involved. So she gotta get dealt with. That bitch really think she is a mafioso or some shit, dragging me all the way out here to leave me. Is she crazy?"

"Calm down, yo. How far out are you?"

"Past the Tanger Outlet!" Yazmine screamed into the phone.

"Me and Peedi gon' come get you. He got the lead foot. We'll see you in about an hour and change. Sit tight."

"Okay," she mumbled.

Blake hung up the phone laughing. "Yo, Londa is wild."

"What happened?"

"She found out some shit about Yaz and left her out in Long Island," he said, not telling Peedi that he'd paid Yazmine to set up Londa.

"Word? What she do? Steal?"

"She ain't say," Blake said, thinking about Londa.

His sister's phone rang again. "Hello."

"Hey, you. You come home and forgot about me?" Londa snapped.

"Nah. Wha's up, partner? Where you at?"

"On my way back to the hood. I had to take care of something. Can I come scoop you up?" she asked non-chalantly.

Blake laughed, knowing what it was Londa just did. He admired her style. She knew how to keep her cool under pressure. That was why he rocked with her in the first place. "Um, me and Peedi about to make a run someplace, but as soon as I get back, we gon' link up. Gimme your cell number."

Londa gave him the number to her dummy cell.

"Hit me up, no matter how late. I need to talk to you about something really, really important, Blake, okay?"

"A'ight."

"Don't *a'ight* me, Blake. Tonight get at me."

"Okay, boss lady. I heard you." He hung up.

When Londa reached the hood, figuring Yazmine wasn't around yet, she called up Mo, who met her on the ave. She rolled down the window as she rolled up on him. "Get in," she said. She pulled off as he barely hopped in. She rolled the windows up and drove a block or two before she started to speak.

"What's up? You creeping through the hood like you trying to catch a one eighty-seven." He laughed.

Londa wasn't in a joking mood. "Mo, I wanna know something. Those girls that come around the way with Yazmine, where they come from?"

"Those dirty girls? Them little young chicks?"

"Yeah."

"I don't know. She said some shit about one of them is her cousin, and the rest was her peoples. Why?"

"So she brought them around, huh?"

"Yeah? Why? What happened?"

"A while back some girls ran up in my house, robbed me, talking about I'm fuckin' they man and all this fugazy shit. I see her with these same bitches weeks later. I just left that bitch in Long Island for trying to play me. She set me up to get robbed a few months back. Bitches ran up in my house and fucked me up, robbed me, but they ain't find nothing."

Mo laughed. "Oh, she called me talking about you on some fly shit and you left her way out in Long Island somewhere." Mo chuckled. "Oh shit. But Yaz doin' it like that?"

"Yeah. And I saw her with the girls, but had to fall back and calm down before I, you know, pull a Rèmy Ma on the bitch and bust a cap. Remember that day you were telling me to watch out for Blake?"

"Yeah."

"It was that day when she was with those girls I saw her."

"Oh, those are the bitches that jumped you? Yaz be with them a lot."

"Can you believe that?"

"Nah. Damn! I was hearing some shit about the nigga Blake setting you up with some chicks, but I was trying to get all the details before I put you on. I had asked her about it, and she brushed it off like, 'Nah, that nigga Blake wouldn't do that. Londa need to slow down. She creatin' enemies and all this shit.' But I know you cool and the gang, so I just brushed her dumb ass off. But don't be surprised if Blake got something to do with it, 'cause the nigga is fucked-up in the game."

"How he fucked-up, and me and him was getting money before he got locked up?" Londa leaned her head on the steering wheel.

"He came to me, borrowing some money, but I ain't give that nigga shit. I don't know what he did with his money."

Londa's head shot up. "He did?"

"Yes. So he has no money, so watch that nigga. He grimy."

Londa reclined her seat back and began rubbing her head out of stress. "Money is the root, boy. Mo' money, mo' problems." She mumbled and laughed. "What am I supposed to do now, Mo? I'm supposed to be meeting Blake later on tonight."

"Just see how he moving. If I hear anything I'll put you on, but watch him. I know he got something to do with it. Matter of fact, when you meet up with him, let me know. I'll tail you."

"Thanks, Mo. I'm so sick."

Mo rubbed Londa's back. "You'll be okay. Get the

fuck outta dodge. I know you got shit set up out of New York." He smiled.

"If I tell you, I gotta kill you." Londa laughed.

"You ain't gotta tell me nothing. You're a smart woman. I admire how you move. Just get away while you can because Yazmine might do some dumb shit out of hurt and anger. And, Blake . . . you know how broke niggas don't want no money . . ."

"They just wanna kill ya," they said in unison.

When Londa let Mo out, she hightailed it to Bushwick to her mother's house to lay low till she heard from Blake, promising to call Mo when she was ready to meet up with him.

Londa was so happy to see her mother. It seemed as if she hadn't seen her in so long, but it was only two weeks. As tight as they were, two weeks was too long.

Entering with her key, Londa walked in and found her mother in her recliner watching *Murder, She Wrote* re-runs. She hugged her from over the back of the chair. "Hey, baby," Londa said, hugging her mother warmly.

Londa's mother was the shit to her. She was so pretty, short and curvy, aging gracefully, her hair in a honey blonde bob. And she kept to herself, a quiet woman with class that could curse you out real bad.

"My baby, what's up? Where you been?" Claudia turned around and hugged her only child.

Londa sat in front of her mother and held her hand. "Mommy, I'm probably going to blow the scene soon, you know, relocate to Atlanta, for good."

"Why?" She sat up.

"You know, I'm just tired." Londa stared into her mother's eyes. She had to tell her something to keep her on her toes. She couldn't just leave her mother up here alone.

⌐ "Tired of what? You living life, girl. You don't seem stressed. What you tired of? Spending money? Running around with these wild cowboys?"

"Mommy, Yazmine set me up to get robbed a while back. I didn't tell you, but they ran up in my house, beat me up. I just found out. I found out that your boy that you love so much, Blake, had something to do with it too."

"What? Are you okay? You can't hide things like this from me, Londa. Are you crazy?"

"Yes, Mommy, I know, but I didn't want you to worry. Blake is home now. I dumped Yaz off in west bubble-fuck someplace, so I know they both are going to try to get at me. And I don't know what they got planned for me. I just left the bitch in Long Island to find her way back home, so I know now it's gonna be on. She feels like she got something to prove now." Londa stood up and stretched.

"I'm tired and I'm done in the streets getting fast money, Mommy. I just want to lay low and live my life now. I'm good. I can go to school, get a job, and chill."

"What fast money? I thought you were having some man take care of you? You know what, I don't even want to know. Well, baby, you know if you go to Atlanta, you're not leaving me up here to deal with your bull-shit."

"I know that, Mommy. Of course. So I tell you what;

pack your shit and go down there. You got the keys. Go down there and wait for me. I'll be there, a'ight?"

"I'll leave a day before you do and *no sooner* than that."

"I love you, Mommy." Londa hugged her mother tight. Her mother in turn tried not to worry.

Peedi pulled over when he saw Yazmine sitting on a bench, her arms folded tight. He shouted her name out so she could walk over to the car.

She got in and slammed the door.

" 'Sup, Yaz?" Peedi said.

"Hey. Blake, we need to talk."

"Not right now. I got a headache. You hungry?"

"Yeah, I'm fuckin' hungry. What you think?"

"Look, don't get mad 'cause you fucking got left out in the fucking woods for being a fucking asshole."

"Some dude left you out here, or some shit?" Peedi laughed.

Blake had already told her not to say shit in front of Peedi.

"I'm not in the mood for jokes right now, a'ight?" Yazmine said, her eyes tearing and her voice cracking.

Saying nothing, Peedi kept driving until they got back to the hood. When they pulled up on Marcus Garvey, Yazmine sat up.

"We need to talk, Blake. Where you going?" she asked, noticing she was getting dropped off.

Blake got out of the car and opened the door for her, and she got out and slammed the door.

"That bitch is gonna get hers, Blakey. Watch."

"First of all, stop calling me Blakey. Who told you that shit sound cute? Second of all, shut up. You ain't no gangsta. Shut up and let me handle it, and don't go running your mouth and doing nothing stupid. Don't make a move till I tell you." He asked coldly, "You got some dough from that nigga Mo yet?"

"Nah. He said he got me in a few days, though. He's going to give me five hundred dollars."

"What good is your pussy that you fucking this rich nigga and you only getting five hundred dollars? You don't have access to none of his funds or nothing?" Blake said, mad as hell that Mo didn't give him the money he'd promised. He put Mo on his hit list. "If Londa was fuckin with Mo? She would have that nigga security code and the whole shit."

Yazmine was thrown with the comparison to Londa. "Fuck you *and* Londa. I'll tell her you set her up, nigga, then what?"

"Then your ass will be a body—How's that? Get ya shit together, Yaz. I'll holla at you later after I talk to ol' girl. Go in the house and cool off. And practice your head skills or suttin'. Get paid for all this fuckin' you doin' to that nigga Mo."

Peedi pulled off before Yazmine could respond.

She held in her tears and walked to her building.

Londa sat in her car watching Blake walk toward her, thanking God she had tints in her car. She was pissed at him and Yazmine. Mo was two cars behind her and across the street in a Lincoln Town Car with two of his boys. She rolled the windows down all cool like, with her seat back.

"This you?" Blake asked, wide-eyed.

"Yeah." She smirked.

" 'Sup? Let me push this," he said eagerly.

Silently, Londa moved over and let him in.

"Damn! How much this set you back? It's paid off?"

"Nah," she lied, "I got a note."

"You okay, Londa?"

"Yeah, my stomach just hurt, is all. 'Sup with you?" She eyed him as he messed with all of the gadgets, like a kid.

"I'm cool. I'm good. Where ya sidekick at?"

"Who? Yaz?" Londa sucked her teeth, trying her best not to let her emotions show.

But it was hard. Yaz had been her only friend for years, since the fourth grade. She had no idea what would make Yazmine betray her after all she'd done for her. And for Blake to be jealous of her, as a man, was downright insane. All of this time they had been scheming on her, when she thought everything was everything. She wondered what else had been done behind her back.

"I don't know where she's at now. Knowing Yaz, she could be anywhere."

Blake smiled wide. "She called me, you know. Why you left her in the trenches like that?" He turned the radio on, a sly look on his face.

Londa paused and took a deep breath. "What kind of games you playing, huh? You acting like you don't know what the fuck is going on, and grilling me? Blake, me and you go too far back for you to give me reasons not to trust you," Londa shouted.

"She said you threw her out the truck because you heard some shit. She didn't tell me why. She just said she was hurt that you believed some shit you heard about her. Then she asked, could I come and get her."

"Well, yeah, it was confirmed to me that she did have something to do with it, so fuck that bitch, real talk. And why you taking up for her anyway? The sex is that good?"

"Ain't nobody hittin' Yaz. Man, you paranoid."

Londa turned to face Blake. "Y'all reading from the same fucking book or something? She said the same shit to me before I tossed her ass out my truck. I gotta toss you too? You think I need this shit, Blake? You think I need to worry about my own friends turning on me?"

"Londa, you need to calm down, yo. Listen, fuck Yaz right now. I got a job for us. Big things," he said, lowering his voice and closing the sun roof.

"Blake, I don't wanna hear 'bout no money or no job right now. I'm a little on edge, and I need time to sit back and re-evaluate some things, Blake, for real. I just found out my best friend of fourteen years set me up to get robbed. I fucking took care of Yaz like a child, like she was my daughter, and I did it happily, you hear me? Happily! And this is the thanks I get? I mean, I'm out there getting money. Why the fuck niggas can't go get money? Why they think it's easier to take mine, huh? I spread love, I don't shit on anybody. I spread love, Blake, don't I?"

"Yeah, you do, but that's the karma, baby. You take niggas' money, and they try to take yours. You know the rules of the game. Because you ain't never hurt nobody physically in this, you hurtin' niggas' pockets every time, Londa. You take niggas' life savings and shit. As far as

Yaz is concerned, I mean, just cut her off then, Londa. What girls she got to rob you anyway?"

"I don't know who they are. I never saw them a day in my life and wouldn't recognize none of them if I saw them again. And that's the scary part."

Blake knew Londa was lying because Yazmine told him everything that went down. He had to watch Londa. She was no idiot, not by a long shot.

"That's not good, you won't recognize them. Were you drunk when they ran up on you?"

"No, it was early in the day." Londa stared at Blake for a while. "You wouldn't set me up, would you?" she asked, playing dumb to get a reaction.

"Me? Set you up? What for? And we getting it together? Come on now, Londa."

"I don't know, Blake. I mean, I just feel a way. Seems like I can't trust nobody, and I don't ever want to feel that way about you. Yaz is my sister, but she is more of a bill than she is any help. You, me, we get money together. That's what we do, and I trust you, Blake." She played it low-key.

"You never have to worry about not trusting me. I'm the last person you have to worry about. So, yo, you down for this last run or what?"

"How much we looking at?" Londa asked, to see if it was worth it.

"I hear between the three of us we can get forty each."

"He is holding like that in his house?" Londa sat up.

"Yeah, man."

"How you know?"

"I got connects everywhere, baby. This is easy fast

money. It can pop off any day now. So get that bitch Yazmine out of your head for a minute, and let's get this money. You can get back to that silly bitch later."

He sounded so sincere, so on her side, but Londa knew damn well Blake was a snake. She just never thought he'd put her in harm's way. But before she bounced out to go to Atlanta, she had a trick for his ass.

Blake called Londa early one Sunday morning excited. "Londa, get up. It's on."

"What's on?" Londa said half-'sleep, her head under the covers.

"You, baby, you. Get up. It's show time," he whispered sinisterly.

Londa sat up and looked at her clock. She sucked her teeth and yawned. "Yeah, but, Blake, it's seven-thirty in the morning, boy."

"Early bird catches that paper. I'll be to you in about, let's say an hour. Bye."

Londa dragged herself to the shower and stood in her closet with her towel on, wondering what to wear. After staring in her closet for about twenty minutes, she pulled out a pair of blue Levi's pants, blue-and-grey Air Max, and a baby blue Gap T-shirt. She sprayed her body in "Dream" by Victoria's Secret, put her hair up in a very tight bun, and decided not to wear earrings.

She waited on a bench about ten minutes away from her house in a park. She wanted to look like an average around-the-way girl and not some hood celebrity.

About fifteen minutes later, like clockwork, Blake, lead-foot Peedi, and a female pulled up. Blake was in the back seat, dressed in a dark denim Sean John suit. He was sipping a Heineken.

"It's nine in the morning. Are you serious?" Londa asked of the beer, rolling her eyes.

"Look, here's the deal—This is Felicia. Felicia, this here is Yolanda."

"Hey," Londa said to Felicia.

"Hi," Felicia said back nastily.

Londa chose to ignore her and wondered why they brought her along. Was this Felicia character supposed to set it on her or something? Her paranoia had her looking at everybody sideways. Felicia looked like one of those girls from the hood that would do anything for niggas. Peedi and Blake both probably hit that. She looked to be about 15 or 16, but her face was worn like she been around a while. She had greasy bangs, greasy lips, and big breasts. She chewed her gum and smiled at Londa naively, but she had a grimy look to her. Londa didn't know who she was and didn't give a fuck.

As soon as Londa sat in the car, Blake began barking out the blueprint. This girl was friends with Val's girl, the guy they were about to stick. Felicia's brother and Val were partners. Through her, because of her brother, Blake knew what Val had in his house. It was sad. You couldn't trust anybody.

"Val's girl is a real live wire, so she isn't gonna back down. You stand there and you argue with the bitch for a minute, Londa. Make something up about her messing with your man or something. I want you to put the drop on Ingrid. Here"—He handed Londa her favorite toy, a .44 long—"I want you to get the cash, run through the house, and just ransack shit. I'm gonna wait out-side."

Londa's mind was still stuck on the words he used when he said for her to make something up about her messing with her man. She thought back to those girls that jumped her. The same thing he ordered her to do is what those girls did to her.

"Londa, get your head out the clouds. You ready?" he said, sipping the last of his beer and setting the bottle down on the floor of the hooptie.

Felicia took Londa's hesitation as Londa being scared or unsure. She had no idea what Londa was thinking.

"You'll be safe. I owe that bitch one," Felicia said, show-ing Londa her burner. "She get the best of you, I'm right there. I got your back." Felicia winked and continued looking straight. "I know where the stash is."

Londa looked back at Blake, remembering the stash that she had in the house. She couldn't bear to think that he sent those girls to her house, but the truth was in her face. The enemy had his hand on her lap. All of the people in this car were her enemies. This is why Yazmine and Blake were keeping in touch. They were in it together.

"I told you I got you, right? I told you that you could trust me. I would never ever do no grimy shit to you," Blake said to Londa.

Londa searched for trust in his eyes and saw none.

All of a sudden a feeling of claustrophobia came over her as she sat in the car. It seemed as if she was going to die at this moment. Like Felicia, Peedi, and Blake were going to all draw guns and tie her up and take her to her house and make her give them all the money she'd risked her pussy and life for. She thought about the rich white college boys, the drug dealers out of town, the many dudes that she went out on her own, seduced, "got to know," and got money from, by herself. These snake bastards around her had no idea how much she risked her life just to live a good life, and right now she felt as if at any moment they were going to take it all from her. She felt it in her gut.

"Londa, you a'ight? You hear me? Get the molasses out yo' ass for a minute and focus. This is how niggas get kilt, thinking of irrelevant shit when they suppose to be on the case," Blake barked. "Stop worrying. I got you."

"Nah," Londa said out loud. *I got me.*

Blake pulled Londa close to him in the back seat and rubbed her shoulders. "You'll be fine," was all he managed to say.

It's all he could say. Londa knew at this moment that he had everything to do with those girls trying to rob her, and there was no doubt in her mind as she stared at Felicia, who looked just as grimy as the girls that came to her house.

Felicia got out of the car and headed over to her "friend's" house.

Londa walked over to Ingrid's house behind her, ready to take all for self. She knocked on Ingrid's door about four times before she appeared at the door laughing. She and Felicia were having jokes about something. The thick ghetto chick stood in front of Londa, hair still in doobie pins, dressed in pajama pants and a camisole, her hands on her hips. Londa stood with her hands behind her back, holding her weapon. She wasn't sure if

Felicia was setting her up, and she wasn't taking any chances. She held her stare.

"Yes," Ingrid said in all her stink-girl attitude.

"You Ingrid?" Londa asked her softly, so that Ingrid could sleep on her.

"Yeah," she said, and shifted her weight to the other side, annoyed.

"You know a Jeff?"

"No, I don't know no Jeff, and I'm sick of y'all bitches stepping to me behind these niggas. Keep ya fucking men in check and you won't have to . . ."

Londa totally didn't argue with this chick as Blake suggested. She was thinking about Yazmine, about Blake, about whoever else was thinking of doing her harm because she was getting money.

This girl had a big mouth, and Londa wanted her to shut the hell up. And she was mad that Blake set her up, so she pulled out her piece and grabbed her wickedly by the throat. Londa put the gun in her mouth and backed her into the apartment. She pushed her down on the sofa and backed up, aiming the gun at her and Felicia.

Felicia was playing her part, acting scared and all, but deep inside, Londa knew that Felicia saw the wild look in her eyes and had no idea what Londa was going to do.

"I'm-a ask you again—You fucking Jeff?" Londa bit her bottom lip.

Ingrid's attitude changed. "I don't know a Jeff." She was humble now. She sat there holding up both her hands.

"Put your hands down, stupid. Who here?" Londa asked, gritting her teeth, looking back quickly.

"Nobody. Just me and her," she said, motioning toward Felicia.

Londa looked around, contemplating her next move. "Get up and go in the room," she told Ingrid. She looked at Felicia, thought about Blake. She decided he wasn't getting shit and that she was going all out. "You want me and you to take this?" she asked Felicia.

"What?" Felicia asked, dumbfounded.

"Fuck this shit! Do you want me and you, we take this cash and split it? We go out in a blaze with Blake and Peedi," Londa asked Felicia, purposely incriminating them.

Felicia greedily shook her head yes, and Ingrid looked at her in disbelief.

Londa licked her lips and gripped her pistol tight when she heard a noise. "What is that?" she whispered.

"My man is here, but he's 'sleep."

"Bitch, you tried to pull a fast one?" Londa lowered her gun quickly and put it behind her back, leaning against the dresser as Val made his way into the room.

Val knew something was wrong when he walked in the room. The air was too still, and his girl looked bothered. When he looked at Londa through the mirror he could see that she had a burner on her. At first he was in shock. Then he stopped to think about who sent her and why she was there by herself. That only meant that she had niggas outside waiting. He went into his room, paged his mans, and loaded his shit, peeking through the window, trying to spot anything suspicious. He didn't want to kill shorty. He knew someone put her up to this, and he just wanted to find out who.

"Ingrid, make a nigga some breakfast before I hit the streets, a'ight."

Ingrid shook her head yes, instead of telling him to kiss her ass and make it himself.

He definitely knew something was wrong then.

Londa had to think fast. Val was up now, so it was hard for her to do anything. But at this point, it was do or die. She had to get out of this house. And if she left without the money, she risked Blake killing her, so she might as well stay and get the money because Val was going to kill her for sure.

Felicia got up, drawing her weapon. "Yo, fuck that! Where the stash at?"

"What stash?" Ingrid belted out. "Lecia, you are trippin'. What the fuck are you doing? We family."

Ingrid looked at Felicia. Felicia looked at Londa.

Londa slapped Ingrid with the gun. "Let's go before ya man comes back out for his breakfast," she whispered.

Ingrid reluctantly got up and lifted her mattress, keeping a wicked eye on Felicia.

Londa walked to the corner of her room and snatched up the big Conway bag in the corner. She then tossed it to Felicia, who began throwing money in the bags. Londa kept her cool, looking at all of the cash that covered damn near the entire length and width of the queen-size mattress.

After all of the money was in the bag, she made Ingrid walk to the front door.

"You gon' walk me outside now," Londa told her.

"Hurry up. If your man starts blasting, you'll be my vest, that's all."

She did as she was told, as Felicia kept the gun to her waist.

Londa got to the front door safely and saw the hoop-tie across the street when Val appeared.

Calmly, Val came walking out of his room, dressed now in sweats and a T-shirt, with his hat on and what seemed to be a vest underneath his shirt. He was on to them. "Y'all leaving already?" he asked.

Londa looked at Felicia.

"We'll be back," Felicia said, her piece in Ingrid's back.

Londa continued to walk toward the car, gun on her side, praying she didn't get shot in the back. She was scared as hell, but couldn't show it. She figured at this moment that Felicia had no love for these people that she was running with. Someone must have done her wrong. When she was a few feet from the car, Blake got out and tried to grab the money, but Londa held it tight. "I got this," she barked. "Just get in the car."

Londa had pulled it off. Blake couldn't believe it. Londa was walking toward him now with a serious look on her face. He could tell she was ready to get the fuck outta there. He didn't want to do it to Londa, but she was getting deaded on this paper. She was eating good enough when he was gone, but she wasn't letting go of the bag. Blake didn't want to argue with her right now about the money. When they got to a safe place, he'd put the drop on her and dead her, and that would be the end of that.

"Let's go now," Londa demanded, thinking she was the boss of shit.

She was pissing Blake off. Before she got in the car, Blake saw Val appear in the doorway, gun aimed. He grabbed Londa by her collar and pulled her down to the ground. Her head hit the bumper as shots were fired.

Val came running out of the house shooting.

Londa started screaming, and Ingrid stood in her doorway yelling.

Felicia ran toward Blake and Londa.

Blake wondered what the hell Felicia was doing with her gun in the air. She was blowing up the spot.

"Yo, let's fucking go!" Peedi yelled. "Get in the car!"

But Londa knew she had to hit Val once before they tried to get away. She had crawled to the driver's side, still holding the bag tight.

It looked like Val was trying to hit her. He ran out of the house and took cover behind a tree.

Felicia ran up to Londa and yelled for her to get in the car. Londa did what she had to, aiming a gun in the driver's side window, shooting Peedi in the arm and in the leg.

"What the fuck you do that for? What the fuck did you do that for, Londa?" Blake yelled.

Londa looked back and saw that Felicia had the drop on Blake.

"Y'all bitches is crazy or suttin'?" Blake asked nervously. He reached in his waistband quickly to draw his weapon. He drew it and didn't know who to aim at, Felicia or Val. Felicia was closer, so he grabbed her by the shirt and put the gun to her head. He pulled the trigger, but the gun jammed. *Fuck!* He pushed Felicia and took cover behind the car.

Val was walking up to the car now, shooting like a madman.

This shit was crazy. Londa didn't want to die. She'd promised herself that this was the last run she'd go on, if God spared her life. Her head was killing her, and she had blood leaking from somewhere. This nigga Val was stopping at nothing. She heard cars screeching and lots of commotion. She pulled Peedi out of the driver's side and yelled for Felicia to hop in. She peeked up and saw Val motioning to his goons with his gun what was going on.

Blake started taking flight down the block, with shots chasing him.

Instantly, Londa did what she had to do. Through her window, she let off two shots. One hit Val in the neck and he instantly stumbled back and fell out against a parked car. The other hit his man that was running up on her in the stomach, and he dropped to his knees. She prayed to God that none of them died.

"Londa, drive this car, girl!" Felicia screamed. "Let's go!"

Londa pulled off, leaving Peedi on the ground and Blake running toward his destiny.

The ride home was quiet and tense. Londa could barely drive, because she didn't trust Felicia at all. They were both armed and on the fritz. Londa had the money tightly between her legs, driving like a bat out of hell.

She pulled over about an hour later, cleaned her gun

with a T-shirt, and tossed it in the sewer. Felicia did the same, as they stood outside the car, both of them nervous as hell and sizing one another up.

"What we gon' do now?" Felicia asked calmly as Londa pulled over.

"Yo, why did you turn on your girl like that? Don't you have to go back and face the music with your brother too?"

"I'm splitting my share with him. He knows what time it is, but he's out of town right now. Fuck Ingrid. I never cared for her too much."

"How do you know Blake?"

"He's from around my way. Me and his sister is cool. Look, we can talk later. Right now, we need to be doing something about this money, you know, like splittin' it."

"Count this money then." Londa opened the bag.

They counted the money separately and came up with $15,000 total.

"This nigga Blake made me risk my life for four thousand punk-ass dollars!" Londa yelled. "I can't believe this nigga. Son of a fucking bitch. Aye, you ever heard Blake talk about sending some girls to some chick house to rob her?" she asked nonchalantly.

"Yeah." She shrugged. "Blake is always doing something grimy, especially to chicks. I heard about him turning your home girl against you. That was you, right?"

"Me what?"

"Something about him getting some girls from around my way to run up in your crib and rob you and he paid your home girl a few thousand to get it done. He tried to get me to run up in your house too. It was you, right? Had to be. He kept referring to you as his partner. Anyway, I told him no that I thought it was foul. Honestly. Just 'cause he was fucked-up in the game, he wanna turn on you? Nah. But your home girl, she needs her ass kicked. He paid her to tell my peoples where you lived. Hey, you think Peedi is dead?"

Londa still didn't trust Felicia, with all of the information she was giving. She realized that she was out for self, black girl lost, money-hungry, and had no loyalty to nobody. Londa thought about where Felicia thought $7,000 was going to take her, especially since she had to split it with her brother.

She shrugged and thought about the money she had. This extra $8,000 was a drop in the bucket compared to the money her mother took to Atlanta with her on her drive down, plus the thousands she had out of town. She had more than enough money to get the fuck outta dodge. There wasn't anything in her apartment worth going back for. She knew Blake would be looking for her, if he was alive by the end of the night. She had made sure her mother was good, as she and Nuny drove down to Atlanta together with the kids, sending all of Londa's personal and valuable things down there with them. Mo took her truck and promised he'd get it down to Londa in due time.

She had a six A.M. flight tomorrow to Atlanta and had to meet Mo in the city so he could pick her up and lay low in his mansion until it was time to bail out. Londa was on pins and needles, wondering if she had a body on her hands, possibly two. She couldn't stand the thought of being in New York another day.

"I think this is where we part," Londa announced quickly, ready to bounce.

"Yeah, I guess," Felicia said, eyeing her.

Londa realized that they were in the Bronx someplace, damn near Yonkers.

"You be good and be safe," Londa said, rolling the Conway bag tight.

Felicia grabbed a paper bag out of the street and put her money in it.

"I'm-a take the hooptie as close to home as possible, then catch the Greyhound or something out of town to go meet my brother. I have nowhere to go, but I can stay in a hotel for a few days until I figure it out. Where you going? I mean, Blake said you're a mean stick-up girl. You think me and you can, you know . . ."

I know this nutcase didn't think she and I would go into business together. I'm done. I'm going to pray to God, live right, do right from this point on. I'm going to get connected with Mo's real estate people, buy a town house, and rent it out. I have no time for this lifestyle any longer, Londa thought to herself. "I tell you what"—Londa dug in her pockets for her house keys. She gave Felicia her address—"This is my apartment. Go there and lay low. Let me go put my money up. Give me your cell number. I'm-a call you when I get someplace safe, and you and I can stay together till we figure out our next move."

Naively Felicia obliged as they switched numbers. Then Londa sent her to the apartment, where she knew Blake would come blazing, ready to kill, as she made her way to Atlanta, tossing her cell phone in a sewer.

She watched Felicia foolishly drive back to the hood in the hooptie with Peedi's blood on the door. She sat in a diner and ate something and took the card for a taxi service off the pay phone.

A car came and picked her up, and nervously she sat inside and gave him Mo's address in Long Island.

"That's going to be at least a hundred dollars or more, miss," he said as he started the meter.

"It's all right. Just go." Londa closed her eyes and sank down in the seat.

Blake managed to get away for now. He made his way to the hood and banged on Yazmine's door crazy.

Yazmine opened the door, covering her mouth at the sight of Blake, who looked dirty, scared, and crazy. "What happened?" she said, letting him in.

He said nothing at first, pacing the floor for a while.

"Come in my room. My mother is here," Yazmine told him.

"That bitch Londa, she's a dead woman walking. Where is she? She came here?" he yelled, his eyes wide and deadly-looking.

"What happened?"

"Never mind that shit," he yelled. "Where is she? She home? I'm-a kill that bitch, her and Felicia, mark my words."

"Blake, you can't go around killing people. We got beef, but I don't want to see her dead."

"You wanna take this fucking bullet for her, Yaz? Where is she?"

Scared for her life, Yazmine stood there trembling like a leaf in the fall. "She didn't call me, Blake. You forgot we aren't talking? I haven't spoken to her in I don't know how long."

"You better tell me if that bitch calls you. Matter of fact, give me your cell phone."

"For what? She don't call me."

Ignoring Yazmine, he snatched up Yazmine's cell phone and ran out of the house like a madman.

Yazmine immediately jumped on the phone and tried to call Londa, but her number was disconnected. She called Londa's mother, but her phone was off as well. She didn't know what to do, so she called Mo, who answered quickly, surprisingly.

Londa was crying on Mo's shoulder. He'd assured her that he'd get her to the airport safely. His girl Nuny was also on the job, helping Londa's mother, Claudine, make her exit. As he sat on the sofa holding a shaken Londa, his cell phone rang. It was Yazmine. "It's ya girl," he said to her.

"Pick it up. She might know something." Londa sat up, wiping her face.

Hesitantly, Mo picked up the phone, knowing that he hadn't spoken to Yazmine in a few days and that she might have some shit to pop.

" 'Sup, Yazmine? What do you want?"

Londa sat up in the chaise. She watched Mo's expressions as Yazmine told him that Blake was on his way to Londa's house, and if he was in the hood, to try to find Londa to warn her, and how Blake was pissed that Mo didn't give him the ten thousand he promised and was talking shit about setting him up through her.

"How long you knew all of this, Yazmine?" Mo asked angrily.

"He just told me just now," she lied, realizing she might incriminate herself.

"He came in here all angry about niggas taking money

from him and him taking dough from anybody that owe him money or getting money more than him. He's on his way to look for Londa now."

"He just left you?" Mo asked.

"Yes, Mo. Please don't let anything happen to my girl, okay. I'm so sorry for even turning on her for that crab-ass nigga. Please find her and keep her safe. And tell her to call me and I love her."

"A'ight, calm down. I'm not gonna let nothing happen to the lil' homie. I haven't seen her, but let me ride around the streets or something, stake out her crib and see what I can find. I'll get back to you. And you need to stay in the house and away from Blake."

"I am. I'm about to pack up my things and go stay with my cousins out in Queens. Blake is acting shifty, and I don't know what he's up to. He took my cell phone and everything, in case Londa calls me."

"Word? He trippin' like that? Okay, I'm not around, but I'll tell the soldiers to look out for her. Call me if you hear anything, and I'll do the same."

"Okay, thanks," Yazmine said and hung up.

Mo walked away, dialing numbers in his cell phone. He was out of earshot, so Londa didn't know what was going on. But she knew it was nothing nice.

He came back out and checked the clock. "Get some rest. Everyt'ing cool," he said in a fake Jamaican accent.

"You are taking me to the airport tomorrow, right?"

"Of course, Londa. Just lay low, stay off the phones, and only answer Nuny's calls. You got it?"

"Yeah."

"You a'ight. Get some rest. You got a new life to start tomorrow." He smiled and began channel surfing.

*   *   *

Blake went back to Brownsville to get ammunition. He also wanted word on Peedi.

When he got to his sister's house, he found her crying in her bedroom. He feared the worst as he walked in slowly. "What, Chello? What happened?"

She looked up at him with a bruised-up, bloody face. "What did you do?" she yelled. "You just got home? What the fuck did you get me into?"

"What happened to you?" Blake asked slowly.

"Some niggas came here looking for you. They killed Peedi, they beat me up, and tore the apartment up looking for money." She got up slowly.

Blake noticed his sister's clothes were torn.

"I gotta get you to a hospital. Fuck!"

"No, you stay the fuck away from me! They killed Peedi, Blake! Oh my God!" she cried as someone knocked at the door.

Blake was feeling sick. He thought Londa had shot him dead, but apparently not. "How you know Peedi dead?" he asked, his voice cracking.

"They came in here talking about how they finished the job, how the nigga Peedi was trying to crawl away. What happened? Crawl away from where? They thought I knew something, and I don't know shit. All I know is, what if my son was here? Huh? What if my son would have seen them do this to me?"

"Let me take you to the hospital. Come on, Chello."

"No, Blake. I can't be around you. Shanda is coming to take me. She should be here any minute."

"I'm so sorry, Chello."

"You need to get out of here before they come back. They're looking for you, whoever they are. I don't know what you're into, but they asked me about Felicia. And they kept asking me who the bitch was with Felicia. You had Felicia with you doing shit? Are you nuts? She's a baby, Blake, a fucking baby!"

"What they say about them?"

"They kept grilling me, asking me, did I know anything and all this shit. Get the door."

"Nah, I'm not getting the door. Go get it, and let me know who it is," he said, jogging into his room to get his burner.

Shanda, Chello's best friend, came in with her brother and his friend. "Oh my God!" Shanda said. "Chello, we gotta get you to the hospital. What the hell happened to her, Blake?"

"I just came in and found her. Take her to the hospital. I gotta go find out what happened," he said and ran out the front door.

Felicia looked around the apartment and fell back on the pretty king-size canopy bed. *Damn! This bitch is living!* She fantasized about going on sticks with Londa and living the life that she lived. Felicia noticed the apartment was rid of any clothes, jewelry, money, televisions, or furniture. Just the king-size bed, a stereo, and some food in the fridge. *This must be her down-low spot.* She lay down and counted her money over and over. She envisioned herself in the mall, shopping crazy, getting her gear up, so she could finally go to school comfortably without being ridiculed. She even thought about Len, a guy she had her eye on. *He would definitely take notice when I go to school in my fly shit.* She didn't even think about the drama she left behind.

With two guns up, Blake jumped out of the taxi, angry as hell, mad ready to kill the woman he shared his secrets with, a woman he used run with, all over money. "That fuckin' greedy bitch," he snarled, running up the stairs two at a time.

Around this time John-John, Smoke, and Percy were pulling up in front of Londa's building.

"What floor she stay on again?" Percy asked.

"Four," John-John said, walking quickly to the quiet building, trying not to be noticed.

The three crooks glided up the steps with ease, looking for whoever was looking for Londa.

With his heart beating fast, Blake reasoned that if he found Londa in the house, he'd fuck her up real bad and take whatever she had in the house. He didn't want to kill her, but he knew she had some heart and would do it to him. So with his thoughts confused, he said a quick prayer and knocked on the door with the butt of his gun.

Felicia jumped up. She smiled. "That must be Londa." She jogged to the door, leaving the money sprawled out on the bed. "Who?" she sang. When she didn't hear an answer, she opened the door anyway, and met the barrel of a gun.

"Where the fuck is Londa?" Blake snarled, backing her into the house.

Felicia put her hands up. "She ain't here."

"How you gon' turn on me, Felicia, when you and me was supposed to get that bitch and leave her for dead out there? What the fuck happened?"

"I don't know, Blake. I just got caught up. I'm sorry. Please don't kill me. I was just trying to get money."

Blake couldn't blame her. He wasn't even mad at her, really. She was an impressionable little girl that would do anything for a buck. He mushed her hard. "Dumb ass, follow rules next time. Where that bitch said she was going? She coming here?"

"Yeah, she said she was dropping her money off and to wait for her. She gave me her keys."

Blake thought about it for a while. "Where the cash at?"

Felicia pointed to the room. "On the bed."

Blake didn't even count the money. He knew it wasn't a lot. "What's that? Like four, five G's?"

"No. Seven."

"How much Londa took?"

"I don't know, but we split it evenly."

"Yo, put it in a bag. Londa ain't coming here. She not sloppy like that. Let's go," he said, rushing to the door.

"Four *C* right here, son," John-John said, about to knock on the door. Before his hand could touch the door, it opened, and there stood two bodies.

Felicia gasped as she saw the three gunmen standing in the doorway, wearing frowns.

Blake went to raise his pistol and met his fate.

Felicia stood there screaming.

"Shut the fuck up!" Percy yelled, pumping bullets into her chest.

Stepping inside, the men looked around to make sure no one else was inside. Smoke snatched up the bag, "A few dollars is in it, son."

"Oh shit, yo. Yo, come on, let's get out of here," Percy said, leading the way.

The three jumped in a black Taurus and hightailed it to their destination, leaving Blake and Felicia bleeding to death.

On the way to the airport, Londa was nervous as hell and quiet. She kept envisioning the feds waiting for her at the gate, with her mother in custody or something wild like that. She wondered where Yazmine was in all of this.

Mo answered his phone and said, "A'ight," and hung up quickly.

Londa didn't bother to ask what the call was about, as Mo switched lanes in his Escalade like he had no worries.

With no luggage, $200 in her pocket and her ID, Londa gave Mo a big hug and was getting ready to walk to her gate.

"Londa, stay in Atlanta," Mo said. "Don't come back to New York. You and Yaz is a wrap, you hear me? Don't call her or nothing."

"I got you."

"You good now. Blake? Gone. Peedi? Gone. Felicia? Gone. Ya dig?"

"Mo, you can keep that dough for yourself, or give it

to Nuny, since I can't travel with it. It's about nine thousand or so."

"Come on, you know I'm good. I'm-a give it to my
mans, since they the ones that did the deed."

"Who did it?"

"John-John and them. Only me and you know that,
you feel me?"

"Aye, you don't have to worry about killing no wit-
nesses over here. I'm done. I'm gonna go pray and start
a new life. I'm done, Mo. I'm done with this shit. I'm
just sorry it had to end like this, you know. I mean,
Blake is dead. Did y'all have to kill him?" Londa started
to cry.

"He was at your crib, Londa, wanting to kill you, girl.
You crazy?"

"I know, but still," she said, trying to pull herself together. "I didn't ask for all of this. I'm just a regular
around-the-way girl trying to make a better life for myself, so I won't get caught up depending on some dude
or living check to check. I never wanted nobody to die
or kill anybody."

"Londa, you ain't kill nobody, so you good. Peedi was
alive. Val and them finished him. You ain't kill him, so
chill out, a'ight. You did what you had to. Val ain't die,
and I ain't get word on his man yet. I heard he in a
coma or something. Listen, all you did was take some
money from a few niggas that had enough to spare anyway. Now go live and send my wife back home in one
piece, a'ight."

Still crying, Londa got her face together and sat up
straight. "I'm a soldier. I'm good." She laughed.

"There we go. Now get on that plane, and I'll see you when I'm passing through, a'ight. Tell your moms I said hi."

"Thank you for everything, Mo."

"Any time, lil' big cahuna, any time." Mo hugged Londa and watched her disappear into the airport.

Londa boarded her flight with a headache. She asked the man next to her for his paper that he wasn't reading.

"Sure, honey," the already-drunk man said and smiled.

Londa smiled back at him. Her smile faded when she read the headlines of the *Daily News:* COUPLE FOUND SLAIN IN BROOKLYN HEIGHTS APARTMENT. Inside, a mug shot of Blake and a picture of an innocent and young Felicia stared back at her. Holding back tears, she closed the paper and handed it back to the man. "Thank you. I'll just take a nap," she said, closing her eyes.

When she opened them again she was at the airport.

She hopped in the passenger side of her silver Infiniti truck and sat quietly next to Nuny. They headed to Sugarloaf, where nobody knew Londa's name or where she was from, and where her mother awaited her with open arms.